"Sherwood Anderson's George Willard shimn
of the Book, an artfully plotted evocation of Chicago in two centuries,
and two aspiring writers deadened by commerce until—for each—an
old love appears to reignite their best and earliest dreams. Porter Shreve
delivers a richly layered hat-tip to Anderson's impact on American letters, and a highly rewarding story at every turn."
—PAULA MCLAIN, author of *The Paris Wife*

"Porter Shreve's *The End of the Book* is a remarkable novel about the
huge promises fathers and sons, writers and readers, books and characters, make to each other, and how we break those promises, and how
still we keep hoping not to break them, or break them again, or break
them completely. . . . Shreve has written some terrific books, but this is
his best yet."
—BROCK CLARKE, author of *Exley* and *An Arsonist's Guide
to Writers' Homes in New England*

The End of the Book is the story of an aspiring contemporary novelist who may
or may not be writing a sequel to Sherwood Anderson's classic *Winesburg, Ohio*.
Adam Clary works in Chicago for a famous internet company on a massive project
to digitize the world's books, but secretly he hates his job and wishes to be a writer
at a time when the book as physical object and book culture itself have never been
more threatened.

Counterpointing Adam's story is that of George Willard, the young protagonist
of Anderson's book, who arrives in Chicago around 1900 when it was the fastest-
growing city in American history. Through alternating chapters, we follow George's
travails, including his marriage to the wealthy daughter of his boss, his affair with
his hometown sweetheart, his artistic crisis, breakdown and flight, and along the
way we see the echoes and intersections between his life and Adam's as they struggle
in two similar Americas through two similar times in the life of the book.

The End of the Book

YELLOW SHOE FICTION
MICHAEL GRIFFITH, *Series Editor*

The End of the Book

A NOVEL

PORTER SHREVE

LOUISIANA STATE UNIVERSITY PRESS
BATON ROUGE

Published with the assistance of the Borne Fund

Published by Louisiana State University Press
Copyright © 2014 by Louisiana State University Press
Manufactured in the United States of America
LSU Press Paperback Original
FIRST PRINTING

DESIGNER: *Mandy McDonald Scallan*
TYPEFACE: *Minion*
PRINTER AND BINDER: *Maple Press, Inc.*

This book is a work of fiction. Names, characters, organization, places, circumstances, and events are the product of the author's imagination, or else they are used fictitiously. Any resemblance to actual occurrences or individuals, living or dead, is coincidental.

Library of Congress Cataloging-in-Publication Data
Shreve, Porter.
  The end of the book : a novel / Porter Shreve.
    pages cm. — (Yellow Shoe Fiction)
  ISBN 978-0-8071-5622-3 (pbk. : alk. paper) — ISBN 978-0-8071-5623-0 (pdf) — ISBN 978-0-8071-5624-7 (epub) — ISBN 978-0-8071-5625-4 (mobi) 1. Fathers and sons— Fiction. 2. Authorship— Fiction. 3. Obsessive-compulsive disorder— Fiction. 4. Families—Fiction. 5. Psychological fiction. 6. Domestic fiction. I. Title.
  PS3569.H7395E53 2014
  813'.54— dc23

                                              2013041043

For Bich, Henry, and Julian

The End of the Book

My father taught at four universities in four midwestern towns, had three sons by different wives, and wrote two books, one published forty years ago and the other, volume two of the definitive biography of a once-celebrated American writer, always on the verge of completion: next month, end of summer, nothing left but the index and a little fine-tuning. Over the years my half brothers, our mothers, stepmothers, and I had looked into his office, a packrat midden of strewn note cards, manuscript pages, newspapers, boxes, overdue books, empty cans of Diet Rite Cola, and airplane bottles of Malibu Rum. Long before his retirement from Central Illinois, everyone in the family but me had moved far away from the town of Normal, whose name my father daily defied. So I was the one who had to drop in to see how he was surviving.

This time was no ordinary visit. I'd made a special trip, and though I told myself not to worry I was growing uneasy. I parked the Prius in front of the *FORECLOSURE: HOME FOR SALE* sign at his curb and climbed over a snowbank. All the neighbors except my father had plowed their driveways and shoveled their walks, so I was up to my knees in snow so soft it squeaked under my sneakers as I high-stepped toward the door. There was his old Mercury Mystique, under a white shell, parked outside the junk-filled garage. It had been three days since Christmas Eve, when a librarian I knew at the university e-mailed, saying she'd heard about the foreclosure and hoped my family was coping over the holidays. I'd seen my father only once since summer, at a diner he liked near campus, but he'd said nothing about trouble with his lender. We talked about the Cubs, as I recalled, whether this would be the season they broke the hundred-year curse. In the end, no such luck: They won ninety-seven games but got swept in the opening round of the playoffs.

When the e-mail arrived I was staying with my wife, Dhara, at the motel her family ran outside Dayton. I called my father that night, but he didn't answer, nor did he pick up on Christmas, so to Dhara's annoyance we headed home the next morning.

"It's nothing. I'm telling you, he's just embarrassed," she said in the car. "My family's going to guilt me about leaving early until we see them again."

"This isn't about your family. My father could be losing his house. For all I know, they've turned off his heat and he's freezing in there. Or worse—"

"Don't get melodramatic, Adam. It's one of your least appealing qualities."

"The man is capable of anything," I said. "No one should be spending Christmas alone."

"He's not going to kill himself, if that's what you're suggesting. He's fine. You'll see. But what you're going to do with him—that's another story."

I dropped Dhara off around noon at our apartment in Chicago, said I might be gone a night or two. She reminded me, though I needed no reminder, that our first anniversary was coming up on New Year's Day, a dinner we couldn't afford at one of the most expensive restaurants in America. I promised to return in plenty of time, then made my way here, a couple hours southwest on I-55.

I'd seen my father fewer than a dozen times since he moved into this split-level, bought four years before at the height of the boom on a zero-down, low-interest loan—*Instant Approval! Act Now!*—that had ballooned beyond the means of a seventy-eight-year-old retiree with a lifetime of bad habits. It was the first house he ever owned. A child of the Depression, he used to pay with cash, buy in bulk, collect the pennysaver. He loved a bargain and drove my mother crazy with Saturday-morning yard-sale rounds where he'd come home with a trunk full of other people's castoffs.

Do we need another popcorn maker?

That one cost me a dollar, barely used.

And what are you going to do with forty-five volumes of the 1961 World Book Encyclopedia?

It's the Braille edition. A classic. I got it for a song.

I couldn't believe my father had bought his own place. The apartment building where he'd cooped up since his last separation got sold to developers who planned to renovate and double the rent, and that's when it dawned on him that if he owned a house no one could turn him out on the street. Instead of steering him toward assisted living or another rental where at least a building manager could keep an eye on him, I'd said there was never a better time to buy—mortgage brokers didn't care about credit history anymore. Infuriating as he'd always been, this man who used to lock his office door and leave an empty chair at dinner or disappear for long weekends on "research trips" to the Newberry, which my mother and I knew was closed on Sundays and Mondays, I felt sorry for my father now, whose career had peaked in 1968, who bore his steady decline on his shoulders like some nearsighted Atlas, and whose failures reminded me daily of my own suspended dreams.

I wanted my father to have something to call his, so when he got the preapproved loan and started driving around town with a realtor who looked like an escort crossed with a mortician, I forgot that he was too dissipated to be living alone, his memory too much like his office: a dusty repository of missing and scattered papers. Before I had much time to think, my half brothers were flying in from the coasts to help with the move. My father hadn't seen Michael in three years, so I arranged a weekend for them in Chicago. I put them up in my apartment and bought them tickets to the Cubs while Eric and I tackled the mess, decided what to take to the curb and what to haul to the new house. In the end, we lost our nerve and moved everything we'd wanted to throw away into our father's garage, afraid that the shock of a clean, orderly space would be too much for his heart to take.

He'd had a triple bypass the year before, and cracks had begun to appear in the walls he'd spent a lifetime building around himself. I'd always been the one to call him, but after the surgery he started phoning me at odd hours, could even turn wistful about the book that had bedeviled him for decades, his parental deficiencies, and his marriage to my mother, whom he called his twin flame and the great regret of his life. Perhaps he was trying to console me, or more likely to comfort himself because my mother was no longer alive, and thus could forever represent the one who got away. But not long after he settled into his new house, rue gave way to routine; he burrowed in, stopped calling or answering the phone, and grew irascible at my unannounced visits.

A smattering of blue-sleeved copies of the *New York Times* and the *Daily Pantagraph*, the local paper, dotted his stoop. My heartbeat quickened as I picked them up, six in all, and brushed off the snow. My father always started his day with the papers, used to read aloud from the obituaries and from local stories that caught his eye—KID LOSES ARM PLAYING

CHICKEN WITH A TRAIN; LOTTERY WINNER GOES BROKE OVER-NIGHT—while my mother rinsed the breakfast dishes and rushed to school to run the library.

I rang the doorbell and peered through the glass sidelights. The hallway was dark and empty. I rang again and heard only the muffled silence of white-blanketed suburbia, post-holiday, woodsmoke brushing the air, my father's house the odd hermitage in a family subdivision. I couldn't hear the bell working, so I tried the knocker. The name of the people who last lived here—*The Fishers*—remained etched in the brass. I wondered why my father wasn't coming to the door, why his newspapers had been growing cold for three days, his walk and car buried under snow, and it occurred to me that I should have gone to the hardware store last time I visited and brought back a new door knocker or, better yet, had one engraved: *Clary*.

Dr. Roland Clary, Professor Emeritus at Central Illinois University, formerly of Indiana University, Oberlin College, and the University of Michigan, author of what might have been the essential biography of Sherwood Anderson, had he only finished. Several major newspapers and journals reviewed the first book favorably. "In this judicious, assiduously researched biography, Mr. Clary reminds us why the author of *Winesburg, Ohio* remains relevant today," wrote the *New York Times*. "The second volume is sure to be anticipated by scholars and literary readers alike."

Why, as I shivered under a purpling sky, was I imagining my father's obituary, and wondering where, if anywhere, it might run? Did the world care about books anymore? Who would note the passing of an obscure academic, chronicler of a mostly forgotten writer's life? A *writer's writer,* my father used to say. Even he conceded that while Sherwood Anderson influenced generations of storytellers and for a time was a godfather to Hemingway and Faulkner, he was not in their league, but for that one odd book about a town of outcasts—*grotesques,* Anderson called them. Believe me: I knew that book well. And I knew my father well enough to realize that by devoting his days to the study of these grotesques he had himself become one.

I banged on the door with my fist. Through the glass I saw the orange tabby, Wing Biddlebaum, round the corner and offer an insouciant meow. I studied the cat's face for signs of trouble, but he had the puffed, squint-eyed look of having just awoken from a long nap. He sat on the hallway tiles, licked his paws, and when I continued knocking, walked away with a vexed switch of the tail.

I took out my cell phone and dialed, and I could hear my father's phone ringing inside. It rang and rang, and still no answer. He was the last holdout against answering machines, voice mail, said cell phones were a swindle and a public menace. A few years before, I had set him up with an e-mail account, but he didn't bother using it. And he called the famous company where I worked *the grand colonizer of the Information Age*. I had to admit I didn't disagree.

Stepping back, I looked up to the second-floor windows. The curtains were drawn, but a single bulb lit one of the rooms, and I felt relieved that his power was still on. At least he wasn't freezing to death in there. But even on my unannounced visits he did always come to the door, slippered and cardiganed, his ashy pallor blending with his incongruously tidy beard.

Why wasn't he answering?

Maybe he was taking a nap. Not that I'd ever known him to do so. But his engine was running down, and he did seem tired last I saw him. *Never felt better,* he'd lied. But if he were napping he wouldn't have left the light on.

Now I was beginning to panic. I pounded the door harder, wondered if I should call the police, see if one of the neighbors had a key.

Why hadn't I thought to get my own key made?

I remembered reading about the Collyer brothers, the reclusive hoarders of upper Fifth Avenue who filled their brownstone floor to ceiling with junk. When a patrolman, summoned by a worried neighbor, broke in through a second-story window, it took him two hours to crawl to the corpse of Homer Collyer, slumped amidst the rubbish in a tattered blue robe. It seemed that Langley Collyer had gone missing, so a search fanned out across the city while police combed the house. Over the course of three weeks they cleared away three thousand books, decades of newspapers, and countless curiosities—a clavichord, bowling balls, an X-ray machine, dressmaking dummies, a horse's jawbone—more than eighty tons of trash before they discovered Langley, long dead, and, it turned out, just ten feet away from where they'd found his brother.

If Dhara were here she'd say I was overreacting. But I was my father's lone caretaker, and he was the closest family I had, so I braced myself for the worst. I trudged through the snow to the back of the house and tried to look in, but the windows were mostly frosted over and the rooms dark. I spotted a ladder beside the neighbor's garage, dragged it back, and leaned it against my father's house.

I climbed to the second floor and rapped on the storm windows, pulled off my gloves and tried to slide my fingers under the frames, but they were cased in ice.

I was blowing into my hands and thinking about breaking a pane with my elbow like a B-grade action star when I heard the creak of the back door opening, then a familiar splenetic voice: "Get the hell down from there!"

In his living room, my father and I had it out:

"What did you think you were doing? Trying to give me a heart attack?"

"Why didn't you answer the door? I've been sick with worry."

"No one's been sick with worry over me since my mother dropped me in the Pensaukee River and thought I was drowned. You think I'm some old sentimentalist?"

"I've been calling for days, Dad. I've been out in the cold for the last half hour trying to get your attention."

"Well, you got it, all right, with your cat-burglar routine."

"Why did you ignore me?" I asked.

"I didn't know it was you."

"Who else would it be?"

His friends had all retired and taken to the skies—celestial, or the fly-ways that end in warm weather. "I've been getting nothing but calls and visitors." He flicked on a light and I saw the tide of unopened mail and papers spilling out of the dining room that he called his office.

I was still in my coat and it was too cold in there to remove it. "What kind of visitors?"

"Predators and harpies, 'cawing their lamentations in the eerie trees.'"

"People from the bank?"

"It's none of your goddamned business."

Manuscript boxes filled the camelback sofa he'd had since the seventies when we lived in Bloomington. The dusty almond aroma of old books mingled with the smell of buttered popcorn, which my father had long subsisted on. I would have sat down, having traveled all day, but there was nowhere to plant myself. Every chair and settee was stacked with books. On his walls he'd hung more photographs, creepy sepia portraits of other people's families, scored over the years at estate sales. My mother had drawn the line on this one fetish. *Your own ancestors I can understand. But who are these people?*

I knew not to push my father, so I looked for a way around the subject of why I was there. "I tried to call yesterday to say Merry Christmas. Merry Christmas, Dad. Did you talk to anyone else?"

He took off his thick-rimmed glasses and wiped them with the sleeve of his purple cardigan. He was slim and fine-featured, his silver hair no less thick and wavy than when he courted his first wife and left her for a classmate, escaped from his second wife into the arms of my mother, and abandoned my mother for a graduate student. "The phone rang a few times," he said.

"You could have picked up. It was only me, and probably Michael and Eric. No one from the bank would be calling on Christmas."

"Don't count on it." With a wobbly hand, he put his glasses back on. "I could use a drink."

"Maybe we should grab some dinner and talk," I said.

The adrenaline from finding me outside the house seemed to have run its course. He leaned over the back of his old fainting couch, curled like an approaching wave.

I took him out to what passed for fine dining in Normal, a cook-your-own steakhouse called Rustler's Grill in a strip mall on the north side. I'd never been before, but I figured it was interactive and primal, a good place for father and son to commune, mutely grilling cuts of meat over an open flame.

Still rattled, I had forgotten about the low-fat, low-salt diet he was supposed to be on. He'd managed to stop smoking after the bypass and claimed he rode an exercise bike, but the seat always seemed dusty, and I wondered if he kept up with the blood thinners and superaspirins, thrombolytics and beta blockers he was supposed to be taking. I couldn't tell him not to eat a steak when I was the one who'd suggested this place, so we ordered top sirloins from a glass case and took our plates to a massive grill in the middle of the room.

My father asked loud enough for others to hear, "Why go out to dinner when you have to do the work?" and I told him no one else was complaining; look at those happy families spearing their marbled Delmonicos. "What's next?" he said. "Butcher your own beef? Raise the herd yourself?"

We were standing there, sprinkling our dinners with mystery seasoning, brushing butter on our Texas Toast, when a man in a cartoon cardinal sweatshirt came up to my father and shook his hand. "Mr. Clary. What a surprise." He had an inland honk and a flattop, the look of an athlete gone to flesh. "I stopped calling you a month ago. We're past the point of no return. Bob Jagoda." He introduced himself and gave me the handshake of a linebacker clinging to glory.

I glanced at my father, who had turned pale and reticent. "Adam," I put in.

"Are you family?" Jagoda asked.

"I'm his son," I said.

"You don't live in town, do you?" His voice carried an edge of judgment.

"I'm the youngest," I felt compelled to explain. "I live in Chicago."

"Well, it's important to have family around in tough times. Season of giving and all," he said.

With a pair of tongs I moved my steak back from the flame and set a baked potato on the grill. My father seemed shrunken and lost outside the walls of his own topsy-turvydom.

"How do you know each other?" I asked.

Jagoda said he was a housing counselor with American Dream Assistance. "We're HUD-approved—legit," he said. "But your Pops took months before agreeing to meet me. Isn't that right, Mr. Clary? And by the time he came to the office, we had the smallest window to try for a loan modification. These banks, I'm telling you. Your pops had the worst mortgage, an adjustable rate that shot up like a rocket."

When my father had signed for that loan I was on business in Ann Arbor and couldn't be there, and though I'd harassed him to go over the terms, asked him to fax me the paperwork and give me the name of the lender, he'd refused my help.

Jagoda jutted his chin at me.

"I had no idea," I said.

My father flipped his steak, which had charred in the flame. "This is a family matter."

"You're right." Jagoda put up his hands. "I'm not in the I-told-you-so business, but after you ignored the court summons and the notice of default, we talked about the seven-month time frame, and you knew all you had to do was say, *Go for it*, and I would have turned the screws on your lender and gotten you a better deal, probably saved your house. I have a lifetime success rate of 80 percent plus, tops in the region." He paused to let this sink in. "But you didn't answer my e-mails or calls, Mr. Clary, and now you're past the Redemption period. Once they sell the place, do you know how long you'll have?"

My father forked his sirloin and dropped it on his plate. "This is enough," he said, and walked away.

I removed my food from the grill, not sure whether to thank the housing counselor for trying at least or call him out for browbeating an old man. I gave him a feeble, "Happy holidays," then headed for the table under a pair of horseshoes where my father slumped over his plate, slowly carving.

"Charming guy." I sat down.

He lifted a piece of steak—charred on one side, nearly raw on the other—into the dim light. "Why did you have to drag me here? You know I don't like to go out."

"Why didn't you tell me your situation?" I snapped back. "It's been months, almost a year. This news came out of the blue."

My father shrugged and took a bite, set his silverware in the bloody pool on his plate.

"What does it mean to be past the Redemption period?" I asked.

"It means I missed my chance at atonement. So much for getting delivered from sin."

"Seriously, Dad. This isn't a joke."

"You're right. Maybe it's not too late. Waiter, bring me a sackcloth and ashes. This flesh is going to need extra mortification."

I knew when my father got this way it was best to let him go, so I ate my potato and looked uninterested. He seemed cheered by his little attempt at humor. When the waiter did come by, he ordered a rum and Diet Coke, and before long was into another. I saw Bob Jagoda leave the restaurant with his wife and burr-headed sons, and when I sensed my father was good and loose, I asked, "How long before you have to move out?"

He pushed his pecked-at dinner aside. "Thirty days after the sale," he said. "*Alea iacta est,* quoth Caesar. 'The die is cast.'"

"So what are we going to do?"

"How about I buy another house? Weren't you the one who said real estate is a can't-miss investment?"

"Don't try to pin this on me."

"What the hell was I doing *investing,* in the first place? I've got one foot in the grave, for Chrissake, and now here we are: end of '08. Worst economy since the Great Depression. I'm making national news!"

"There's no sense looking back," I said. On some level I knew that my father was right, that I had urged him to buy a house when I should have realized that it was too late for him to make that kind of commitment. In a flare of guilt, and thinking neither of the consequences nor of Dhara—whose nickname for my father was Vritra, the Hindu god of drought and destruction—I said, "Why don't you come and live with us?" I knew it was a mistake even as I formed the words, "Dhara and I can help. We have an extra bedroom. You don't have to stay forever, just long enough to sort things out."

2

Eight years ago George Willard came to Chicago green as a sprout, and now to his surprise, he had risen to near the top of the city's leading ad agency. His campaigns had reached households across the land, and his large-windowed office on the fourteenth floor of the Monadnock Building looked down on the workers and vendors, horses and drays, omnibuses and cable cars crisscrossing the Loop. At twenty-seven he made a higher salary than his father had ever dreamed of, and were he to return to his hometown of Winesburg, Ohio, he could buy one of the finest houses. But he knew there was no going back. He had made a promise to his mother before she died that he would leave for the city and not follow the path of his father, who even now was patching the walls of the gloomy family inn and promising that the New Willard House, that husk by the tracks in a dying town, would one day be filled with guests again.

When he left Winesburg in spring 1896, George had planned to find a newspaper job, and after that to become a writer. But he'd arrived in the fastest-growing city the world had ever known only to find that this place of a thousand tongues had one universal language: commerce. You could breathe it in the air, a devil's brew of sweat and rotting vegetables, pine and turpentine and something deep and earthy, like steam off a rendering pot. And you could see it at every corner: brokers gathered under lampposts discussing the price of wheat, seamstresses hunched over tables in basement windows, salvagers peddling iron from the backs of rickety wagons, newsboys shouting bulletins. George had wanted to write those bulletins, but an accident, an actual collision with fate, had made him a writer of a different sort, a persuader for profit: a copywriter. And though he wanted to believe that he was still a kind of artist and his work had the same aim as a novelist's or story writer's—to communicate, one soul to another—he'd been growing restless, and was sometimes gripped with a worry that for all his outward success he had lost his way.

From his half-open door he could hear the voice of his boss, Alfred Lazar, in conversation with the vaunted Clyde Kennison. They were talking, as they had been for months, about Kennison's new ideas.

"You're the future of advertising," Lazar was saying now. "I want you to teach the whole firm your philosophy. From today until spring that's your only assignment. We need scores of Clyde Kennisons here."

George stood up from his swivel chair and closed the door, then sat again behind his polished cherry desk. He had no one to blame but himself for the arrival of Clyde Kennison. One June evening six months ago he had been in Lazar's office planning the next installment of his Tidy Town campaign. He'd made his reputation with Tidy Town, a mythical place where the citizens polished everything clean as pearls, from floor to ceiling, with Nuvolia Soap. George had invented all the characters and written all the jingles, had helped make Nuvolia America's top-selling cleanser. But other brands were gaining, Nuvolia had dropped to third behind Ivory and Gold Dust, and though George did have one hidden advantage, a trump card he'd been reluctant to play, he knew he was falling out of favor at the agency.

He remembered that day in his boss's office when a courier had knocked on the door and delivered a note. Lazar had grabbed it and read aloud: *Not a man in your firm knows the first thing about advertising. Not a man on this spinning earth knows, either. But if you want to know, tell this courier to send me upstairs. I'm waiting in the lobby.*

"Would you believe the nerve?" Lazar had said.

George had taken the note and read it himself; even the bold handwriting had the mark of audacity. "But aren't you a little curious to meet this fellow?"

"Oh, go ahead, if you're so interested." Lazar commanded the courier to send the man up.

Kennison introduced himself, and Lazar told him it was getting late—he had five minutes to make his case. More than a decade older than George, Kennison had keen, close-set eyes and a chevron mustache that barely concealed his supercilious mouth. He said he was a copywriter in Milwaukee who had led successful campaigns for Dr. Shute's Restorative, Wheatabits Cereal, and the Royal Shoe Company. He'd once been ad manager for Hudson's Bay in Winnipeg, but his truly formative experience had come during his years as an officer of the Royal Canadian Mounted Police, when he used to travel alone on horseback across the northern snows thinking of advertising day and night, meditating, like some capitalist monk, on how to reach the largest number of buyers. What he came up with was so simple that it could be summarized in one sentence, which he delivered at the end of those first five minutes: *Prove They Need It.*

That single line had piqued Lazar's interest enough to ask Kennison to explain, and for the next four hours the Canadian paced and gesticulated and went over his concepts point by point. Ads should be unadorned, easy for the average person to grasp, and must avoid cleverness and art, anything to distract from the argument that the product is essential and no reasonable human being should be without it. "Advertising is sales on the page," he said. "Pretty pictures and rhymey jingles and silly made-up characters are useless because they make only the most general claims." George took umbrage. "Perhaps you've heard of Tidy Town?" But Kennison was unimpressed. "The tidy farmer, the tidy grocer, the tidy maid and the lot? No offense, sport, but Tidy Town will soon fall off the map."

George had bristled at this prophecy, but he should have been alarmed when Lazar failed to defend him and allowed the meeting to go on until close to midnight. George couldn't have known then what he was beginning to realize now, that advertising was changing, that the soft sell, which had made his career thus far, would soon be eclipsed by *Prove They Need It,* that the meeting George himself had made possible would go down in business history and launch the agency so far into the firmament that one day Alfred J. Lazar would become known as the father of modern advertising.

George put on his coat and hat and left his office. He wasn't sure where he was going, only that he wanted to get out of the building and feel the December air on his face. On his way to the elevators he nearly sailed into Lazar, who was stepping out of the Service Department into the hallway. Everyone dreaded the Service Department, where an enormous wall chart displayed due dates for the firm's assorted campaigns. Lazar was notorious for setting the dates weeks ahead of clients' schedules in order to keep his workers under continuous deadline pressure. This, and his habit of firing 10 to 20 percent of his employees every couple of years in what he called a regenerative act of nature, kept everyone buzzing with anxious efficiency.

It had been a while since the last purge, and George had grown used to the look on his peers' faces: *you might be dead weight, but certainly not me.*

"Where are you going in such a hurry?" Lazar asked.

George stood a head taller than his boss, but Lazar had dark eyes under a heavy brow and a thistly posture that magnified his presence. "I was headed to lunch," George said.

"But it's four in the afternoon."

"I've been so busy I plumb forgot to eat."

Lazar rubbed his chin. Slender and young-looking for forty-nine, he was obsessed with grooming and had been known to interrupt meetings in order to run down to the barbershop for a midday shave. "Well, I want you back here soon, d'you understand? I've been meaning to tell you something."

Those words wedged in George's mind like pebbles in a shoe, and as daylight dissolved into the smoky haze that forever hung over the city they gathered a sense of foreboding. He walked up State Street amidst the mad scurry of workers and Christmas shoppers and tried to imagine what Lazar might want to tell him. Nuvolia had recently signed a new contract running through the end of next year, and George had taken this as a vote of confidence that though sales had been slipping of late his future was secure. So many products had entered the market—cleanliness had become the imperative of the age—it was all one could do to keep up. But what of that overheard conversation: *We need scores of Clyde Kennisons here?* George was a writer, not a salesman, and couldn't imagine being remade into a bloodless advertising machine. Lazar knew this, and it was his company, so what would keep him from saying to George, perhaps this very afternoon, *Thank you for your time, but we no longer need your services?*

There was a contest within George between the pursuit of art and financial security. His mother was a failed artist, his father a failed businessman, so George had much to compensate for. Elizabeth Willard had wanted to be an actress and travel the world, but never managed to leave Winesburg, and the disease that made her the hollow figure haunting the New Willard House went undiagnosed but might have been called disappointment. George shared his mother's sensibility and knew he had come to Chicago in part to avoid the trap of unrealized dreams. At the same time, he had grown up in that bedraggled hotel, and each year the hallway outside his room, dimly lit with kerosene lamps, had grown quieter as travelers continued on to the next town or sought more welcoming accommodations. Tom Willard lived in denial of the failure that surrounded him; he walked briskly along Main Street twirling the ends of his black mustache, and greeted his fellow citizens with a mayoral air. At first George had resisted the path of wealth that his father had urged him toward, but Chicago was a dynamo that sucked him in, and now the thought of losing his income and falling from his comfortable perch among the Monadnock "cliff-dwellers" made him shudder.

It was the Friday before Christmas. Lights illuminated every window, voices rose with the clatter and grind up skyscraper walls, and George was swept by the convulsion of people past Adams, Monroe, and Madison Streets. Crossing Washington, he forgot to hold onto his pearl-gray homburg, and a crosswind off the lake sent the hat airborne. As it spun toward the ground, a girl with an armful of flowers dropped what she was carrying and caught the hat in both hands.

George rushed over to where she was standing in the middle of the street. "Thank you," he said. "But look what's become of your flowers." Her chrysanthemums lay scattered about the macadam, trampled under the boots of indifferent passersby. The girl bent to gather the few salvageable blooms, and when she looked up George saw the dark rings under her eyes and her pale dreamy face and recognized her as one of the many flower girls, immigrants from central Europe who went about the city's corners and saloons singing popular ballads or playing concertinas or sticking carnations in buttonholes with the entreaty, "Give me whatever you please."

The traffic was encroaching on either side, drivers yelling, "Hurry up already! Out of the street!" George took the girl's arm and hustled to the curb. "What do I owe you?" he asked, pulling his hat tight over his head. "I'm terribly sorry."

Under the lamplight her face had a consumptive pallor. She couldn't have been more than eighteen. "It's no trouble, sir." She brushed the sooty slush from the petals of her drooping chrysanthemums.

"I want to buy the whole bunch from you." He removed his billfold and took out ten dollars, two weeks' earnings for someone in her work.

"It's too much," she said, but George pressed the money into her small gloveless hand. She thanked him and, before she turned to leave, pinned a flower to the lapel of this topcoat.

When she had disappeared into the crowd like a snowflake on pavement, George found himself under the great clock of Marshall Field's, drifting past the brilliant Christmas display windows, each as elaborate as a theater stage—this of a fire-lit living room and bright spangled tree, that of a couple riding a sleigh across a winter moon. George wondered if he would be spending Christmas alone or at the office or having dinner with his landlady's family again at the Cass Street boardinghouse that she ran like an orphanage. Though he made salary enough to buy his own flat in one of the finer residential districts, he sent a good portion of his money to his father for renovation projects and lived a simple existence between the office and his third-floor room. He found comfort in the transience, even the dowdiness of Ma Kavanagh's place that reminded him of home, and for a while enjoyed the feeling of living in two worlds: up in the clouds with the ballyhooers and down in the streets among the hungering folk.

But work had come to so dominate George's life that he could no longer name most of his fellow boarders, and where he used to walk the mile and a half to and from the Monadnock, taking in the faces he passed on the street or stopping to chat with waffle vendors, newsboys, laundresses, market gardeners, now he took the grip to the office and stared into middle space, avoiding commuters' eyes, his thoughts fixed on selling soap with his Tidy Town cartoons. Ma Kavanagh had half-jokingly threatened George with eviction. "I'd be doing you a favor, son. You haven't had a date since Hector was a pup. How can you meet a nice girl when you're living in a room with a slanted floor over a tobacconist?"

When he had boarded the train in Winesburg with a trunk and his father's warning, "Be a sharp one. That's the ticket. Don't let anyone think you're a greenhorn," he never would have imagined that upon reaching the downslope of his twenties he'd still be unmarried, unattached. He had assumed he would get together again with his adored Helen White. But it seemed a lifetime ago that Helen had gone east to Cleveland for college, and George had made his way to the "Gomorrah of the West." He hadn't heard from Helen in four years, had lost touch with those in Winesburg who would know what had become of her. She might have continued east, to New York or Boston, and settled down with some high-nosed stockholder her parents would approve of. Funny to think that George had reached a position where Banker and Mrs. White might finally say he was good enough for their daughter. Maybe Helen had children and had forgotten that night at the empty fairgrounds, how she and George had run laughing down Waterworks Hill, then picked themselves up and walked home in regardful silence.

George fled the cold, following the crowd into the main entrance of Marshall Field's. The flower girl and Helen White, his worry that his days at the agency were numbered, and a dread now flooding him that he would spend the rest of his holidays alone were like hands guiding him into the vast shopping emporium, past the Christmas tree that seemed to soar clear up to the gold-domed ceiling, past the bough-strung perfume counters and the carolers singing "Joy to the World." Until, puzzlingly, here he was, leaning over the sparkling glass of the jewelry cases.

A saleswoman in an absinthe-green dress asked, "May I help you?" Thin as a stem, with her white hair swept up, she resembled a tulip at the end of the season.

"Yes, I'm looking for an engagement ring," George heard himself say.

And that's when his mind finally turned to Margaret Lazar, his boss's daughter, who two weeks ago at her twenty-first birthday party had confessed to George that she believed she might be in love with him. They were in her parents' library at the time, and the news had come as such a shock that all George could manage in response was, "You can't be serious."

Margaret grasped his wrist. "I know it's unconventional for a woman to say such things to a man, but these are different times, and I'm old enough now to make my own decisions."

"What of all your suitors?" George gestured toward the other room, where sons of the Lake Shore Drive elite had arranged themselves in polite antipathy.

"Prigs and fops, all hand-selected by my mother," Margaret whispered.

"But we hardly know each other," George said. Which was true and not true. He had always thought of her as the daughter of Alfred Lazar, a frequent visitor at the office and sometime summer employee. When he'd first met her she was just thirteen, and though she had filled out her satin dress, traveled to Paris, Vienna, and Florence, and attended the University of Chicago, he had never considered her a peer, let alone a potential match.

"Really, you must have known," she said. "I've been sending you cues from the moment my father ran you down in the street."

George laughed uncomfortably. She was referring to the accident that had led to their first meeting. In Chicago for less than a week, he had been trying to land interviews at the city papers. Having made little progress he was wandering the Loop in that somnambulant state of so many new arrivals from Midland villages. He had yet to stand on the shoreline of the lake, had only seen it from a distance, so he was walking toward Michigan Avenue and the great expanse of shimmering blue beyond.

He remembered it was an uncommonly temperate afternoon for April, how just before he stepped into the street the voices and crowd fell aside and a ribbon of sunlight seemed to spool over the water. George had never been in a boxing match, but one second he was walking toward the lake and the next he was on his knees in the Michigan Avenue mud, feeling as if Jim Corbett had knocked him out with a single vicious punch to the slats. He looked up, seeing stars, then into his line of vision a girl's face emerged.

"My God. Are you all right?" she cried. The ginger springs of her hair trembled with panic. "Father, come quick."

George sat up slowly and clutched his ribs. He tried to catch his breath as the girl moved to touch him. When he winced, she pulled her hands back as if from a hot stove. Behind her appeared a man in a swallow-tail suit.

"He stepped into the street." The man pointed with his cane. "It could hardly be avoided."

"He did not!" his daughter declared. "You drove up onto the curb!" She turned her attention again to George. "Say something. Tell us you're not injured."

George took a deeper breath this time and grimaced at the stabbing pain in his midsection. "That was a sockdolager," he said. "But I think I'm okay." He began to stand up, and as the girl put her hands under his arm to assist him her curls brushed his ear.

"Go on, father. Don't just stand there like a statue."

"I'll be fine," George said. But when he rose to his full height he had to bend down again.

"Shall we take you to the hospital?" the girl asked.

"Look at him," her father said. "Not a spot of blood on his shirt."

"I told you we shouldn't be out in that contraption until you've mastered it. You see—" She gestured to George. "You have the singular honor of being one of the first automobile accidents in the city of Chicago."

The man in the suit and cane added, "This is one of only twenty Duryeas in all Illinois."

"It's no time to boast, Father. If you can't control the thing you shouldn't have it out on the road."

The man was inspecting the chassis of the Duryea with his swank malacca cane. George had never seen an automobile before. It was a simple two-seat carriage, like a phaeton, only it had a tiller in the middle, a sputtering box beneath the bench, and seemed to be propelled by the ghosts of horses. A crowd had begun to gather, and behind the Duryea traffic had stopped and drivers called curses into the air.

"We have to get a move on." The man climbed into his seat and took hold of the tiller.

"We're terribly sorry," the girl said to George. She introduced herself as Margaret Lazar, got the name and address of his temporary lodgings, and promised to have something sent over. After they parted, George figured he would never see her or her father again, but two days later, while he was still nursing his bruised ribs, a note of apology arrived along with an invitation to dinner.

Inside the grandest house George had ever stepped foot in, Margaret's mother treated him like an uninvited guest, but her father perked up when George told him about his work at the *Winesburg Eagle*. Alfred Lazar had always loved journalism, had started his own newsletter in St. Joseph, Missouri, at the age of fourteen, edited his high-school paper, and spent the first six years of his working life as a reporter in Cape Girardeau and Kansas City. But his father called the career impractical and pressured him into business, urging an old friend at a Chicago advertising firm to hire his son. Lazar promised himself he would return to writing one day, but instead rose swiftly at the company, from office boy to traveling salesman to full partner and general manager, until at thirty-six, upon the founder's retirement, he bought the company and renamed it after himself.

He hadn't forgotten journalism, however, and made his success by hiring the best copywriters he could find. He had hoped his own son would join the company and one day take over, but Charles had fled to New York City for college and work, and almost never came home. Lazar had been looking for a protégé, and for seven years, until the arrival of Clyde Kennison, that might have been George. He started out cleaning cuspidors and running errands, but Lazar, seeing something of himself in the go-getter from small-town Ohio, had ushered George steadily along.

Now, at the jewelry counter of Marshall Field's, George refused to admit

that he was standing here not because he loved Margaret Lazar or had imagined a life with her, but rather to avoid a precipitous fall from the cliffs of the
Monadnock. He had climbed too high, come too far. Drumming his fingers
on the glass, he asked the white-haired woman in the absinthe-green dress
to bring forth her finest box of rings.

3

He'd lost his house; his retirement plan brought in half of what it used to; he'd run his only credit card to the limit until he could no longer make mortgage payments; he had late fees, collection fees, his credit rating was nil; his pension and Social Security could cover rent, but what about debts and expenses? I brought all this up when at first he refused my offer. *Do you really have a choice?* I asked, and he told me to let him sleep on it. So that was what I did, though *I* couldn't sleep, not on the yard-sale daybed that smelled like a golden retriever after a swim in a toxic creek. I sat up much of the night thinking of Dhara, of our own money troubles, or rather *my* money troubles. I owed twenty thousand dollars for that most impractical of degrees: a Master of Fine Arts in Creative Writing.

I knew I shouldn't have gone to an MFA that wasn't paid for, but I applied to four schools and the only place I got in was Lakeside, the Big Ten stalwart just north of Chicago where the buildings look Ivy League but little ivy grows. Instead of a fellowship I was offered a work-study that came nowhere close to covering rent and tuition, so I had to take out loans. What had I done with my MFA? I'd written a 128-page thesis called *A Brief History of the Fool*. I wanted to say it was a novel, because that sounded more impressive than what it really was: a sampler of sketches in which each chapter tried out a different voice, running with it until it slowed and put up its hand, doubled over trying to catch its breath, then limped to the finish line. *You have a problem with endings,* I used to hear in workshop. I had a professor who believed so strongly in voice—*Style is all,* he kept saying—that in my effort to impress him I parroted a different god—Kafka, O'Connor, Calvino, Carver—each time I turned in a story. *Keep casting around for that voice,* he wrote in the margins. *Listen hard enough and you'll hear it.*

My thesis advisor was the one who said I should call the book a novel.

The short-story market is toast. If you don't link up the pieces you might as well apply to law school now. Story collections sell about as well as poetry. Who am I kidding? he said. *The novel is a dying animal, too. In twenty years no one will read books anymore. I'll be food for worms, but what are you going to do?* Such words of inspiration cost me over ten thousand dollars a year. This same advisor hadn't published a book in a decade, but he had tenure and lots of opinions, so I took my cacophony of voices, my tales of fools and outcasts trying to find a home in the world, put them all in the same small town, gave them jobs at the five-and-dime and the local bar, and in the last story—"The Conflagration"—threw them together at a party at the town hotel, where a fire breaks out and my heroes are forced to act or flee. It's a cheap ending to a ragbag of a book, which is why *A Brief History of the Fool* sits under a pile of sweaters in the darkest corner of my closet.

Little did I know that the work-study Lakeside arranged for me would become my safety net. In my third semester there, in 2004, I got assigned to pull and load books into trucks for the monolithic search engine Imego, which had chosen Lakeside, among other universities, as partner in the Imego Library Project. Soon I was working evenings and weekends at the Imego warehouse in West Town. It seemed innocent enough at the time. We unloaded books, ran them under robotic scanners, or shipped them off to Bangalore to be scanned and returned on the cheap, then sent them back to the libraries they'd come from. And though friends from my MFA co-hort needled me for speeding the demise of the physical book, I didn't care because the job offered full-time summer work and opportunities beyond graduation—and if it weren't for the project I never would have fallen in love with Dhara Patel.

As regional coordinator for Imego Books, Dhara played a role in her company's plan to digitize over thirty million volumes from twenty-five thousand libraries around the world—pretty much everything ever bound and printed on paper. She traveled from the warehouse and her office in downtown Chicago to universities around the Great Lakes to make sure that libraries were sending their books and people like me were moving apace. We kissed for the first time to the sound of the robotic scanner turning the pages of John D. MacDonald's *Ballroom of the Skies*. On our second anniversary as a couple, I tracked down a copy of the book, a sci-fi novel from 1952 about an intergalactic romance. We read lines of stilted dialogue to each other as we drank champagne and fell into bed. The following year we had much to toast. Dhara was promoted to affiliate sales manager, continuing her rise up the ranks; she convinced management to hire me into her old position; and on January 1, 2008, we were married, at her family's motel, in a watered-down Gujarati ceremony.

I had hoped, by the time I turned off I-55 onto Lake Shore Drive, almost home after five full days in Normal, to have mustered the courage to confess, but I still couldn't bring myself to tell Dhara about my father's decision. "We're still working on it," I had said as late as that morning, talking on the cell phone with one hand while instructing movers with the other. I'd called some assisted-living places around Normal and Chicago, but couldn't imagine adding three thousand dollars a month to my debts. I'd tried the rental office at Harbor City, the iconic downtown towers better known as "the Honeycombs," where Dhara and I lived, and considered signing a lease on the only available one-bedroom apartment. But I had no idea how I could afford another twelve hundred dollars a month, or the two thousand I'd have to pay the graduate-student movers who even now were packing the foreclosed house and hauling the contents of the junk-filled garage to a storage locker in Little Italy.

Though my father was the stubbornest man I knew, I assumed he was out of money and options and had no choice but to agree to my offer to stay at Dhara's and my apartment for a couple weeks or a couple months or for however long it took us to make a permanent plan.

I left the Prius with the attendant and took the elevator up to thirty-seven. When I arrived at our apartment, Dhara was already getting ready for dinner. She stood at the bedroom mirror in a creamy silk slip, blow-drying her hair.

"Happy anniversary," I said. "You're looking awfully nice."

"I'm in my underwear."

"So you are—have I told you how much I missed you?"

I went to embrace her, but she stuck out her hair dryer like Barbarella's space gun. "I missed you, too, but maybe later. You look like you hopped off a garbage truck."

I had dust streaks on my waffle shirt, a week's growth of beard, and still smelled of golden retriever. "Fair enough." I gave her a quick kiss and ducked into the shower.

By the time I'd washed away the grime of moving my father's life into boxes and out the door of the only house he'd ever own, Dhara had already shimmied into the black Diane von Furstenberg dress I had bought her for Christmas. Or, rather, the four-hundred-dollar dress she saw in a boutique window on our way to lunch in Wicker Park and that I bought, wrapped, and presented to her with her family as witnesses. I knew that at the end of the month *her* checking account would pay the credit-card bill, but Dhara had always wanted me to give the appearance of breadwinner. So I picked up the tab with *my* card, though it was all for show—she made the higher salary, had worked steadily since seventh grade, had a business degree, and had invested well, even protecting most of her assets through the current crisis, unlike me, with my debts and my personal albatross otherwise known as Professor Roland Clary.

"How did it go?" Dhara asked. "What did you decide to do with him?"

I continued to buy time. "I'm still making calls. But at least I got him to move most of his junk into storage."

"Who have you called?" Dhara wrapped the hair-dryer cord around the handle and put it away.

"Nursing homes. Those kinds of places. But they're criminally expensive."

"Are your brothers pitching in?"

"Not much." I'd phoned them the other day. Michael offered a hundred bucks a month. Eric claimed he couldn't afford half that, even if he wanted to. Both agreed that whatever they contributed, our father didn't deserve it.

"It's not fair how they stick you with everything," Dhara said with irritation.

I wasn't quick to defend my brothers. They lived in New York and Boston, so I saw them once a year at most, and we rarely made more than a nominal effort. Our father was our only link, one we too often forgot. But I couldn't forget him at the moment, not when he was moving into this very apartment a couple days, a week, too soon from now.

"Why is this your responsibility? You're the youngest. You're supposed to get a free pass." Dhara swept her hair into a ponytail, then pinned it up in a bun.

"It's the same old story. They live far away and have too many kids." Michael had three and Eric four. They both married only children and got to breeding in their twenties, to compensate for lonely childhoods. Their kids slept two to a room; space was so tight at Eric's apartment that he turned a closet into a bedroom for his youngest boy, who slept on a tiny mattress and decorated the walls with decals of spaceships and planets. My brothers were priced out of the East Coast, on a public defender's and assistant principal's salary, and neither had any room at the inn. So it was all on me, and Dhara knew this, but that didn't stop her from asking *Why?*

"So I heard there might be a vacancy at corporate coming down the pike," she said. "One of the top marketing people got hired away by MirrorMirror. If the job gets posted, I think we should talk California again."

I let out an audible sigh. We had talked California before; it was our greatest sticking point. To Dhara, the Midwest, though she'd been born and raised here, had always seemed a foreign place, a flat horizon with no reward at the end of it, and California the land of gold and poppies and a great bridge over the bay. To me, the Midwest was home, a parchment on which I might write stories; to leave would mean abandoning my material, letting go of my claim. "We can talk about it later. The timing isn't great, with my father's situation," I said, and now shuddered at the thought of inviting him to move in: Vritra, the god of drought and destruction, Collyer Brothers Professor of Chaos, coming to Chicago to share our eight-hundred-square-foot apartment, where we didn't have space for our own worldly goods. Our bedroom closet was so cram-jammed that I had to wrest my shirts off the rack; our storage cage, on the twentieth floor, was stacked higher than an ossuary; and most of our wedding gifts still sat in a vacant room in my in-laws' motel. *What had I got us into? How could I tell Dhara?*

The most expensive restaurant in America had no sign out front. You could walk right past the gray brick townhouse and not know this was Alchemia, the five-star, *Gourmet* number one, James Beard Award–winning toughest reservation in town. Ever the long-term planner, Dhara had called a year ago, the day after our wedding, to get us a table. She'd been looking forward to this night ever since, reading blogs, checking online forums, downloading Alchemia's changing menu of magical molecular gastronomy.

A lone doorman greeted us with a cunning smile and swiftly admitted us, as if into a Cold War hideout. Inside, we were alone in a long purgatorial hallway, lit orange and seeming to narrow to nothing but a wall. But as we neared the end of the corridor an automated door whispered open and a glimmering host and hostess appeared. "Mr. Clary. Ms. Patel," the host said, "happy anniversary," and took our coats. The hostess led us upstairs and seated us by a corner window in the white-walled, vase-and-stem-lined dining room. In the center of the table she placed two fresh sprigs of rosemary anchored and held aloft by metal cylinders. When she walked away, the scent of rosemary stirred in her wake.

Dhara asked if I wanted to go for the twelve-course tasting menu or the twenty-five-course tour. "They're small bites," she said, "like tapas for the gods." I knew this was my first test of the night, so I said the tour, of course, ignoring the price—$250—and when she asked about the wine pairing, which was an additional $250, I held my tongue. All told: a thousand dollars for both of us. "Tour with pairing," I said to our waiter, and snapped the menu closed.

A problem I had with upscale restaurants was that they made me feel like I was at church, on punishment, or a fraud. My suit felt wrinkled and secondhand. I got fidgety, like a boy, and quaffed the wine I was supposed to save for the first two courses. At the table next to us, four businessmen worried aloud about future junkets in the coming age of government oversight. They swallowed their food without pausing to admire how each piece was a mini postmodern sculpture.

Dhara and I were not the kind of couple who sat in silence across a table. Since I had her old job and we worked in the same office, with the same collection of wannabe-hipster engineers, we could have talked shop all night if we'd wanted to. But I found myself at a loss for words. And she seemed edgy as well. About California, no doubt. How I'd dismissed that conversation, kicked it down the road.

"Aren't you forgetting something?" Dhara asked.

Our waiter arrived with the first course: char roe with parsnip cream, licorice foam, and ginger. The roe, we were told, had been retrieved from the Arctic by a friend of the chef, flown in overnight, and removed from the char in the Alchemia kitchen.

Ordinarily I couldn't stand the first three ingredients, yet together the taste was miraculous, like a whole fish distilled into a single pearly bite. I realized I'd forgotten to raise a toast. "To the best year of my life," I said.

Dhara narrowed her eyes. "Are you sure about that?"

"I've never been happier." I lifted my glass higher.

Dhara's glass didn't leave the table. She tipped it in my direction. I lowered my glass to clink hers. "You look gorgeous," I said.

And she was pretty, even with a scowl dulling her diamond face. And smart and quick, and she knew what she wanted and nobody got one past her. I didn't deserve Dhara, and worried sometimes she'd wake up one morning and realize she could do better.

"It took you long enough," she said. "I've been wearing this dress for hours."

"I'm sorry. I was distracted." And I left it at that, though I was wondering again about my father, telling myself not to ruin this, of all nights, when I found the next course—tips of white asparagus, which the waiter said took two years to grow—arranged on a plate in front of me like a side street in a city diorama.

Then we were halfway into dinner, and the meal was so transcendent that thoughts of my father and the stridor of the businessmen had fallen away. Each plate was custom-made to fit the course it was serving. Atop a stand the size of a chess piece sat a tidy square of pork belly. Along a plate in the shape of a winding river, sprigs of ice fish, horseradish, and parsley seemed to move as if swept in a current. Each glass of wine had a story. *We're going to take you now to the coast of Italy, outside the village of Praiano, where the vines grow on seaside walls and harvesters descend the cliffs on ropes, suspended high over the crashing surf, to pick the grapes.*

Our waiter placed pillows in front of us and explained that they'd been filled with lavender-scented air. Atop each he rested a plate of slow-poached duck, wine-braised turnips, and mango puree. As we lifted each bite from the plate, the air slowly escaped the pillows, infusing the space around us with a soft lavender aroma. It was in the middle of this, the best course of the night, that Dhara said, out of nowhere, "Lucy called."

I hadn't heard from Lucy since graduate school. Last I knew she was still in Boston working for a big publishing house, climbing the rickety editorial ladder. She had e-mailed to say she'd begun to acquire books and I should keep her in mind when the time came to look for an editor. I knew she'd be disappointed to hear that I hadn't written a word since my MFA and was working for the company that had become the bane of all print publishers. Still, I was curious to hear what she was up to.

"Did she say what she wants?" I asked.

"She left a message on the home phone." Dhara lifted her napkin, folded it, and returned it to her lap.

"That's strange. I'm sure she's looking for someone's number. We have friends in common."

"How did she know where to reach you?"

"She probably assumed I'm still in Chicago and called directory assistance."

"So you haven't been in touch with her?"

"No."

"I thought we agreed we wouldn't keep our exes hanging around."

"*She* called *me*. I haven't spoken with her in years. She was my high-school girlfriend, Dhara."

Two waiters, one at each end of our table, nimbly removed our plates and pillows and were gone too fast to cause a timely interruption.

"There's no such thing as an innocent ex," she continued.

"I haven't a clue why she'd be calling," I said.

I had rarely seen this side of her—jealousy over someone from so long ago. Perhaps *I* had reason for insecurity, but not Dhara. I wondered if she'd had too much to drink. But her eyes were sharp as pins.

When we first met, she was still grieving her mother, who had died of ovarian cancer in her fifties, and she was furious with her father for marrying a receptionist at the motel two years after burying his wife. Dhara and I had both lost our mothers and were baffled by our fathers, and she knew that just as I'd been around for her when it mattered, Lucy had been around for me. Could that explain the outburst?

"You once told me that Lucy was the love of your life," Dhara said.

"I don't remember saying that. When?" I asked.

"Before we were dating, during the confessional stage of the mating dance."

"Well, if I ever said such a thing, I was wrong, because *you* are the love of my life. Isn't it obvious?"

"Should you have to ask?"

"Dhara, listen to me: We're in one of the finest restaurants in the world, in the city where we met. It's New Year's Day 2009, the year of *Hope*," I said. "And it's the first anniversary of our marriage, which was the best decision I ever made in my life."

"Was it your decision?"

"It was our decision."

"Do you ever wonder if it was the right decision?"

"What's gotten into you? We shouldn't be talking about a meaningless phone call. We should be talking about our wedding. Remember after the ceremony when we played that game?"

"You don't even know what it's called."

"Give me a minute." I hesitated. The name wasn't coming to me.

"*Aeki-Baki*," she said.

We'd limited the number of rituals and games at the wedding, but this one got a great laugh and had become a running joke with her family. One of the bridesmaids mixed a pot of water with milk and vermilion and threw a ring and some coins into the cloudy broth. Dhara and I were told that the first of us to fish out the ring four times would be the dominant one, ruler of the roost. While I kept coming up empty or with a useless coin, Dhara plucked out the ring four times in a row.

"You're the empress and I'm the serf," I said. "So why are you acting like this?"

But she'd lapsed into silence. She slid a palate cleanser onto her tongue. I sipped my wine, and my ears filled with the sound of the businessmen ordering single-estate cognac. More courses came by and we finished them without a word, and since the spell had been broken, the evening lost—all of this, I was quick to assure myself, through no fault of my own—I said, "My father's moving in with us."

She sat back in her chair.

"It's only temporary. I need more time to get him situated. A month. Maybe two."

She plunked down her glass of dry salted caramel, a space-age confection that expanded and softened in the mouth.

"We can't afford a nursing home," I continued. "But these last few days have made me realize he needs a nurse, or at least someone to make sure he's taking his Coumadin."

"*We* can't afford one of those homes?" Dhara's bottom lip was quivering. "You want to move him into *my* apartment?"

"Yes, *we*. We're married. Not *your* apartment. *Ours*."

I went on, trying to make my case. I said he was the only family I had and she of all people should understand that no matter what a thorn in the side he'd been, he was my father, and I couldn't allow him to waste away because that's what he'd do if I put him in some transient apartment in Normal. When I'd asked if he'd been to the doctor lately he'd laughed and said he was trying natural remedies, as in *Let nature take its course.* "And no, Dhara, I'm not overdramatizing when I tell you he's never looked worse. Having a father is not like having a cat; they don't just wander off when they get old, crawl under some neighbor's porch, and exhale their last breath. Abandoning him now is something I refuse to live with."

Dhara stopped me right there. "If your father moves in, I refuse to live with you."

"Be reasonable." I reached for the bill.

"It's him or me," she said. "Your choice."

4

George never did go back to work that Friday. Lazar's request that he return soon because "I've been meaning to tell you something" faded into a quiet corner of his mind. At the jewelry counter he wasted little time choosing a one-and-a-half-carat Marquise ring with a brilliant diamond in the middle and sparkling clusters at the edges. He paid five hundred dollars, a third of his annual salary, and exhausted most of his savings account. But no sooner had he bought the ring and called a coachman to take him and his precious cargo home in the safety of a covered landau than he began to worry that the ring was not impressive enough for the likes of Margaret Lazar.

At the boardinghouse he climbed the narrow staircase and sat at his desk. He took the ring from its velvet box and held it to the single gaslight that illuminated his Spartan quarters. The saleswoman had urged him to consider a larger diamond, of superior color and clarity, but given his uncertain future at work in the regime of *Prove They Need It,* he could not afford to go into debt. Though the ring might not have been the most expensive in the case, here, in George's room, it glittered like an animate eye looking back at him. As the light ricocheted from facet to facet he told himself that of course the ring was good enough. How could Margaret expect anything more from one of her father's employees, a salary-earner without name or fortune?

At the birthday party he had wanted to ask what she saw in him, but he was thrown by her confession, and such a question would have been foolish, anyway. She grew up with money; he grew up with none. No sense drawing attention to the fact. He would ask her to marry him, and she would say yes. He was good enough for her, good enough for anyone. But after he climbed into bed and pulled the layers of wool blankets up to his eyes, trying to warm his bones in these shoddy quarters that put up only the frailest resistance to the Chicago winter, he was beset with further doubts.

Through the thin walls a man and a woman—a streetcar conductor and his pregnant wife—were having an argument. They had gone at it before, and weren't the only quarrelers at Ma Kavanagh's. George had long ago learned to tune out his neighbors' voices when he'd come home from work still adrift in the cartoon world of Tidy Town. And Ma, who lived in a top-floor apartment with her unmarried daughter, only rarely thumped her broom handle on the planks or yelled into the stairwell: *Keep it down!* Everyone turned a deaf ear to fights on the property, even to the sounds of men striking their wives, of plates crashing to the floor, and of the metronomic creaking of bedsprings that so often followed, like defective apologies.

I told you we're not leaving early, the streetcar conductor said. *I put in for the weekend shift, and we can't afford to give up the wages. Your mother will have to wait until Christmas Eve.*

But we promised a longer visit this time, his wife said. *You never let me go back to Belle Plaine.*

If you had a job we wouldn't be in this spot. But you're too good for factory work. Like some kind of princess.

Some princess I am in this tenement, living with a man like you. Twenty-nine and already a curmudgeon.

You'd be one too if you worked my hours and put up with a thousand stinking straphangers after you with the push. But no, you sit by that window all day flipping through the Ward catalogue, decorating your mansion in the clouds.

At least I have a few dreams left, she said. *When we met I thought you had ambition, but you're all talk.*

I'd find something better if I didn't have to work morning and night. And now look what you've done: an ankle-biter on the way. Just what we need!

What I've done?

That's right, he said. *I took every care.*

You took what you wanted and always have. You're no better than a barnyard animal.

Something shattered. A picture frame? And a great scrambling could be heard, followed by the thud of an upended chair.

I never should have married you! she screamed. *You're the mistake of my life!*

A door slammed. Heavy footsteps resounded in the hallway, then the falling scales of the conductor hustling down the stairs and out into the bitter night.

George lay awake wondering over the future of the child curled inside his neighbor's belly. He would grow up in a boardinghouse so hastily constructed for the World's Fair that cracks veined the walls and splinters widened dangerously in the sagging floorboards. The building should be condemned, George thought on freezing nights like this, and wondered anew why he continued to live in such a place, this scruffy urban cousin of the New Willard House. The streetcar conductor and his wife might well have been George's own parents, squabbling over the vacancies and paths untaken. He clutched the velvet box beneath his pillow. Marriage. Was this what he had to look forward to?

Three days later he took his seat at Christmas dinner with Ma Kavanagh, her skittish, snaggletoothed daughter, and seven other boarders at the Cass Street table. He had spent the weekend pacing his room and gazing out the window toward Michigan and Superior, wanting to venture into the city but leery of the cold and the thieves lying in wait to relieve him of the contents of his pockets. The Alfred J. Lazar agency was closed for the holiday, and George pushed away the thought of how he would be received upon his return to work. He had fled, and Lazar had not bothered to send over a note or call after him. Perhaps he was as good as finished at the agency, and no amount of pleading, even a proposal of marriage to Lazar's daughter, would save his job.

He cast his eyes around the table at the other boarders, only half of whom he knew by name. There was Tiptoe Joe, whose heels never touched the ground on his daily walk to and from the West Side bicycle factory where he worked as an assembler. Across from him stooped Ostrinski, a bouncer at a LaSalle Street resort who stood at least six and a half feet tall but wore the abashed, tentative look of someone hoping not to be noticed. Next to him, adjusting his peacock-blue cravat, sat the dandy of the building, the ancient widower Harry Quincel, who seemed unaware of his stained clothes and spent most of his days sitting on a bench outside the tobacconist's tipping his hat to pretty girls. And setting out dinner at the head of the table was Nellie Kavanagh, who looked a good deal older than her thirty years, due in part to her work as chambermaid, cook, and caretaker of her mother's boardinghouse.

George imagined himself out of a job and back at street level, where he'd lived his whole life before coming to Chicago. The candles and gaslight cast a lambent glow about the room. A fire crackled in the hearth. Ma Kavanagh took her place and raised a Christmas toast. Cream-of-oyster soup made its way around, then Nellie selected George to carve the goose. Her fingers trembled as she passed him the knife and wiped her hands on her aproned hips. When he had finished carving she gave him a quick smile, the candle-light flickering in her eyes. He had never noticed her regard before, and wondered if she had seen the ring while cleaning his room and was drawn to the sparkle of the diamond, the romance of an imminent proposal. Then he realized, of course, that he hadn't let the velvet box out of his sight, had barely ventured out of his apartment in days. He touched the pocket of his dinner jacket, felt the jut of the box, and smiled back at Nellie before taking his seat.

George felt an upsurge of kinship for his fellow diners. He only knew them coming and going, but their presence here, the warmth of the room and the headiness of the spiced wine, made him nostalgic for something he couldn't quite name. He'd always been the person anyone could come to, the reporter, the writer in the making, and it occurred to him as he passed the browned sweet potatoes to Nellie, who sat on one side of him, and the creamed onions to a doleful-eyed man who sat on the other, that before long a decade would have gone by since his train pulled out of Winesburg. Yet this ragtag group of strangers felt more familiar to him, more like the people he knew growing up, than any of the cliff-dwellers he saw and bantered with every day.

He tried to dismiss the thought as the sentimental longings of one far from home, and pictured his father cutting into a turkey or saddle of venison at precisely the moment George had been carving this Christmas dinner, 280 miles between them. Last time he went home for Christmas, three or four years ago, his father had purchased more than enough food to satisfy a teeming dining room, but the only guests to show up that night were a small convergence of melancholy bachelors from town, a starry-eyed young couple on a long haul to California, and a family from Monroeville whose matriarch had recently passed away and couldn't bring themselves to do the holiday board. Most depressing to George was the sight of his father the next morning examining the larder full of food that would soon spoil, and the way he announced, with false cheer, "How's that for a king's ransom?"

These are my people, George thought for a fleeting moment. Though he knew he could not return to Winesburg, even if Helen White herself were to summon him back, he felt more at home than he had in years. The ring in his pocket was like a weight in his heart, and he decided he must return the diamond to Marshall Field's as soon as the store reopened after the holiday. He had been foolish and impetuous. He was not in love with Margaret Lazar. He was merely afraid.

But before long the room fell into silence. Silverware scraped on plates; the fire hissed and the mantel clock kept time. There were chewing sounds and gulping, an almost desperate hunger to the way people ate and drank. The dandy widower Harry Quincel picked the apples out of his Waldorf salad one by one, licking the pieces, then crunching into them with little moans of satisfaction. No one, apparently, had a word to contribute by way of conversation, so Ma Kavanagh said, "Let's get to know each other," and began asking questions. People went around the room saying where they were from; not surprisingly, everyone had arrived from the Midlands or overseas.

Nellie leaned toward George and whispered, "My mother has no shame. You see, the man sitting next to you is a great mystery, and this whole charade is meant to unmask him." She said she was surprised the doleful-eyed man had come to dinner, when no one so much as knew his name, and though better rooms had been available, he had requested the one farthest back on the top floor. He shut himself in there for the entire day and toward dinner could be seen furtively leaving the property carrying what looked like a cashbox under his arm. After being gone all night, he would slip in the front door around breakfast time. He voluntarily paid extra rent—for the inconvenience of his odd hours, he said. "My mother thinks he has something to hide and is trying to buy her silence."

After everyone answered where they were from, Ma Kavanagh circulated a new question—"And what work do you do?" It came around to Nellie, and she said, with an effort at humor that had the edge of a sneer, "I'm mother's little helper." Then it was the doleful-eyed man's turn, and he said simply, "I work in a Turkish bath. I'm the resident chiropodist."

"Come again?" pressed Ma Kavanagh.

"He removes plantar warts," Tiptoe Joe put in.

"Mostly corns and bunions," the chiropodist clarified.

Ma Kavanagh seemed flustered at having her conspiracy demystified in front of her daughter, and perhaps to hide her embarrassment she didn't prompt George about his job, but rather answered for him. "Young Mr. Willard is a very successful man," she said. "Top brass at one of our city's finest advertising agencies. Makes a pretty penny, he does, yet he lives right here in a little room with a sink and table. I keep telling him: Get out of this place, buy a house, find a nice girl. You're better than the lot of us. He doesn't listen, just goes about his business. But really," she asked, "why do you stay? What's keeping you here?"

George looked around the room at the faces—suspicious, wary, confused—all turned in his direction, and froze where he sat, reaching inward for some kind of answer.

By New Year's Eve, George was determined to begin 1905 in dramatic fashion. He had not come up with an adequate answer for why he was still living in a tumbledown boardinghouse, and Ma Kavanagh's challenge had compelled him to make a change. He told her that he would soon have an announcement and she might as well begin to look for his replacement. He did not return the engagement ring on the day after Christmas. Instead, he went into the office intent on recommitting himself and patching up any misunderstandings with his boss. But Lazar was apparently gone for the week, so George spent his workdays looking out his window at the clotted streets, taking the ring from its box and tumbling it around his fingers, and trying to read the expressions of his fellow employees. Did they know something about his future that he did not?

Late that week he steeled himself and dropped into the office of his rival, who was always eating breakfast at his desk as George came in to work and dinner at his desk as George was leaving.

"Why, if it isn't the runaway come home!" Kennison exclaimed. "Where have you been, sport? Mr. Lazar was looking for you."

George could hear the false ring in his voice as he said, "I had an appointment."

"You didn't send word. We waited for you past eight on a Friday, and now Mr. Lazar is in New York taking meetings."

George had heard nothing about that trip. Had he fallen so far that no one bothered to update him anymore? He made a pretense of knowing, anyway. "Yes, right," he said. "When is he coming back, again?"

"Middle of next week." Kennison twitched his mustache and leaned back in his chair. Facing outward under his table lamp sat a picture of his younger self, in profile atop a horse, in full Mountie uniform.

"And remind me: what is he doing in New York?" George asked.

Kennison seemed to enjoy offering only the smallest crumbs of information. He took a long drink of water and tapped his tobacco-stained fingers on the desk. "Among other matters, he's discussing the Nuvolia contract."

"But we only recently drew up a new arrangement with them," George said.

"There have been developments. I probably shouldn't be the one to fill you in."

"At least tell me what you know."

"I should let Mr. Lazar handle that. It's really not my place."

George was furious with Kennison, but he left the older man's office with a tip of the hat. Within an hour he had sent a messenger to deliver a note to Margaret Lazar expressing his interest in seeing her on the day after New Year's. She replied the next morning, and they agreed to meet in the Demidoff Collection at the Art Institute, where George had decided to ask for her hand surrounded by paintings of the Dutch Masters.

The Demidoff had been his sanctuary soon after he'd arrived in Chicago. Those days had been so bewildering; he could hardly believe he'd come this far. How many times had he nearly been shouldered into the street as he wandered over the worm-eaten sidewalks from one hopeless newspaper interview to the next? Ma Kavanagh's looked like the Palmer House compared to the coal-blackened hotel at the thundering heart of the rail web where he spent his first weeks in the city. He remembered climbing the crumbling steps, pulling the loose doorknob to let himself in, how the clerk had burst out laughing when George had asked for a view of the lake. The view, in fact, was of a filthy alley. The windows opened over the hotel's garbage box, and his room was dark and cramped, with damp, yellowed linens. The whole building felt damp and greasy, and he cursed his father, who had recommended the place. But what did Tom Willard know of Chicago? He had barely left Winesburg his entire life.

George had happened upon the Demidoff Collection by chance. In much the same way that he later collided with the Lazars' Duryea, George had been wandering abstractedly along Michigan Avenue one day when he saw a crowd of students, palettes under their arms, headed up the lion-flanked steps of the great Beaux-Arts building. He followed them in and up the marble staircase to the Dutch Masters' room, where he sat on a bench eavesdropping on the art teacher's lecture about Rembrandt, Jan Steen, Pieter van Slingelandt, and Hans Holbein the Younger. There were landscapes and historical paintings and pictures of rustic and social life, maritime and rural settings, secular and religious subjects, scenes that took place in bawdy taverns and in the drawing rooms of the aristocracy. George used to come here every few days for a respite from the hurly-burly. The democracy of the collection appealed to him, the way it showed the full panoply of Dutch life, and he was especially drawn to the portraits of the common people, the ragged, scarred, and overlooked: Rembrandt's *The Child of the State,* Slingelandt's *The Hermit,* Holbein's *Portrait of an Ecclesiastic.*

He planned to make his proposal in front of Jan Steen's *The Family Concert,* which showed the painter strumming a lute while his wife sings along and the rest of the family gathers around, talking and playing instruments. It's a portrait of domestic leisure and marital harmony, the only tension an amusing standoff in the foreground between the family cat, who is enjoying the lion's share of table scraps, and the family dog, who is looking on in abject frustration.

But on the appointed day when George met Margaret at the front entrance of the Art Institute and was leading her toward the staircase, something caught her eye. She grabbed his hand and took him to Galleries 25–30, on the first floor, where a new exhibition—*Portraits of Influence: Chicago and the World*—was on display. The opening reception had happened the month before, and though she hadn't been able to attend, many of her friends had gone. It was the talk of the town, she said, and added: "I have a surprise for you."

"But wait." George hesitated. "I have a surprise for you."

"Ladies first," she said.

Margaret was a curious blend of youth and sophistication, tremulousness and confidence, and though she spoke with sympathy about the working classes she could not disguise her pedigree. She was young-looking, with soft ginger curls playing about the pale, translucent skin at her temples. In her Nile-green tea dress and long white gloves she rushed through Gallery 25, scanning each painting before moving on to Gallery 26. "There's Nettie McCormick." She pointed to one of the portraits, of a silver-haired woman in a red velvet toque with teal feathers. "She's looking awfully stern."

"You know her?" George asked.

"She's been to the house many times. She's actually a lovely woman, one of the city's great philanthropists. Her late husband, Cyrus, invented the grain harvester. As you might imagine, she's richer than Croesus."

"And look," she continued. "It's Valerie Root! I recollect the very day she sat for that portrait. We were in school together, and she broadcast the news unabashedly. A bit of a spoiled girl. Her father was the architect John Wellborn Root."

"I know that name," George said.

"Of course you do. He designed the Monadnock Building. You work every day in one of his masterpieces." George was six years older than Margaret, but she had a way of making him feel as if their ages were reversed. She went on, "Father says that John Wellborn Root would have been the finest architect of his generation had he not died young. Valerie has some talent, too. She's quite good on the piano. Just the other day she sent us a wedding announcement. She'll be marrying a Mr. Edgar Fletcher of Winnetka. I can't tell you how many of my schoolmates are getting married this summer."

"It appears you're at that age," George said. "I've been thinking a lot about marriage myself—"

"And over there is Marshall Field." Margaret glided across the threshold to the next gallery and stood before the portrait of a nattily dressed but dyspeptic-looking man who held his cane and hat in a way that suggested he was eager to get to his next appointment. "Have you met the great man?" Margaret asked.

"I've shopped in his store." George had removed the ring from the box this morning and nested it in an inside pocket. He touched his coat to confirm that the ring was safe.

Margaret held up her hand to whisper, "He's rather intolerable. And if the rumors are true, his first wife was a drug addict and died in France under mysterious circumstances. He had a longtime affair with his best friend's wife. And his son, Marshall Field Jr., is a well-known habitué of the famous Everleigh Club."

"The bordello?"

"Yes. I hear it's very posh. Have you been?"

George reddened and shook his head. "Certainly not!"

"I've embarrassed you," she said with delight, then whirled around the room browsing the other portraits.

George was about to cross into the last gallery of the exhibition when Margaret extended her arm to stop him. "Not another step," she said. "Now put your hands over your eyes. No peeking! The surprise is in this room."

George did as he was told. Margaret's behavior gave him pause, and reminded him acutely of their different origins. How could she consent to marry the son of a small-town innkeeper? And even if for some curious reason she did say yes, he had to wonder why he would want to spend the rest of his life feeling like a hanger-on. His every accomplishment from this day forward would be attributed to his marrying well. He could choose not to work another day in his life or, like the Canadian Mountie, spend all his waking hours at the office, and the perception would be the same. He felt as if the eyes of the elite were following him from room to room, impressing upon him that he had no business consorting with the only and eligible daughter of Alfred J. Lazar.

George had a passing wish to be back among ordinary people, the hermit and the child of the state, the bouncer and the night-shift chiropodist, the lonely souls he remembered from home: Wing Biddlebaum, who never left his porch but had the most expressive hands; the dissipated Doctor Parcival, who had few patients and once told George that "Everyone in the world is Christ and they are all crucified." He thought of Helen White, daughter of the richest man in Winesburg, but who never gave him the sense that she dwelled in some Pantheon; the sphere of influence in that town reached no farther than Banker White's lawn.

His eyes still closed, George felt a hand take him by the elbow, an arm entwine with his, and he imagined it was Helen, leading him blindly toward some new and astonishing place. The eyes of the elite no longer scrutinized him; he stepped into the darkness, heard footfalls call and respond across the floor, and he believed for the first time something he had always doubted: that his restlessness was curable, and he could achieve the greatest freedom, not alone, but in the company of another soul.

He stopped when he heard the words, "Now you can open your eyes," but instead of looking up at the two portraits Margaret had been wanting to show him, he reached into his pocket and brought out the ring. Without a pause or catch in his voice he said, "Will you marry me?"

"George!" she exclaimed, then glanced about, as if to be sure they were alone.

Her self-consciousness only emboldened him. "Remember what you

told me in your parents' library, how you might be in love with me? Well—"
He advanced the ring toward her, and heard himself say, "I have no doubt
that I'm in love with you."

She looked away, and he followed her eyes to the wall where, presiding
over the occasion, in frozen judgment, were the portraits of Alfred Lazar
and his wife, Harriet.

"So that's what you wanted to show me?" George asked.

"I guess your surprise trumps mine," she said.

"Well, Margaret? Will you have me?" He knew he couldn't keep this up
much longer, this show of authority and confidence. He remembered how as
a boy he used to test his balance by walking on the railroad tracks that ran
alongside the New Willard House. This moment gave him the same feeling,
as if he might lose his footing, or a train might barrel out of nowhere and
lay him flat.

Margaret fixed her gaze on the portraits of her parents—one blasé, the
other imperious. With her gloved hand she brushed curls away from her
forehead. "Have you talked to my father about this?"

"What do you mean?"

"Have you asked for my hand?"

"Was that the expectation?" George was teetering. He knew little of the
social codes of Margaret's class.

"So you haven't made an official request?"

"No," he exhaled, figuring all was lost.

"Why don't you talk to him now? He's right here." She pointed to the
portrait. "Go on."

And so George did. He asked the oil painting of Alfred J. Lazar for his
daughter's hand in marriage. When he had finished speaking, Margaret said,
"There, see, he approves, just as I suspected." Then she smiled and pulled off
her long white gloves. She put out her left hand, and as if by reflex George
slipped the diamond ring onto her finger.

5

Everyone wanted to work for Imego. At the main campus in Silicon Valley, where Dhara and I went on business three times a year, employees had all the perks they could imagine: cafeterias serving gourmet meals; snack rooms stocked with fresh fruit, candy, protein drinks, and cappuccino; gyms; a swimming spa; decompression capsules; on-site masseuses and physicians; day care; language classes; laundry; dry cleaner; a twenty-four-hour concierge. Workers dressed purposefully casual and the techiest engineers got loose in Chuck Taylors and Battlestar Galactica T-shirts, and, though the sun rarely kissed their skin, cargo shorts. Imego knew that to keep the children happy work had to feel like fun, so we had fire poles and slides connecting floor to floor, foosball, pool and ping-pong tables, video games and lava lamps in primary colors, and along each wall, whiteboards where the inspired and punchy alike jotted down formulae, graphs, and assorted nonsense like the quote I could see from my office desk that day: *Spandex: It's a privilege, not a right.*

Dhara loved Imego and couldn't understand why I called it The Cruise That Never Ends. On the nights when she came home at 1:00 a.m. and I was in bed struggling to keep my eyes on a novel I'd been trying to read for a month, I asked her how many hours she'd worked that day, that week. I could understand what kept the engineers haunting the hallways at three in the morning, talking embrangled algorithms. But I worried that Dhara racked up hours just to be noticed or because she preferred to be at work rather than anywhere else. When she got hired out of Ohio State's business school she bought the apartment where we lived now, not because Harbor City was an architectural landmark or in the heart of downtown, but because all she had to do was take the elevator to the lobby, walk a single block up State Street, turn left, and there she was, at the glass gates to the mother ship.

I asked Dhara once if she wished she'd been around at Imego's initial public offering, when twenty-five-year-olds woke up instant millionaires, and she said no, if she'd gotten that rich she might have cashed out early and started her own business, but it would have been a mistake to leave such a company. *It's like family,* she'd said, then asked me, *What would* you *do with all that money?* And though I was pretty sure I would get a good robe and slippers and dust off *A Brief History of the Fool,* or begin writing a *real* novel, I said *I'd quit and figure things out from there.*

What a pretty dream, I was thinking now, in our first week back to work after the New Year. If only I had that cash on hand I wouldn't have worried about taking on another twelve hundred dollars a month. Dhara's ultimatum left me no choice but to rent my father the apartment on the thirtieth floor of the east tower, across from our place. From our frozen balcony I could look down on his room. *You wanted to keep an eye on him,* Dhara said. *Now you have your wish.* With a pair of binoculars and a lot of time on my hands I could have played Jimmy Stewart in *Rear Window.*

Tomorrow was the big move-in day, so I was distracted and restless at work. I'd been on the phone all morning with the rental office and the movers and my father, who would be driving the Mercury here—or at least that was the plan. I had tried to talk him into selling the car, but he said *What's next? My body for science?* I wouldn't have put it past him to get to the signs for I-55 and decide to head south toward St. Louis, then down along the great river, to Cape Girardeau, Memphis, through Mississippi, all the way to New Orleans, where someone would find him on a park bench in Jackson Square.

I would have gone to Normal and driven him myself, but I was off the road that week because we were having a videoconference with the poobahs at corporate HQ, and we'd all been asked to stick around. Dhara knew I had little desire to rise in the company. I was happier traveling the flatlands and daydreaming than I was pasting on a smile at work, where the hipness was purchased and I was forever reminded that I was an old-economy, creative-writing flake who couldn't tell his OS from his El Torito. And everyone knew that I wouldn't have been hired were it not for my popular wife, who moved with ease between the techies and the sales force, exerting all the charm of an innkeeper's daughter.

Dhara was good enough to swing by my desk to say the meeting had been moved to the cafeteria. Since her promotion, she and I worked on opposite ends of the floor; I was the lone generalist thrown among software designers who were fine-tuning the mobile-book-search project; Dhara headed up the sales team, who unlike the vainglorious engineers at least saw Imego for what it was—the world's wealthiest advertising company. As much as the techies liked to think they were driving the future, they forgot that the purpose of their eighty-hour weeks, the end result of all their striving, was to bait as many people as possible to click on those little ads.

I was following Dhara toward the stairs when we ran into engineering manager Eddie Hartley. A trust-fund kid from Rhode Island whose full name was Edward Billington Hartley III, he wore the uniform of the working class: Carhartt boots and a Stag Beer cap—*It's smooth. . . . It's dry*—pulled tight over his unruly curls. He was cheery and coltish and an unabashed flirt. *He's part boy, part wolf,* I told Dhara once. *Jealous?* she'd said, the color rising in her cheeks.

"Lord Byron," he greeted me. He had nicknames for everyone in the office. "Did you catch my quote of the day?"

"Was it something about Spandex?" I indulged him.

"That's right." He grinned at Dhara.

They had a laugh about the movie *Hackers,* traded some choice lines, while I tuned out. Eddie took the fire pole down to the cafeteria, Dhara trailed him, and though I was loath not to use the stairs because this was a job, not kindergarten, I slid down, too.

"Look at Lord Byron work the pole," Eddie applauded.

Phony S.O.B., I wanted to say.

I followed them to a table to settle in for the meeting.

Onto the video screen came the company's CFO, a more impish Mister Rogers and one of the few Imegoers who wore a tie. "Hello, Chicago," he began and got right to the point.

I'd spent all weekend trying to convince Dhara that with the markets in a tailspin I shouldn't sign a yearlong lease when my father could stay in our apartment for free. But she stuck to her warning—*It's him or me*—and said Imego stock was well above three hundred dollars a share. *Half what it used to be,* I reminded her. But now it seemed I had reason to worry, as the CFO was telling us that in light of current circumstances the company would be cutting back on perks. A few months before, the Tuesday tea and Wednesday chair massages had abruptly disappeared, and complaints had been heard around the microkitchens that inventory wasn't what it used to be.

The CFO trotted out an array of mixed metaphors. *We're headed up a rocky road, but we're going to wade through it. Even the leader of the pack has to tighten his belt once in a while.* But after the screen went blank, one line stuck with me and with everyone else in the room: *We need to be more efficient, and in this time of fewer resources we're going to have to feed the winners and starve the losers.*

We all looked around wondering which of us fell into which category.

"I'm hitting the trough," Eddie said. "This winner's gotta eat. Anybody with me?"

Dhara got up, but I stayed where I was. Somewhere along the way I'd lost my appetite.

On moving day I kept sneaking out of the office for fifteen minutes at a time to monitor the progress at my father's apartment. Imegoers whispered that cutbacks could be around the corner, so I wasn't about to make myself scarce when Big Brother might have been watching. Word around the ping-pong table was that recruiters would be the first to go because of the hiring slowdown. Engineers assigned to newer projects would migrate to more established ones. The software designers in my bullpen convinced each other their work was secure; too much money and too much hype had gone into Imego Books already. I had enough to worry about, so I assumed my job was safe.

During one of my quick escapes I checked the voice mail at home to retrieve Lucy's number. Dhara hadn't got rid of it, but I wondered if she wanted me to delete or save the message. If I erased it she'd assume I'd called and was back in touch, but if I left it the reminder would always be there. I decided to press delete and hope the subject would just go away. Lucy's voice hadn't changed, still high-pitched and a little quavering, girlish for someone now past thirty. "I'm trying to reach Adam Clary. I hope I've got the right number," she said. "It's Lucy. Lucy Youngblood. If you get this message it would be great if you'd call me back." She left her number—617, still a Boston area code—then hung up.

I took a breath and dialed, but the call went to voice mail after a few rings. *I'm away from the phone right now,* she said. *I,* not *we.* I couldn't imagine she was still single, bright and attractive as she was, but I remembered the last time we spoke she complained that it was tough out there for a Harvard girl. Though she grew up, like me, in gosh-golly Indianapolis, and would have seemed right at home at a bake sale, she'd said that mentioning her job or where she went to school had a chilling effect on conversation. She regretted not dating in college, because at least back then she lived in the same building, shared meals and classes with other singles who didn't find the word *Harvard* intimidating. I knew in part why she'd told me this: We went out through her junior year; she'd fly back and spend weekends in my dorm room in Bloomington, and I made a couple of trips to Boston as well. She burned the days with me, in other words, when she could have found someone else.

Now I wondered why she was calling me. We hadn't spoken in five years. Was she married? Engaged? I doubted she had any idea about Dhara beyond the *we* and *us* on our voice mail. I decided to leave a message. "This is Adam," I said. "Haven't heard from *you* in a long time." I gave her my cell-phone number so she wouldn't try me again at home, then hung up assuring myself I'd done nothing wrong.

By the end of the day, my father's furniture was in place; I'd paid and tipped the movers and was lining his shelves with books. He directed me from the couch with a green umbrella printed with the logo of the bank that seized his house. "Don't bother with alphabetical. I've got my own system," he said. "Handle with care, Mr. Internet. Some of those books are more valuable than you know."

When he first accepted my offer he seemed melancholy and fatalistic, but arriving at Harbor City seemed to have got his vinegar up.

"Why won't this couch go flat against the wall?" he complained.

"It's not the couch." I blew dust from the spine of an ancient copy of Edgar Lee Masters's *Spoon River Anthology* and explained that the walls were curved because the building was round; the elevator shaft ran up through the core, and the apartments fanned out from there, like petals from a stem.

"Well, it's an absurd design. Completely impractical." He tapped the umbrella on the parquet floor. "Who wants to live in a round building?"

To impress Dhara once, I read up on Harbor City, so I knew that the architect didn't like square apartments because *In nature there are no right angles.* "He thought cylindrical high-rises were more efficient."

"A lot of good that did the Tower of Pisa." My father looked around, no doubt for further flaws. "And the balcony—it's a suicide trap. I guess you weren't thinking of Wing when you signed me up for this aerie."

The orange tabby, Wing Biddlebaum, crouched in an empty box.

"He'll be fine," I said.

"Does he look fine?"

The cat's ears were clamped to his head, and when I met his eyes he gave a long, plaintive meow.

"He has acrophobia," my father said.

"Cats aren't afraid of heights."

"Tell that to your local fire department. Never heard of a cat stuck in a tree?"

"I'm sure he'll be fine."

"You should have seen him walk up to those sliding doors. That's a three-hundred-foot drop. Wing got vertigo in his tracks."

"Most people *want* the balcony," I said. "This whole design—the way the apartments open up—it's supposed to feel like a movie theater. When you walk onto those great balconies it's like stepping into the picture. There you are, above it all, the whole city at your feet."

My father thrust his umbrella toward the ice-encased balusters. "You want to go out there? Be my guest."

"Wait till spring and summer," I said. "You'll thank me then, I promise."

The idea of my father expressing anything like gratitude was my own private running joke. Forget that I'd bailed him out, moved him here, and become his de facto guardian. He wouldn't have thanked me if I raised Sherwood Anderson from the dead, set him up in the apartment next door, and made him collaborate on volume two of the great biography that never was.

That first week I went to my father's place at every opportunity, made him an appointment with a Chicago cardiologist, brought him healthy dinners from Whole Foods that he called too bland, too spicy, meager, *crapulent*. Over the first couple weekends I helped him unpack but felt as though we were making little progress. I wondered if he was putting his books and papers back into boxes, little by little. He complained all the time that he couldn't find this letter or that first edition, and I told him if he'd only finish moving in he might see where everything was. *I can see it now*, he said. *It's riding in the back of a truck headed to the McLean County landfill.*

I wasn't sure whether he resented me for my intervention or if he had been calling for it all along. How could a mortgage lender take him in so thoroughly when he'd spent the first seven decades of his life inveighing against the credit system? I wondered if he stopped making payments because he was out of money or for some other confounding reason. When he lived in the walk-up by the Normal depot he had a landlord around to make sure he paid rent. But I couldn't imagine even my father allowing his bills to gather on his desk and then slide to the floor unopened. And why didn't he call my brothers or me when the bank came after him? I could have said it was stubborn pride—it wouldn't be the first time—but he followed the news, and knew what would happen if he didn't send those checks. Bob Jagoda had given him every opportunity, yet he hadn't gone through with renegotiating his mortgage. Perhaps a part of him had wanted all this to go down. Maybe he hoarded discarded objects and filled his walls with random old portraits to create the illusion of company, of life. And clattering around in that house, the shut-in from whom young neighbors kept their distance—*Don't play in* his *yard*—only increased his isolation. Was the foreclosure sign a distress signal, a flag of surrender? I wondered if I'd ever know.

It was in the middle of one of these unpacking sessions that Lucy called my cell phone.

My father was going through old papers, his desk already a sloping heap.

Lucy sounded out of breath. "I'm sorry I didn't call you back right away. I'm in the process of moving."

"Me, too, as it happens," I said. "My dad just moved to Chicago. I'm in his apartment right now." Across the room he lowered his glasses and peered over the rims at me. Though I was only in a long-sleeve T-shirt, I slid open the balcony door and stepped outside so he wouldn't overhear. The wind whipped across my face and whistled into the phone. I tucked my free hand under my arm and huddled in the corner to try to stay warm. I was thirty stories up in the Windy City on an overcast, ten-degree afternoon.

"That's a coincidence," Lucy continued, "because guess where I am?"

"You must still be in Boston."

"Last week, yes. This week, no. I'm in Chicago. I just settled into an apartment in Lincoln Park. I was calling to see if you'd lend your brawn, but I realized it was too much to ask, so I got some pros."

"So you're here. Right now. How about that?" I paced the balcony.

"I got a job at the University of Chicago Press," she said.

"Great. That's amazing." I could hear the ambivalence in my voice, clear as my own breath forming a cloud and disappearing. I peered over the railing at the gray mosaic of the frozen Chicago River, and felt vertiginous—at the thought of my father looking down from this balcony, of Lucy less than a mile away. "So tell me about the job."

"Long story. You really want to hear it?"

"Sure." I glanced across the way, at the west tower, and tried to find Dhara's and my apartment. I spotted our patio chairs and the red Weber grill that she bought for my thirtieth birthday but I rarely used. At first I couldn't see her, but then a shadow moved across the glass and I worried she'd look over here and catch me talking on the phone in the freezing cold. How odd, she'd think, and would interrogate me when I got home.

"Adam?" Lucy asked. "You sound like you're in a tunnel. What kind of apartment is your father living in?"

"I had to step outside. We've got a couple more things to move here, then we'll be done. I wonder if I can call you back. Or—you know what might be better: we could meet, get a coffee or something."

"Sure," Lucy said. "Name the place. This is your city."

I suggested the Art Institute, at the end of the week. We agreed on two o'clock at the entrance to European Painting and Sculpture, my favorite collection.

"Good luck with the move," she said.

"Same to you."

Back in my father's apartment I rubbed my arms to get warm.

"What were you doing out there?" he asked.

"Had to take a phone call."

"You don't want me in your business?"

"You were working. I thought I'd give you some privacy."

"Who was it?" he asked.

It wasn't like him to show any interest in my life. He'd had to drag himself to my wedding, might not have gone without pressure from my brothers. "Someone from the job." I put my hands over the heating vent.

"Someone from the job, eh?" He gave me an annoyingly conspiratorial look, which I ignored.

"I could use a cup of tea," I said. "Want me to get you something?"

"Diet Rite, two rocks, and a splash of Malibu."

"That's not exactly what the doctor ordered."

"A drink or two won't kill me."

"It's three in the afternoon, Dad. You might at least wait a couple hours."

"Are you with the Temperance Union?" he said. "Well, my order has a different motto: 'He who does not love wine, wife, and song will be a fool his whole life long.'"

He had wine and song covered, but a little trouble loving his wives—or at least one at a time. I put the water on to boil and fixed the rum and cola. Wing jumped onto the desk, stepped gingerly over the drift of papers, then curled up in my father's lap.

"I think you're going to like it here," I said. "When the complex went up in the sixties, it was advertised as a city within a city, to lure suburbanites back to the Loop. This one block has anything you'd want: grocery, dry cleaner, four restaurants. Even the laundry room, on twenty, has 360-degree views. There's a fitness center, a bowling alley, a hotel, and I'm sure you'll be a regular at the Boombox."

"I've already complained to management," my father put in.

The Boombox was a club/music venue and a magnet for testosterone-addled drunks that occupied a small stand-alone rectangular building. Before and after concerts we heard rebel yells, wolf whistles, fights breaking out, women screaming *Get away,* the pop of sirens, and warnings over bullhorns caroming between the towers and rising into the atmosphere.

The kettle whistled, and I poured hot water into a cup. "We're not far from the Newberry. It's a quick ride up Dearborn on the 22 bus," I said. The Newberry Library, home of the Sherwood Anderson Papers, including books, manuscripts, correspondence, scrapbooks, artifacts, sound recordings, and photographs, used to be my father's summer retreat. I remembered as a child taking the train to the city and staying at a slatternly Howard Johnson's, spending afternoons with my mother at Oak Street Beach.

"I'm done with the Newberry," my father said. "There's nothing in that place that I haven't seen, duplicated, and read a hundred times. Look around you." He swept his arm—everywhere, books, papers, half-empty boxes. "I *am* the Sherwood Anderson Collection."

I stirred my tea and dropped two cubes of ice into my father's drink.

"You seem to be staying busy in your retirement. How's your work coming?"
I brought him his rum and cola.

"It's an accumulation." He coughed into his fist. I came around behind
him, startling Wing Biddlebaum out of his lap. He leaned over his papers
and crabbed his arms to cover the manuscript pages, like a star student
shielding a test from a flunky's prying eyes. "If you don't mind—" he said.
And because this seemed such curious behavior, I couldn't help focusing on
the papers on his desk. I set down the rum and cola, and my eye fell on a
page half-uncovered by his liver-spotted hand, a title page with the words:

> *The Book of the Grotesque*
> *A Novel*
> By Roland Clary

My father, a novelist?

Impossible, I was thinking on the elevator up to Dhara's and my apartment. Perhaps he was now calling his endless biography *The Book of the
Grotesque*, which had been Anderson's original name for his one great
classic. My father hadn't cared for the title the publisher had insisted on—
Winesburg, Ohio felt too quaint and regional, *like antimacassars or a fish fry,*
he'd once told me. *We're talking about one of the most yearning-filled books
of the twentieth century, far sexier than anything those dull pornographers
Henry Miller and Anaïs Nin ever wrote.* Winesburg *teems with repressed
desire. Its citizens are a constellation of unfulfilled dreams and communions.*
I remembered asking him, *What's sexy about* The Book of the Grotesque?
He'd said that to Anderson grotesques were not outwardly so much as spiri-
tually deformed; the culture of materialism had so warped and corrupted
them that they'd lost touch with each other and with what it meant to be
human. Yet they were the most beautiful characters, most deserving of our
sympathy, and in their isolation were the most like us.

I was trying once more to picture what I saw on my father's desk before
his arm moved over the title page and I retreated with my cup of tea. Had
I really seen the word *novel,* or was I projecting my own frustrations onto
my father's manuscript? Perhaps biographers wrote in their subject's voice
from time to time, as an immersive experiment. I could bring this up, but
I knew my father would never answer me straight. All I'd get was the old

evasiveness—unless I did some digging on my own.

Dhara had cooked a tomato pasta and was twirling noodles on a fork at our swag-leg table.

"I thought we were going to have dinner together," I said.

"You were supposed to be home more than an hour ago." She set down her fork. "How long does it take to move into a six-hundred-square-foot apartment?"

"You're right," I said. "But he's like a magician doing a hat trick; he pulls out rabbits, bouquets, one thing after another from those boxes."

"If it's so entertaining, maybe you should move in with him. You're paying for the place. Might as well get some use out of it."

"Dhara—"

"So did you call back the love of your life?" She got up with her plate and scraped the remainder of her dinner into the trashcan beneath the sink.

"Stop it, for Chrissake. And what makes you think of that anyway?" I asked, though I could picture her checking the voice-mail messages to see if Lucy's had been saved or erased.

"Just wondering." She rinsed her plate and put it in the dishwasher.

I knew I should have told her that Lucy had moved here. I should have admitted I was going out for an innocent coffee. But then it occurred to me that of all Chicago landmarks, of all places to meet, I'd chosen the European Collection of the Art Institute—the place where, on a bench with a view of Gustave Caillebotte's nearly life-size oil *Paris Street; Rainy Day,* I had asked Dhara to marry me. I decided to say something true and something less than true: "I listened to the message, and I did call Lucy back. It was just as I thought. She wanted a phone number for an old friend."

"Who?" Dhara asked.

"You wouldn't know him. We went to high school in Indianapolis, lost touch years ago. I couldn't be very helpful, in other words."

I made myself busy cleaning the stovetop, where Dhara had left a portion of pasta in a saucepan. Before sitting down to eat, I threw away the tomato seeds and garlic skins, rinsed and dried the cutting board.

"What else did you talk about?" she asked.

"Nothing. It was a short call."

"What's she doing now?"

"She's still in publishing," I said. "Like everyone else, she's worried about layoffs."

"Well, I hope this will be your last conversation." Dhara fetched her coat and scarf from the closet.

"*She* called *me*, remember?"

"I thought we agreed to leave the past in the past." She bundled up and pulled on gloves.

"Where are you going?"

Back to work," she said on her way out the door.

6

Alfred J. Lazar did not approve of his daughter's engagement, but she was headstrong and one of the few people over whom he exerted little control. It would soon become clear to George that she got what she wanted, and no amount of cajoling or threatening could distract her from her aims. Upon his return to work he was called into a meeting in Lazar's capacious office overlooking Jackson Boulevard. Family pictures—of his wife and daughter, of his son as a boy, and of his father, who began his career peddling tinware from a rattletrap wagon in rural Missouri and made his fortune in the wholesale grocery business—hung on the walls. It struck George that he was about to marry into this family, and photographs like these would adorn his house. He had never lived in a house, had always shared space with strangers passing through. But now he had committed to a settled life, and this man, his boss, pacing in front of the window, would soon be his father-in-law.

"I understand that Margaret has accepted your proposal," Lazar began. "I had no idea you were part of the cattle call. Harriet is rather beside herself. My wife does not take well to surprises."

George sat stiffly in a bow-arm leather chair. Out of deference he made a point to sit down when Lazar was standing so as not to tower over him. "I assumed that Margaret had told you her feelings. *My* feelings, as well."

"At the office nothing gets past me, but at home I'm the last to know. D'you understand?" He often paused midthought with this rhetorical question, and George had learned to give a look of assent and allow Lazar to continue. He didn't like to be interrupted and spoke in commanding streams that left no room for disagreement. He stopped before a mirror and examined his trim sideburns and meticulously shaven face. He had installed full-length mirrors on opposite walls so when he sat at his desk he could see himself in multiple dimensions. "I have to say this is most unexpected." His voice carried equal measures of chagrin and disappointment.

"I had wanted to ask you first," George said, "but you were away in New York. I never knew you were going on a trip."

"I would have told you on the Friday before Christmas, but you vanished. What's gotten into you, George? I used to come into the office and you'd be asleep on the conference-room divan, up all night finishing a campaign. Now you're hauling off early to start the long weekend?"

"If you must know, I left to buy your daughter a ring."

"But I told you to come back."

"And here I am. I'm sorry it's taken until now."

George had feared Lazar was going to fire him, that he would fall victim to one of those "regenerative acts of nature" that had his coworkers skittering about like cats on hot bricks. Though he would not admit this to himself now or for years, his trip to Marshall Field's was more detour than destination. He had stumbled into the place, in the throes less of romance than of professional anxiety—of what turned out, moreover, to be unfounded professional anxiety: All Lazar had wanted to talk about, or so he said, was a new department he was setting up at the agency. He'd visited Chicago clients throughout December, and had gone to New York to announce his creation of a "Performance Department," a grand new selling point for the firm.

"Kennison's idea, of course," he said. "I told him he should come with me and give the briefing, but he's against soldiers taking credit, d'you understand?" From now on, he continued, all of the agency's clients would be turning in weekly sales reports to show how well each ad was performing. Within the month he'd be hiring six accountants to record and calculate the returns for all seven hundred clients on the pulling power of five thousand newspapers and magazines. "I'll know the number of replies for every ad in every retail and mail-order campaign, and by the end of each week I'll be able to say what's working, what's got to go, and who takes the checkered flag."

Lazar had become an aficionado of the growing sport of auto racing, and was an investor in Barney Oldfield's "No. 999," which won the Manufacturer's Challenge Cup. He took every opportunity to pepper his talk with racing analogies and automotive terms.

"There you have it," Lazar said. "First I cried out, 'What's the future?' and an echo came back: 'Prove They Need It.' Now, with the Performance

Department, we'll have all the evidence necessary to reach the most consumers. We'll know who they are and what they want. It's not the craftiest driver that wins the race, but the best-built machine."

After the meeting George knew he should have felt relieved. He hadn't lost his job, and though Lazar never gave his consent for George to marry his daughter, he didn't refuse, either. In fact, he was oddly silent on the subject, more invested in the firm than his family. Perhaps he chose to ignore George's impending role in his life, or George's position at the firm was indeed never in jeopardy. Kennison had told him that among the boss's errands in New York was discussing the Nuvolia contract, but when George asked about this, Lazar said all seven hundred contracts were being revised to include the Performance Department. It was just like Kennison to mislead a perceived adversary, but George was going to be part of the family—heir apparent, untouchable.

Despite Harriet Lazar's protestations, the wedding was set for July. Seven months seemed an unusually short time to plan, but Margaret was graduating from the University of Chicago in spring and saw no point in waiting around for the rest of her life to begin. Harriet spread the rumor that her daughter was speeding up the schedule out of fear she might come to her senses, and George had a similar worry, accompanied by another: that *he* might change his mind. He wondered if he ever would have proposed had he known his job was safe. Or, perhaps, it had not been safe, and Lazar only kept him on grudgingly after learning of the engagement. Regardless, George had committed to marriage, and even while he told himself he could love this woman and spend the next half century by her side, bone of his bones, flesh of his flesh, there were days when he thought of catching a train east and going where no one knew him, to start another life.

The months blurred by like a blizzard off the lake. Winter dragged into May; ice ensnarled the river, and pedestrians crowded over sidewalk grates to warm themselves in the steam. George had planned to move to better lodgings for the swan song of his bachelorhood, but hadn't found the time. Talk at the boardinghouse turned from the weather to the factory protests, the strikes by the garment unions against Sears, Roebuck and Montgomery Ward. By spring, picket lines, ten thousand bodies long, snaked around the city, up Rush Street to Huron, just short of Ma Kavanagh's door. And on a bitter day in April, riots broke out between the strikers and armed police.

Ostrinski and Tiptoe Joe and other labor men in the building knew George worked high in a corporate skyscraper and had heard from Nellie Kavanagh, who read all the society papers, about his engagement to Margaret Lazar. At the breakfast table and passing on the stairs, George felt the hostility of his neighbors and wanted to remind them where he came from, let them know that he was one of them. But instead he took the grip to the Monadnock and the elevator to fourteen, and when the scorn grew intolerable he finally moved his few belongings to a well-appointed room in the Palmer House, an easy walk to work.

Margaret seemed of two minds about his new accommodations. Now she could tell her mother that her betrothed had a *soigné* address. But at the same time she claimed to support the strikers, even those who slugged nonunion workers for crossing picket lines. George felt off-balance around his fiancée, who was proud of her privilege, aflutter at the public portraits of her wealthy friends, and also quick to declare her allegiance with the man in the street. George had promised himself that sometime before the wedding he would ask Margaret what she saw in him, but May gave way to June; the labor strike moved from the streets to the courts; the Performance Department put the firm on high alert; and George's soon-to-be wife and mother-in-law were so embroiled in their contentious wedding planning that he could barely get a meeting with Margaret, and certainly not alone.

Before he had come to Chicago, the biggest house George had ever seen belonged to Banker White—a new stone mansion on Buckeye Street that was the pride of the town. But the Lazar estate on Lake Shore Drive was grander still, with its rusticated walls, masonry arches, three stories, two towers, and front yard of vast blue sparkling lake. Harriet had tried to insist on a traditional church wedding at Lincoln Park Presbyterian, but Margaret refused and after much debate rallied her father to her side, convincing him to host the ceremony on North Avenue Beach, with cocktails in the house and the reception on the back lawn. Harriet was furious and said her friends would be scandalized: *Home weddings?* Outdoor *weddings? They simply don't happen in our society; you didn't grow up among gypsies, you know.* Margaret called her mother a mid-Victorian, accused her of knowing nothing of modern customs, and seemed to relish the victory, as Lazar made arrangements with the Twenty-First Ward alderman to set up a temporary altar on a bulkhead so the bride and groom could be married with Lake Michigan at their backs.

But on the morning of the wedding day, July 15, 1905, dark clouds scudded across the sky over the Lazars' property. Around noon a light drizzle fell, and by the time the first guests were arriving the weather had turned ominous. Then, at the appointed hour of two o'clock, as if the fates were amusing themselves, the rain began in earnest and the ceremony was delayed. The shower continued; the altar stood abandoned like an empty frame. The photographer tried to gather the family for formal pictures, only to be rebuffed by a flustered Harriet Lazar, who had the staff and ushers corral the guests into the ballroom, which had been set up with chairs in the event of bad weather. The string trio played, the processional began, the minister, bridesmaids, and groomsmen took their places, and George walked down the aisle to Handel's "Largo," the city's social register a blur in his peripheral vision. In the ornate room, festooned with vines and white roses, he stood before the soaring limestone fireplace and waited for the bride.

In his mind there was a silver lining to this unfortunate turn of events. The bride's side had two hundred guests compared to three on the groom's side, and in the confusion of changed plans he felt less exposed and outnumbered. He had sent twenty invitations to friends from home, and should not have been surprised that so few attended. By leaving he had rejected Winesburg, and though everyone had said they knew he would go, even urged him to set forth and make his way as a writer, now they took his abandonment personally and no longer wished him well. He couldn't blame them, really, when, to his own regret, he so rarely visited home and with each year ventured less frequently into the attic of his memory.

But Will Henderson, his editor from the *Winesburg Eagle,* had come. And so had Seth Richmond, once his rival for Helen White's affections. Of all people he had most expected Seth to send regrets, yet here he was next to the third guest on the groom's side, George's father, Tom Willard. Because Margaret had eight bridesmaids, resplendent in pink organdy with tiny wreaths of lilies of the valley in their hair, George had asked his party of three to join the processional and stand nearby for the vows.

By the time Harriet strode down the aisle and took her seat in the front row she had managed to compose herself and put on a face of false serenity. A stout, square-chinned woman, she looked a good deal older than her husband, who went to such pains with his appearance. She wore a dark-gray satin gown with a beaded collar, and her white hair capped her forehead like snow on an imposing peak. "Gracious me," she said aloud, unable to hold her tongue. Only those up front could hear her. The rest had their heads trained toward the ballroom door, awaiting Margaret's entrance. "Would you look at the time—" Harriet gestured toward the mantel clock.

She had a curious relationship with the Central Time Zone. A Boston Brahmin, she kept her watch and all clocks in the house set an hour ahead. George and the bridesmaids knew about Harriet's eccentricity. She was forever complaining about Chicago, calling it "a pestilential bog," and longing out loud for the better people of Boston and the salt air of Cape Cod. But Tom Willard, upon seeing that the clock read four, double-checked his pocket watch and said, "Has it really been two hours?"

George leaned over to tell his father that he would explain later, and it was at this point that Lazar appeared at the entryway, arm in arm with his daughter. Margaret wore white, a beautiful silk taffeta and crepe de chine gown. A wreath of orange blossoms crowned her head, and her hair fell in plaits down her back. Two flower girls, grandnieces from New England, scattered rose petals before her, and her father looked after her long train as she made her way down the aisle.

Standing in the presence of all those people, his odd assortment of groomsmen shifting from foot to foot, Margaret and her bridesmaids shining in their regalia, George found his attention drifting as he repeated his vows. At some point in the service he followed the minister's eyes to the bank of ballroom windows, where the clouds parted and the sun cast a shimmer over the wet green lawn. The wedding-goers raised a collective *Ah*. The minister said *Now there is a sign,* and for a moment laughter filled the room. Soon the music was playing again, and George was walking out of the ballroom, Margaret's arm entwined with his. People he had never met before shook his hand—*Well done,* they said. And *Aren't you a lucky one?* Then he was in the parlor with his wife, and surrounded by the Lazars, then with his father, flash-lamps aflame in his eyes. *You look stunned,* Margaret would later say when they went through pictures to choose which ones to hang.

The newlyweds circulated through the ample rooms, and George caught up briefly with Will Henderson before his former editor wandered off to order another sloe gin fizz. He had an awkward conversation with Margaret's brother, Charles, a pale and rabbity art dealer who had aggrieved the family by leaving for the East Coast and losing all touch. Charles had come home on this occasion only because he knew Margaret would never forgive him if he missed her wedding. He said as much to George, but when the former reporter asked about life in New York City, he turned chary, then vanished into the crowd, leaving George face to face with the city's elite. Margaret introduced him to Bertha Palmer, widow of the hotel magnate and grande dame of Chicago society; the great architect Daniel Burnham, who designed the White City at the World's Fair; and the philanthropist Nettie McCormick, in a similar toque and feathers to the one she'd worn for the portrait now hanging at the Art Institute.

It was all George could do to pull his father away from Mrs. McCormick. Tom Willard was known for being a talker, and he had the kindly philanthropist boxed into a corner in the drawing room. He must have recognized her name, because by the time George swooped in, his father was crying up the growth potential of Winesburg and its proximity to Cleveland and Lake Erie, and enumerating the many improvements needed at the New Willard House.

"I'm looking for an investor," he was saying. "A town like ours needs a first-rate hotel, but we're still getting over the depression of '93." He twisted his mustache, which he wore with the ends turned up. "We're right on the B&O line. We've had patrons from Maine to California. Canadians. Europeans. We're just eight miles to the lake, twenty to Sandusky. You'll find all the recreation you could imagine right at our doorstep, plus the charm and hospitality of a village. I like to say that people are our top attraction."

He leaned back on his heels and smiled at Margaret, who had met him for the first time at dinner the evening before and seemed not to know what to make of him. His Prince Albert suit looked faded, and some of the threading at the collar had come loose. George recognized the coat as the one his father had worn to his mother's funeral a decade ago, and felt a mixture of sorrow and pique. Mrs. McCormick congratulated the bride and groom, and Margaret took the opportunity to lead her away, no doubt to apologize once out of earshot.

Tom Willard knitted his brow and seemed about to scold his son for the interruption when Seth Richmond came around. He looked unchanged since George knew him as a youth, still hangdog and melancholy and a conversational challenge. George asked if he was still living in town, and Tom answered for the young man, who spoke in short sentences that trailed off, sometimes unintelligibly. "He's living in Columbus, went to the state university for a couple years there, didn't you?" Tom said, and Seth nodded. "And you're a mechanic, isn't that right? Working on—what is it? Automobiles?"

"My father-in-law is a motor man," George put in, trying to find some common topic. "I should introduce you."

This line of questioning continued for a while until Tom Willard grew bored and began scanning the room, with its profusion of luxuriant fabrics and furnishings, carved moldings and winking crystal. When Tom had slid away, Seth turned to George and without ever making eye contact asked, "Did you invite Helen White? I was sure I'd find her here."

The idea had crossed George's mind. On the one hand he had wanted Banker and Mrs. White to come to Chicago and see this house and all his success. And he wanted to impress Helen, as well. But there was a history between them, and it didn't seem fair to Margaret or, more to the point, to George's memory, where he maintained an image of Helen White as a standard of perfection. "I didn't invite her," George said now. "We've fallen out of touch. I don't even know where she lives."

"Why, she's right here in Chicago," Seth exclaimed. "She's been a year and more. I thought surely you'd have heard."

"It's news to me," George managed.

And as the cocktail hour came to an end his mind began to drift again, while the rain resumed its pitter-pat upon the reception tent in the Lazars' back garden.

In months to come George would try to make light of the terrible weather that marred the wedding, how the drizzle on the tent grew to a great downpour that muffled the toasts and drowned out conversation. He couldn't recall the few audible words, only the suspended feeling of his father's speech dragging on, the tent's roof growing heavy with rain, the caterers furiously sopping the floor with towels, his new wife reaching her hand to her hair to make sure her tiara of orange blossoms had not fallen.

On their first wedding anniversary, in July 1906, George and Margaret had dinner at Henrici's on Randolph, in the Theater District. They had spent a pleasant afternoon together, walking in Lincoln Park and reading under an umbrella on North Avenue Beach.

"Why didn't we have this weather a year ago?" Margaret asked.

"If we had, there wouldn't have been a story," George put in, and repeated something he'd overheard a farmer say at Biff Carter's Lunch Room in Winesburg: "Rain and pain are both for growth."

"You're quite the philosopher, George Willard." Margaret wore an off-the-shoulder evening gown of dark heliotrope and had grown her ginger hair long, some swept up and the rest a cascade of curls down her shoulders and arms.

A year into the marriage, George found himself for the most part content. He had gone into the arrangement in such a headlong manner that the morning after the wedding he had woken up disoriented, wondering how he had materialized in the bridal suite of the Morrison Hotel, his clothes a tangle on the floor and lying next to a girl he hardly knew. He was still just becoming acquainted with Margaret Willard, getting used to his name affixed to hers, and perhaps the gloss of novelty was the key to his well-being. He spent longer hours than ever at the office, steering between the Scylla and Charybdis of the Service and Performance Departments. So he enjoyed coming home, having a late dinner with his wife, and relaxing before bed with the essays of Ralph Waldo Emerson, whose writing about self-discipline and "the infinitude of the private man" calmed his whirling nerves. And he looked forward most of all to turning in for the night, having spent the better part of ten years sleeping alone on a straw mattress in a grubby boardinghouse. Though it was still the fashion to sleep apart in twin beds, now George lay down on a horsehair mattress between the finest cotton sheets. For months his nightly ritual was to climb into Margaret's bed and stroke her hair, touch her hip and shoulders, and more often than not she would take him into her arms. Though lately, it was true, she turned him away with greater frequency, complaining of fatigue or the summer heat or the bed built for one. *Wouldn't you rather talk?* she'd ask. *I haven't seen you but for a minute all day.*

Margaret's talk consisted mostly of society matters that didn't much interest George. She complained endlessly of her mother's active social calendar but was quick to take up the latest gossip. She knew who'd been prowling the resorts of the vice district, who'd given up children for adoption before marrying well. She knew of fortunes gained on the backs of the poor and of secret memberships in covens and cults. A year out of the university, she had no apparent prospects or plans for the road ahead. She came into the office two days a week as a creative advisor on her father's campaigns, and George endured the derisive looks of his coworkers. He wished she would find a permanent position in a theater or a gallery—she had a passion for the arts—but as much as she groused about her parents, she could not disentangle herself from their lives.

George had expected that he and his new bride would own a house by now, in Lake View or one of the areas along the Lincoln Avenue streetcar line. He pictured an unassuming greystone with deceptively grand interiors in a neighborhood of new arrivals from Ireland, Luxembourg, Nebraska, Indiana. As a child he used to make believe that the New Willard House was a palace, that he was crown prince and the guests all functionaries of court. But when he stepped into the streets of Winesburg he drifted toward odd-jobbers and millinery-shop workers, those whose best days were behind them or would never come. He felt at times that two different George Willards were battling within him: the striver after money and position and the solitary figure at the margins of the world. Perhaps this explained his restlessness, his enduring dissatisfaction: He wished to be a deserter from his own internal civil war.

Yet he had not so much as escaped his in-laws' backyard. After the honeymoon in Lake Geneva, he and Margaret moved into the carriage house behind her parents' mansion on Lake Shore Drive. It was meant to be a temporary solution, since there had been no time to find a house amidst their sped-up wedding planning. Margaret's father thought nothing of dropping in with an armful of extra work, and her mother had taken up gardening and could be heard spading the dirt and pruning the bushes outside their bedroom window. When George would say *We can't live here forever,* Margaret would agree: *You think I want my mother pawing through my bloomers?* But nothing happened. George would bring home the real estate ads, press the subject too far, and Margaret would call him a nag and walk away. Now should have been a fine time to talk of the future, but George was not going to risk upsetting his wife, who looked ripe as a peach in high summer, on this of all nights.

George ordered the Diamond Jim cut steak and Margaret the whitefish on a plank of fragrant hickory. They toasted themselves with champagne and shared a bottle of Château Margaux with dinner. After the waiter filled their glasses with the last of the bottle, Margaret asked, all at once, "So why did you marry me?"

George took a long drink of water and carved at the gristle of his steak.

"No, really, I want to know," she said, her mood shifting from chirrupy to earnest. "It occurs to me I've never asked you."

"Well—" George put down his silverware. "The harder question is why you married me."

"I can answer that without any trouble. These questions aren't supposed to be difficult in the first place."

"I thought we were having a fine time. Is this some kind of test?" George asked.

"No, just something I should have asked a long time ago. Why did you marry me?"

George picked Vienna roll crumbs off the table linen and dropped them on his plate one by one. "You shouldn't have to ask," he said, then, digging himself in deeper, added, "I don't know what to think about couples who steal kisses in public and talk of their mutual affection with the regularity of coffee and toast. Speaking of love diminishes it. Holding it in the heart makes it grow."

"I disagree," Margaret said. "Do you really believe that?"

"I do."

"Well, this isn't any other day." Margaret tapped her fingers on her wine-glass. "If I didn't know better I'd say you were stalling for time."

The waiter passed nearby, and George summoned him.

"Another bottle?" the waiter asked.

"Sounds like a swell idea," George replied, but Margaret said, "That won't be necessary. You could bring us the dessert menu instead."

While the waiter was away the couple sat in silence, surrounded by the jocular din of Henrici's patrons, most coming or going from the theater. Until two nights ago Margaret and George had tickets to see *In the Bishop's Carriage* at the Powers, but the show had been canceled without warning, apparently due to a dustup between the playwright and the theater owner over the use of "mistress" to describe a lady friend of the main character. Harry Powers refused to allow such a word to be uttered on his stage, and the playwright acceded for the first few shows, then defiantly returned to his original script. Margaret and George had run out of time to make alternate plans, in the opening act of what was turning out to be a most disappointing anniversary.

George wondered what had gotten into Margaret to ask such a question, particularly late in the evening, when George's mind was addled from too much food and drink. He saw nothing wrong with daily confessions of love, fancied himself a converser, even a romantic at times, one who knew his heart's core. So he couldn't understand what had come over him, why he hadn't answered straightaway: *You're smart and beautiful and sophisticated.*

You're all this small-town boy ever dreamed of, lying in his room late at night listening to the trains running off to better places. I'm lucky as loaded dice. But his tongue had frozen, as if he didn't believe what he hadn't been able to say. Whatever the reason, it was too late to go back and fill Margaret's ears with sweet nothings; the moment had passed, perhaps unalterably.

He glanced across the table, but she was looking away. He fixed his gaze above and beyond her shoulder, and there, in the distance, talking animatedly to the bow-tied maître d', stood a woman the very image of Helen White.

The host stepped away for a moment, and the woman turned so that George could see her straight on. He felt a shiver of recognition and grew certain it was the girl, now woman, he had once loved. She had the same slim figure, in a pouter-pigeon blouse and trumpet skirt, her hair combed up and pinned in a bun. George had half a notion to dart over and greet her, but then the host returned, a stack of boxes in his arms. When the woman— Helen, or her double—turned to profile again, George began to wonder if his eyes were deceiving him, or if he were somehow conjuring her. Though striking, she was humbly dressed. It would be unlike Helen to wear the costume of the middle class, especially here, in one of the finest restaurants in Chicago. The host handed her the boxes, she bowed her head to thank him, he held the door open for her, and she vanished into the night.

The waiter returned with dessert menus. Margaret ordered the German almond cake, George the chocolate mousse and a cup of café noir. He decided to buck up and try to salvage the evening, but just as he was getting ready to apologize and make some excuse about not feeling quite himself today, she put an end to the thaw between them. "You know what," she said, "I'll go first, if that would make it easier. I'll tell you why I married you. Maybe that will help loosen your tongue."

George had been curious about the source of her affection ever since her startling confession at her twenty-first-birthday soiree. He'd waited for this moment, had not known how to draw the story out of her, and now here she was about to tell him. But instead of hearing every word he was thinking about the woman he'd just seen leave the restaurant. It had to be Helen. Seth Richmond had said she was living in Chicago, and wouldn't it be the ultimate sign that in this city of two million souls they would both end up here, of all places, of all occasions? He remembered sitting with her on a cold night in late fall under the grandstand at Waterworks Hill, the reverential feeling that swept over him as she nestled close and he placed his hand on her shoulder. The thought he had then returned to him now: *I have come to this lonely place and here is this other.*

But when he looked across the table it was not Helen White but Margaret Lazar, his wife of one year. And the room was so boisterous that it took a great effort of concentration for him to make out her words: "When I saw you in the street that day of the automobile accident I felt the strangest sensation," she was saying. "It was something I'd never experienced before or since. Mind you, I'm no Florence Nightingale, but from the very first time our eyes met I wanted to take care of you."

"But you were so young," George said, slipping out of his reverie.

"I know," Margaret continued. "But in that moment I swear I saw the future." She spoke of the years that followed, how she almost never saw him but would tune in at the dinner table whenever her father mentioned the tall young man from Ohio and his talent for business, his innate understanding of people's moods and needs. Margaret would see him each summer when she worked part-time for the agency, and every year George's workspace marked his progress, from cubby to desk to interior office to window office with a sweeping view. "Growing up the way I did," she said, "I had never met a self-made man who was anywhere close to my age. I remember pointing you out to friends from school and their saying, 'Now that's a man, all right. The rest of your admirers have never had to lift a finger. Boys, Margaret, the whole lot of them.' I agreed, but I didn't tell my friends that I saw something of the boy in you, as well. The openness, the sensitivity, the part of you—I don't know how to describe it or where it comes from—that needs caring for. It's that combination, man and boy, that brought me to this place."

George picked up his dessert fork, then set it back down.

"There—" Margaret exclaimed, raising her empty glass. "Happy Anniversary."

"I'm speechless," George said, though he knew full well that his turn had come.

7

Dhara was not usually jealous. At work or at parties, she didn't appear threatened by other women. Only people I knew from long ago caused her to act this way. It was as if our lives began when we met and we were only allowed to live for the future. Our building looked straight out of the Jetsons; we'd furnished our apartment with austere modern sofas and chairs. Dhara knew the names of the designers and how to distinguish the Neo from the Portola Collection, an Arco floor lamp from an Orbit sconce. We worked for the company that had contributed more than any other to the death of print, the end of the book. I wondered if Dhara secretly hoped that I'd give up my dream of writing a novel, because storytelling was an act of memory. She never talked about her own childhood, and her attention drifted when I talked about mine. Besides two or three visits home each year to Dayton, she rarely brought up her family. What I knew about them had come not from her but from listening at the table over the Christmas holiday or during the annual festival of Diwali.

Dhara grew up in the Dynasty Inn, at the crossroads of Interstates 70 and 75, in the middle of Middle America, and spent her childhood watching weary travelers headed north or south, east or west, always looking down the road toward somewhere else. The thought that a family lived here, in this motel, must have seemed as strange to the parade of people passing through as the aroma of curries that Meera Patel cooked on a portable stove in the back room office. From an early age Dhara tried to mask the smell with vanilla-scented candles, and over time she, too, saw her family as strange. She and her younger brother, Ajit, were among the few South Asian kids at their school. To combat the taunts and exclusions, Ajit took bodybuilding supplements and spent hours in the weight room until he resembled a comic-book henchman, and Dhara survived on charm and good looks. *We called her Indian Barbie,* her father liked to say. *Her hair was so tall she had to duck to get through the door.* She rode in a float as homecoming queen, won a scholarship to Wittenberg, and would have waved good-bye to Ohio for good had her mother not grown ill her senior year in college. Dhara finished school and returned to Dayton to work at the Dynasty and help care for Meera, whose cancer eventually went into remission.

Then September 11 happened, and travelers, upon seeing brown faces behind the desk, would turn on their heels and head to the next cheap lodging. Jagdish Patel bought a flagpole and raised the Stars and Stripes. On the marquee out front he hung the words AMERICAN-OWNED MOTEL and, after the deployments, WE SUPPORT THE TROOPS. If the rooms or the service weren't perfect, customers could grow hostile. One St. Patrick's Day a college kid told Ajit to hop on his magic carpet and fly back to his own country. Ajit wheeled around the reception desk with pointed finger, saying *I'm Indian, you fool,* and got his nose broken with a single lucky punch. Dhara tried to clean her brother's blood out of the pale carpet, but her scrubbing only made the stain grow. That year she applied to business school, and though she got into a couple programs in California, her mother convinced her to go to Ohio State. Dhara did not regret it, because in the winter of her first year her mother's cancer came back, and at least she could drive home weekends. By summer's end her mother was dead, and too soon after that her father fell in with the Dynasty's receptionist. When Dhara left for Chicago and a new job, she promised herself she would not look back.

I loved my wife, but we did have this fundamental difference: In order to leave she had to sever ties, while in order for me to get on with my life I had to go back and repair them. Every day I brought my father lunch, smuggled into my shoulder bag from Imego's gourmet cafeteria. Dhara reminded me I shouldn't abuse the free food in times like these, but I needed to cut costs, and a man can't survive on buttered popcorn alone. On one of these visits I arrived an hour earlier than usual because I had an afternoon meeting in Madison. When he didn't answer the door, I let myself in with my extra key.

I looked around the apartment—no one there but the orange cat, failing to camouflage himself on the battered office chair. I put the sandwich I'd brought into the refrigerator and went to my father's desk to write a note— and there was that title page again, with the words *A Novel by Roland Clary.* But beyond this one piece of paper I saw no further evidence of *The Book of the Grotesque.* I peeked under the pile, careful not to upset the disorderly order, but all I found were scores of typewritten pages of what seemed like disconnected fragments—impressionistic character portraits, details of city life from a century ago—mixed with reams of handwritten notes on index cards and legal paper, page after page scattered about or stuffed into manila folders with labels such as *Leaving Winesburg; Turn of the Century Chicago; Anderson and the Chicago Renaissance; The Golden Age of Advertising;* and *Secondary Characters and Other Grotesques.*

I opened the thickest folder, marked *George Willard,* and thumbed through my father's notes. George Willard is the central recurring character in *Winesburg, Ohio,* the young reporter who has a gift for drawing even the most alienated townspeople out from the shadows. I leafed through articles my father had written about the death of George's mother, his strained relationship with his father, the shabby hotel his parents run, and how, in nearly every tale in the book, different characters seek George out, as if they've waited their whole lives to tell him their stories. My father had written notes, mostly about George's habits and background:

He sometimes talks aloud to himself, and his mother used to kneel on the floor outside his room listening to his soliloquies and thinking that within her son "is a secret something that is striving to grow . . . the thing I let be killed in myself."

His room, on the second floor of the New Willard House, has one window looking over an alleyway and another looking across the railroad tracks. Of course George has a view of the tracks leading out of Winesburg. He shares that common small-town affliction: an unyielding restlessness.

As the sole reporter at the Winesburg Eagle, *he carries a notepad with him everywhere, but what he wants to write most of all is a love story. In "The Thinker," he tells Seth Richmond just whom he's going to fall in love with, too: It's the banker's daughter, Helen White—"the only girl in town with any 'get-up' to her."*

I was about to close the folder when I saw, on the inside flap, that my father had written more notes to himself in his shaky hand:

There are questions that linger after Winesburg, Ohio, *and we can only guess at the answers. In the final scene of the book, George Willard boards a train. He has said good-bye to his beloved Helen, so their love story, for now, is incomplete. It's the last years of the 19th Century, and he is headed for the great, teeming metropolis of Chicago. All we know is that "the young man's* mind was carried away by his growing passion for dreams." Kate Swift, his former teacher, had once told him, "You must not become a mere peddler of words. The thing to learn is to know what people are thinking about, not what they say." She was urging him to become not just a reporter but a writer, one who can see into people's hearts and minds. And by the last page of the book we glimpse a portrait of the artist as a young man now coming into focus: "He thought of little things—Turk Smollet wheeling boards through the main street of his town in the morning, a tall woman, beautifully gowned, who had once stayed overnight at his father's hotel, Butch Wheeler the lamplighter of Winesburg hurrying through the streets on a summer evening and holding a torch in his hand, Helen White standing by a window in the Winesburg post office and putting a stamp on an envelope."

But questions remain: What became of George Willard in Chicago? Did his love affair with Helen White continue or come to an end? Would George have been drawn by the siren song of commerce, as Sherwood Anderson himself was, living in Chicago at the dawn of the 20th Century? Or would he fulfill the great hope that he would one day become a writer?

I was standing at my father's desk asking myself these same questions when I heard rattling keys and then the lock turning. I quickly closed the folder and said, "Hello," in my most unthreatening voice.

"What are you doing here?" my father asked.

"Just bringing you lunch." I hurried to the refrigerator and put the sandwich on a plate, then explained why I was early. I expected him to berate me for letting myself in and keeping a key of my own, but he seemed distracted so I asked where he'd been all day.

He took off his gloves and Cossack fur cap, draped his coat and scarf over a chair. He leaned on a ball-handle cane that I'd never seen before. "I've been on a walk," he said, his voiced tinged with melancholy. "I used to be a regular flâneur in this city, but now I'm a wheezing, jangling sack of bones. I'm lucky to cover ten blocks round trip." He caught his breath and sat down heavily on the sofa. "I can't remember the last time I strolled Wabash Avenue. So much has changed." He rested his cane on the coffee table.

"Before the bubble burst we had a lot of construction. I'm sure you've seen Sceptrum Tower next door. Ninety stories, nine hundred million dollars, and a massive shadow over Harbor City. So what took you outside on this perfectly dreary morning?"

He dabbed at his forehead with the back of his hand and kicked off his shoes, the insoles spilling out like tongues. He said that Wabash Avenue used to be called Cass Street, and Sherwood Anderson wrote the *Winesburg* stories at 735 Cass. "He worked as an advertising copywriter at the Critchfield Company in the Loop, and used to cross the bridge right down there." My father pointed beyond the balcony to the Chicago River. "He examined the faces of people he passed, holding them in his mind as he walked home. Then he climbed up to the third floor of the rooming house where he lived—alone, a thirty-eight-year-old man who had left his family in Ohio to become a writer—and sat down at a long table lit overhead by a bare electric light. And in what he described as a series of feverish sessions in 1915, he wrote 'Hands' and then the rest of the stories on print paper he'd copped from the office."

"What's become of the boardinghouse?"

"I'd been wondering that myself. Last I checked the building still stood, worse for wear, but you could look up and see that third-floor window and imagine Anderson working into the night. But now the building's gone. Nothing there but a fenced-in parking lot."

I wanted to ask my father about *The Book of the Grotesque,* see if there was more to this novel he was writing than a title page, sketches, and haphazard notes. I hadn't seen him this expansive since the months after his heart surgery, when it seemed, however briefly, that we could talk about anything. But if I admitted I'd been riffling through his papers, he'd shut down and demand my key and I'd lose his trust completely. So I asked what year he last saw the old rooming house, and he said it must have been a couple decades ago. And then he was off reminiscing about Chicago summers with my mother and me, and mooning as he always did about how she was his twin flame and single greatest regret.

Soon I had to get on the road to Madison, but the next day I brought lunch at the same time and again he was gone from his apartment. The windchill had dropped below freezing and the sidewalks were treacherous, so I worried about a seventy-eight-year-old setting off on these excursions, though I knew there was nothing I could do to stop him. While he was away I pored over his notes, about the dawn of the age of advertising, the theater scene at Jane Addams's Hull House, and at night in bed next to Dhara I reread *Winesburg, Ohio.* By Friday I was so swept up by the notes and my father's missing manuscript, which I'd scoured his apartment looking for, that I nearly forgot my two o'clock meeting with Lucy.

She was waiting at the entrance to the European Painting and Sculpture Collection. Dressed down in stretch pants and a soft, hooded sweater, with little makeup and her sandy hair pulled back in a band, she was attractive and rangy, though leaner, more angular than I remembered. I was both relieved and a little disappointed that she looked more like someone on her way to a yoga class than out on a date. But who was I to flatter myself, and why was I thinking of this afternoon as anything other than old friends catching up on lost years?

We hugged quickly, and I felt short beside her. She was an inch taller, and just as she always used to, she stooped to compensate.

"You look great," I said.

"You too." She glanced at my left hand, at the wedding ring Dhara and I had bought from Overstock.

I saw that she wasn't wearing a ring. "I'm married." I held up my hand. "Dhara and I just had our first anniversary."

"Congratulations!" she exclaimed, though she seemed unsurprised by the news. We were past thirty, after all, and hadn't spoken more than a handful of times in the last ten years. She asked how Dhara and I met, and I told her about Lakeside and tried to avoid the particulars of the book-scanning project, but Lucy asked, "She works for Imego?" And I said, "Yes, I know. But it's quite a company—they take good care of their people." I couldn't bring myself to admit that I was one of them.

She forced a smile as we stepped inside the gallery. In front of us was Caillebotte's *Paris Street; Rainy Day*, and to our left was the bench where I proposed to Dhara. Overcome with self-reproach, I said, "I asked my wife to marry me here. It's one of my favorite places in Chicago." When Lucy reddened I remembered how I used to tease her that I knew when she was embarrassed because the blood would rise just to her chin, like a crimson collar. As a distraction, I talked about the painting of the man and woman walking arm in arm by a cobblestone intersection near the Gare Saint-Lazare. The man, in long coat and top hat, holds an umbrella over himself and the woman, who is wearing a black frock and netted cap. I told Lucy what I loved about the painting: how, like a frame on a reel, it captures a moment in the lives of this couple—sheltered from the rain, looking off in the same direction—but also, somehow, their entire past and future.

"You sound like an old romantic," Lucy said.

"That's me. Don't you recall?"

"My memory must be failing me."

"Oh, come on." I touched her elbow.

"I like the painting," she said, "but maybe we should talk somewhere else."

In the Art Institute cafeteria we got coffees and a corner table and I asked what brought her to Chicago. "I was downsized. Can't you tell?" She slumped in her chair, then told me the story of her eight years working for H. Davenport, the venerable publisher of some of the finest writers of the past century. She'd taken the Radcliffe publishing course out of college, Xeroxed, opened mail, read slush, caught her big break at twenty-eight and begun making acquisitions. At first she was allowed to buy one or two books per list—narrative nonfiction only. But when another young editor took maternity leave, Lucy volunteered to pick up the slack, and for a short while she had the best job in the world. She was buying fiction, memoir; one of her novels became a finalist for the National Book Award, and she discovered a lost classic from the Davenport archives that became a surprising best seller. But around this time a thirty-five-year-old European financier got in his mind the foolhardy idea that serious books could turn a profit in a country where at best a small city's worth of people—say, the population of Des Moines—read anything approximating literature. He took out massive loans to buy the company, then lured another respected publishing house into a doomed marriage. Not long after the merger, the editor who had returned from maternity leave received a pink slip, as did dozens of other editors, publicists, and salespeople.

"I survived the first purge," Lucy said. "But six months later we learned that our whiz-kid financier was seven billion dollars in debt thanks to his spending spree, and now, with the world economy going belly-up, he was desperate to cut his losses. Soon after that a company spokesman none of us had met announced a freeze on acquisitions. The next day my boss quit in protest, and on December 1, known around the publishing world as Black Monday, nearly half of our depleted staff was let go."

"Including you—"

"I was given until the end of the week to pack up my office."

"That's brutal."

"Surely it's worse at GM or Alcoa or in the one-company towns all over the country where there's no hope unless you pick up and move. I'm just lucky to have a safety net."

We never used to talk about Lucy's safety net. Her father was a top executive at the pharmaceutical megacorp Bowen & Leary. She grew up in a mansion on Meridian Street, three houses down from the governor of Indiana, and though she had always tried to hide her privilege, her safety net was threaded with twenty-four-carat gold. I never liked going to her parents' house and sitting through their noisy dinners where her mother, Yvonne, threw table scraps to their Vizslas while complaining in her husky voice about the provincial Midwest. She was brought up in Richmond, Virginia, which couldn't have been much different, but she assumed a queenly air and sat on more advisory boards than anyone in the city.

I never thought she liked me, for all the typical reasons—I was beneath her daughter, had no great plans; I was taciturn and didn't kiss the ring. Yvonne was fascinated by my mother, though—a relatively young woman who had never remarried and was raising me alone. She would ask prying questions about my mother's personal life—*Does she date? Is she still in touch with your father?*—in a falsely intimate way. Even if I had trusted Yvonne I had no news to share. My mother had found a lump in her breast not long after we moved to Indianapolis; she'd been ill off and on ever since, and didn't have the energy to go looking for companionship. She put all she had into running the school library and covering up signs that something might be wrong. She forbade me to tell friends she was sick; only her sister, Kathleen, knew. Even Kathleen's kids, my younger cousins, who lived a couple miles north of the little rambler we shared off the Monon Trail, were in the dark.

I figured that Lucy's mother persisted because she sensed, somehow, that all was not well, and she wanted me to surrender what little I had: a secret. The Youngbloods had everything: private school, a live-in maid, a summer house in Lake Geneva, four kids, boy-girl-boy-girl; they were the flawlessly orthodontured family you find in purchased picture frames. I resented them, even Lucy, who volunteered at soup kitchens, made her own money at the Broad Ripple Beanery where we first met, wore thrift-store clothes, and drove an old Honda festooned with progressive bumper stickers. The only time she ever talked about money was on the rare occasion when I would bring it up.

My mother died toward the end of my junior year, and I moved in with my aunt. That fall I applied to the best school I could afford: Indiana University, where my father had once taught but left under unpleasant circumstances. When I got my acceptance and asked Kathleen where I should go to take out loans, she said I wouldn't need much, because Lucy had given her a check for twenty-five thousand dollars to go toward my college fund. Kathleen had broken her promise not to tell me, and since Lucy had been covert about the money I didn't mention it until years later when we were having one of our long-distance arguments. She was complaining that I never visited her in Boston; I said I couldn't afford the ticket, and as always she offered to pay my way. But we'd begun to grow apart; our calls and visits had become less frequent. It was late on a Saturday night, and I'd had too many beers at a party where everyone else was coupling up. So I asked her about that twenty-five thousand, and she said she'd meant to tell me but didn't want to make a big deal of it. I explained that my mother had life insurance; I was eligible for loans; I already worked thirty hours a week; I wasn't a charity case. But Lucy knew from my aunt that the policy didn't yield much, that my father couldn't be counted on, and that my aunt and uncle had limited income and their own kids to worry about.

Lucy said she had raised the money along with a bunch of friends. Everyone pitched in what they could. I pressed her for the names and amounts of those who contributed and said the least I could do was write them thank-you notes, even years after the fact. Lucy said I was missing the point. The donations were anonymous, given out of sympathy—just be grateful and forget it. But I had to know where the money had come from, and when Lucy refused to say, we fought through the night and for weeks afterwards. I called our mutual friends, and they said they'd given what they could, but certainly not thousands. That summer before her senior year at Harvard, Lucy studied abroad in Venice. I received a few postcards but never replied, and that August we met at the old coffee shop, and she asked if I thought we should take some time off. I didn't bring up the college fund again, and instead put the blame on the universal fall guy, geographical distance, even though we'd made it three years and had just one to go.

Maybe we can try again later, she'd said.

If only we lived in the same city. . . . My voice had trailed off.

Now, twelve years later, here we were.

I wondered if she was thinking: *This is my old boyfriend, who I put through college.* I still believed that nearly all that money had come from her, that she had drawn it from the small fortune she'd be coming into right about now, one of those trust funds that kick in after age thirty. I didn't know what to think about Lucy's gesture: Was it genuine, done out of compassion, as she'd claimed? Or was I the face on the *Save the Orphans* box that she could stuff full of bills to ease her rich girl's guilt? I used to believe it was an act of control, a way to ensure that I'd be forever in her debt—yet years had gone by; if a job hadn't come up in Chicago, perhaps we never would have seen each other again.

"Enough about my woes," she said now. "What have you been up to?"

I didn't want to talk about my job, my role as termite in the house of the printed word, so I asked about her new position at the University of Chicago Press. She said it was small and she'd have more autonomy, and though she'd mostly be doing academic titles she did convince the editorial board to start a new fiction series. "How's your writing coming along?" she asked.

"My writing?"

"I have a confession," she put in. "Sometimes when I read the industry circulars about forthcoming books I look for your name. Did I miss something?"

I sipped the sugar at the bottom of my empty coffee cup. "I'm still working on it."

"You better be. You've got talent, Adam. I've seen my share of manuscripts, and I can tell within the first page, the first paragraph even. You know how to see beyond the surface of things. Remember the open-mic night we started at the Beanery and how I pushed you to share your stuff and you were so shy and nervous you practically read in a whisper? But everyone was riveted."

"That was a long time ago," I said.

"I still have a piece you wrote called 'The Oldest Man in the World.' Remember that one?"

I did, but I never thought much of it. The story was based on a walk I used to take through the cemetery near our house in Bloomington. I'd cut through the graveyard every day on the way home from elementary school with a girl from the neighborhood named Talia Kuplinski. She was my first crush, and to impress her I'd make up stories about the people buried there, particularly the ones who died young or lived to a very old age. One day we came across a mossy stone with the names of a husband and wife: Nathaniel and Leonore Rose. They'd both been born in 1845, and though the year of Leonore's death, 1903, was listed, there was no year of death after the dash under Nathaniel's name. I did the calculation: it was 1985, so Nathaniel Rose would have been 140 years old if, as the tombstone showed, he were still alive. In the story I imagined that after his wife died, Nathaniel moved to Chicago to try to escape the memories. He eventually remarried but kept a secret stash of pictures and mementos of Leonore, who was, as my father would say, his *twin flame*. He couldn't bear to remove his name from her tombstone, so he never told his second wife that a plot had been reserved for him a few hours away in another state. When he died she had him buried in a cemetery on the North Side under a stone with the dates 1845–1932. She eventually joined him there, not knowing he had left a symbol etched in stone in Bloomington, Indiana, that his love for Leonore would go on forever.

"It was a maudlin story," I said. "I used to specialize in those."

"Well, I thought it was sweet, the way the old man couldn't let go and even in death was living a kind of double life. What are you working on now?" Lucy asked. "Imagine that you're writing a query letter. What would it say?"

"I've never been good at that kind of thing."

"How about the title at least?"

"Okay, that I can do," I began, but the name of my graduate thesis, *A Brief History of the Fool,* the only "book" I'd written, was not what came to mind. "It's called *The Book of the Grotesque,*" I said.

"A Gothic novel? I didn't know that was your thing."

I explained Sherwood Anderson's idea of the grotesque and reminded her about my father's lifelong work. "He's still plugging away at that second volume. Forty years in the making, and you know he's never going to finish." I asked when she last picked up *Winesburg, Ohio,* and she said not since high school when we read it together one summer. "It's a surprisingly steamy book. Those small-town dreamers just bursting at the seams. Anyway, at the end of *Winesburg,* if you remember, George Willard boards a train for Chicago in the hope of becoming a writer. My novel picks up where Anderson left off."

"I'd love to read it," Lucy said.

"I should have a draft by the end of summer."

Later that afternoon, headed north on Lake Shore Drive for an appointment at the Lakeside library, I thought of my father at his desk, scribbling his endless notes about George Willard in Chicago, and tried to imagine how his missing manuscript, his *Book of the Grotesque,* might unfold.

8

On the afternoon following the anniversary dinner, George tried to clear his head of the specter of Helen White, but it begirded him like the thick summer heat, and instead of heading home after work he took the grip to the Theater District and found the host at Henrici's. The slight, fastidious man wore the same bow tie and waistcoat from the night before, and seemed in a hurry, though no other patrons appeared to be waiting for him.

"I have an odd question," George began. "My wife and I came in for dinner last night, and I saw you speaking with someone who might be an old acquaintance of mine. Do you remember handing some boxes to a woman fairly late in the evening, around ten o'clock?"

"And what was the name on your reservation?"

"Willard," George said. "You seated us at that table over there."

"Yes, of course. I recognized your wife. Her father has dined with us on several occasions."

"I work for him."

"Right," the host said, as if he already knew.

George cautioned himself not to share more information than necessary. This fellow had a high-hatted manner and seemed just the kind of gatekeeper who would continue to ask questions if given the opportunity.

"Those boxes. . . ."

"Bread for the poor. We give all the rolls we don't use to Hull House. They have a bakery over there, but can't keep up with demand."

"And the young woman—do you happen to know her name?" George asked.

"She told me once, but I've forgotten."

"Was it Helen? Helen White?"

"There's always a chance, but I doubt it. Part of my job is to recollect names, and that one's ringing no bells."

George thanked him and caught the grip at the corner of Randolph and Dearborn, and all the way home he recounted this exchange. He knew Lazar had been to Henrici's on a few occasions, but was surprised that the host could pick Margaret out of a crowd. It was also curious that he couldn't name this other woman who came into the restaurant perhaps every day. Was he so wonder-struck by automobiles and finery that charity workers slipped beneath his notice? Or was he withholding the mystery woman's name, for some reason? He did seem the dissembling sort, and George wondered for a moment if he would soon be reading in the society pages that the son-in-law of the city's top adman was looking to rekindle an old flame.

Impossible. Even if it was Helen, the host couldn't recall her name, so how would he know the first thing about her? And why all this hand-wringing? George had done nothing wrong, had not so much as entertained a wayward desire. He thought he'd seen a friend from his hometown and it was only natural that he'd want to say hello.

By the time he stepped onto the sidewalk at Lake Shore Drive he had convinced himself that the woman at the restaurant was not Helen White, after all. In a rare moment of marital tension he'd seen a chimera in a perfect stranger, an employee of Jane Addams's Hull House. That night he recited to Margaret an Elizabeth Barrett Browning poem, "The Best Thing in the World," which the speaker defines as *Love, when, so, you're loved again,* and by month's end George had read nearly all of the sonnets aloud.

He had struggled when Margaret asked his reasons for marrying her, but in the pressure of the moment he recalled that she'd been a member of the Browning Society at the university. In his first months in the city, when he was hoping to become a writer, he had made himself memorize a famous poem every few days, and among those that he had learned by heart was Browning's Sonnet 43. So when it came time to tell his wife why he had married her, he let the verse do much of the talking: *How do I love thee? Let me count the ways. / I love thee to the depth and breadth and height / My soul can reach, when feeling out of sight / For the ends of Being and ideal Grace. . . . I love thee with the breath, / Smiles, tears, of all my life! / and, if God choose, I shall but love thee better after death.*

Margaret was impressed, and well beyond their first anniversary she and her husband would read to each other every night before bed. Years later, when George would write his first book, he would credit these hearth-bound evenings with helping him hear the music out of which all stories flow.

Summer 1906 would prove a tranquil time for the couple. George would get his wish when Margaret agreed to leave the carriage house. Harriet made it clear that her financial contribution would depend on propinquity to 814 Lake Shore Drive, and so, far-flung neighborhoods having been made less appealing, they moved just seven blocks west. Margaret and George got a considerable bargain on a three-story brick townhouse on a leafy Gold Coast street where at least Harriet Lazar wouldn't be following them like a sunflower across the garden. "Five bedrooms!" she exclaimed on her first of what would become daily visits. "A fair amount of space, but you know what they say: 'Nature abhors a vacuum.'"

"If you're talking about children, Mother, you might learn a bit of patience. I'm twenty-two, and unlike some people I intend to have a life before any little shavers arrive on the scene."

"I had a life before your father abducted me. Have you heard of Beacon Hill?" She turned to George. "Our house was on Louisburg Square. We had Vanderbilts and Cabots for neighbors. 'The Swedish Nightingale,' Jenny Lind, was married a bouquet's toss from our front door."

"If that's what you call having a life," Margaret put in. She reserved her harshest words for her mother, something George would come to be grateful for. And Harriet never backed down. "As if you're any better, Margaret. Your every action is a reaction to mistakes you think I've made. But you're making them all over again, in ways you'll only realize when there's nothing to be done."

"I have no idea what you're talking about."

"You will in time, dear."

Margaret and her mother could be laughing one moment or talking about the wallpaper; then the mood would turn, and they would rage at each other, swift and furious as a summer storm.

"You chased away my brother. Are you hoping to run me off, too?" Margaret went on. "The only reason you want me close by is to have a sitting target."

"I wasn't the one who chased Charles away. He couldn't stand Chicago, and really, what's to recommend it? The reek of the stockyards? The slums and gambling houses? The world's most notorious vice district? The bloody strikes? The muddy streets? The unrelenting winters?"

"That's not why he left, and you know it."

"We're first in murder again this year," Harriet said. "Every day I read about a bar brawl where one factory worker cuts another's throat. Can you blame your brother for not wishing to live among savages?"

"You made him hate it here. You, with your clocks set to Boston time."

"I'm not the issue, Margaret. This won't come as news to you either, George, but Charles wanted no part of the business. You should hear him rail against commercial art and advertising—as if we haven't given him every privilege in the world. His schooling, his hobbies, the roof over his head. Even now, though he barely speaks to us, we keep his business afloat and foot every bill so he can flit about New York like a popinjay."

"And yet George and I can't live where we want to," Margaret said.

"So you don't want to live here?" Harriet stood in the dining room, where the eight-arm chandelier floated over the table like a glass octopus. George had never imagined in all his years that he would live in a house this grand.

"It's fine," Margaret said. "But why does the good daughter get so little and the prodigal son so much?"

"Do you really get so little?" Harriet asked. "If I were you, George, I'd take offense at that comment."

Margaret laid a hand on her husband's shoulder. "I meant nothing against you, darling. But sometimes the world just isn't fair."

September 13, 1906. He would always remember that date, his twenty-ninth birthday. A Nuvolia representative named Richard Trumbull had come from New York to review the Performance Department and report back to his bosses. Lazar, Kennison, and the chief accountant had spent the morning with the client behind closed doors, and when George asked his father-in-law during a break between meetings why he hadn't been invited, why in fact he hadn't known about Trumbull's visit until that very morning, Lazar said, "You must not have seen the latest numbers. We're going to be making changes with this account."

"But Nuvolia has been my client for years," George said. "Shouldn't I have a place at the table?"

"We can talk about this later." Lazar steered him out of his office toward Kennison's, where the Mountie and Trumbull were taking in the view of Dearborn Street. "George, be a good man and take Mr. Trumbull on a tour of the city. Show him the sights. It's a glorious day."

Trumbull crossed the room and shook George's hand. A large man with a teetering walk, he had thinning hair of a silvery brown that matched his wool sack jacket.

"The Thomas Flyer is waiting out front," Lazar said. "It's the 1906 model, just came in last month from Buffalo. Four-cylinder. Fifty-horsepower, d'you understand? It's the only tonneau in the world that can be owned and maintained without a full-time chauffeur."

"I hope you're not putting Willard behind the wheel," Kennison said. "Have you ever driven a car, George?"

Lazar laughed, and George could only shake his head.

"I'm glad to hear you're retaining your driver," Kennison said. "There's the rest of the fleet to keep in mind."

"Are you a car man, Mr. Trumbull?" Lazar asked.

"I don't own one myself, but a man can dream."

"I've heard rumor around the racetrack that an engineer in Detroit is working on an automobile for the masses. Could be the future."

"Imagine. A car for every curb," Kennison put in. "And we'll be first in line to sell it."

George gave an inward groan—at his rival's relentless need to impress, and at the sense he kept having of being left in the dust, too slow to adapt to the times.

Soon he was snug in the button-tufted seats of the Thomas Flyer, crowded into a corner by the ursine Mr. Trumbull. "Where to?" asked the chauffeur, a stoic veteran of the Spanish-American War named Virgil Reed.

"A fine question. Let me put it to our guest."

"How about the stockyards?" Trumbull said. "Isn't that what everyone wants to see in Chicago? The pure spectacle of it?"

"Oh, I don't know." George shielded his eyes from the sunlight, which beat down on the macadam and the black leather seats. "On a hot day like this, with the wind coming in from the west, you can smell the place from here. I wouldn't recommend it."

"Half the city's business ties back to the stockyards. It's the biggest game in town."

"Have you read *The Jungle*?" George asked. Upton Sinclair's novel had caused a sensation when it was published earlier in the year. People were horrified at the stories of exploitation, of workers falling into rendering pots and getting mixed into Pure Leaf Lard.

"Who's to say it's not all bunkum?" Trumbull put in. "Tubercular beef makes headlines. That doesn't mean the claims are true."

"I've been to those cattle pens and killing floors, and I'm not surprised by the accounts. With all due respect," George said, "there's nothing appealing about the world's largest slaughterhouse."

"Well—" Trumbull sat back in his seat and produced a pack of Beemans Gum from his jacket pocket. "Take me where you like, then. I can see the yards on my own time." He tucked some gum into his mouth, then put the pack away without offering any to George.

Virgil, the chauffeur, had been a Buffalo Soldier, serving in Cuba under Pershing; he had papery skin and the countenance of one who had seen it all. "Where to?" he asked again, and George suggested Lake Shore Drive. The Thomas Flyer sputtered into motion, and as they inched toward the lake through midday traffic George remembered the time, six summers ago now, when his father came in on the train for a visit—one of only three in the whole ten years—and how, the very morning of his arrival, he had insisted upon taking the commuter rail to the stockyards.

It was a hideous place, with holding pens and ramps, smokestacks and brick buildings as far as the eye could see, and muddy, rutted streets and a katzenjammer of terrible sounds that Tom Willard talked right over. "It's an assault on the nose, but I could live with the profits. I heard the Armours are worth some sixty million. Can you imagine, George? What would you do with sixty million?"

They were waiting in line at the slaughterhouse on the grounds of the Armour plant. A tour guide stood at the entrance under a sign—*We Feed the World*—and all around them train tracks brought in cattle and pigs and sent out beef and pork, day after day, around the clock. At the time George was the golden boy at the Alfred J. Lazar Agency. He'd been given a raise and an interior office and creative freedom on his first big contract, but he had never entertained the idea of one day earning millions, hadn't pictured himself among the Armours, Palmers, McCormicks, and Lazars. He still dreamed of becoming a writer then, so when his father asked what he'd do with all that money, the first thing that crossed his mind was to pause his life and revisit the people and stories that had once so stirred his imagination. But Tom Willard, who thought only of business, would never understand. So George turned a mirror on the question and asked, "What would *you* do with sixty million?"

The tour guide announced that the doors would soon open; please enter single file and stay to the left.

"Do you really want to know?" George's father said, all too happy to talk about himself. "I'd tear the New Willard House down. I know what you're thinking—what would your mother have wanted? But I've put my life into that place—and a king's ransom, too. I can't go on fixing a few rooms here and there, trying to keep up with the maintenance. If I had sixty million I'd build a grand hotel on the site, with a big staff and all new everything. And I'd call it The Elizabeth, for your mother, that's what I'd do. People would flock there for parties and conventions. And I'd give the better part of my fortune to Winesburg, for a new library, opera house, historical museum, and parks full of fountains and flowers. Our town would be the new Saratoga. Resorts would line the road straight up to Lake Erie. Everyone would know Tom Willard, then, and with that kind of influence I'll tell you what: Sandusky County would finally send a Democrat to Congress. What would you think of your old man then?"

The doors opened. The tour group entered the slaughterhouse. Squeals and shrieks rang through the room. George had no reply, only wished that his father would go on and not stop talking. The smell burned his nostrils, made him light-headed, coated his tongue with a repugnant glaze. The tour guide's mouth was moving, but George couldn't hear. In the near distance, the pigs entered the slaughterhouse one at a time. A man in the final pen looped a chain over the rear leg of each pig, jerking the animal into the air and pinning it upon a revolving wheel. When the pig was upside down, a hook at the top of the wheel moved the animal onto a trolley, then along to a butcher who ended its life with a ready stab in the throat.

George tried to look away, but the scene fixed him in stunned horror. He'd been a townie so had spent little time around animals, though he did occasionally wander down a back alley where the day laborers of Winesburg lived. Women in calico dresses washed dishes at kitchen windows. Children raced around ramshackle houses, and pigs rooted in small, grubby yards. George had always thought all pigs were the same, but as each one approached its execution he realized he'd been wrong. Some lowered their heads, resigned to their fate; some scrambled backwards and put up a struggle; some huddled close to their companions, shivering, sniffing the air; some kept silent; and some let out terrified screams, sounds that if he closed his eyes George would swear were human.

Later it would occur to him that if no two pigs went to their deaths the same way, then each pig must be an individual. And if being an individual was the essence of being human, then what could be said of pigs? Of the steer that took a sledgehammer blow to the skull, then dropped through the pen's false bottom into a trolley bound for a meat locker?

These questions were taking shape in George's mind when he sat down with his father for dinner at the Stockyards Inn. They had finished the half-day tour, witnessed the slaughter of pigs, cattle, and calves, and seen women in white hats and aprons from Greece, Lithuania, Poland, Germany, and every other corner of Europe package the by-products of the operation that Phillip D. Armour had boasted uses "everything but the squeal." George had no appetite, and the very idea of sitting down to a steak brought bile up to his throat.

The inn was an island of opulence in a sea of gore. The half-timbered building contained beautiful antique furniture and china, and the restaurant teemed with traders and cattlemen toasting their yield. Scanning the tables, set with crystal and white linen, Tom Willard proclaimed, "Now *this* is my idea of a proper dining establishment." He filled the air once again with his unreachable dreams, and George wished his father would stop talking when the moment called for silence and say something when the moment called for conversation.

Tom Willard ordered a sirloin and marveled aloud at the efficiency of the workers, the choreography of the slaughterhouse line. This was before *The Jungle,* before the true working conditions had made the papers. George knew that something was wrong, could feel it in his senses—in the smell of the place, the way the livestock met their ends, and the effect the yards had on the people who worked there. Pushing a potato around his plate, he thought of the man who killed the pigs, his paleness, the detached look in his eyes. The animals had more life in their final moments, and George wondered if each plunge of the blade made the butcher a little paler, a little further adrift from the shore of his humanity.

The experience at the stockyards had marked George to this day, and it bothered him that Richard Trumbull seemed to be sulking on the car ride along Lake Shore Drive. Perhaps the Nuvolia representative should have been forgiven for wanting to see where soap comes from, but George was not in an accommodating humor on this hot day when his father-in-law was treating him like an errand boy and his father had returned in memory, dismaying as ever. When Virgil pulled over beside a lagoon near the end of Lake Shore Drive and asked, "Where to now?" George's snap reply was, "Take us to Hull House."

"Are you sure?" Virgil asked.

"Is it such an odd request?"

"Hull House?" Trumbull said.

"Wouldn't you like to meet the extraordinary Jane Addams? I hear she receives visitors right off the street."

"I hear she's a socialist." Trumbull mopped his brow with a handkerchief.

"Perhaps you should take your coat off," George said. "We're getting no break from the sun."

Trumbull returned the handkerchief to his pocket. "I'll be fine, thank you." He sniffed.

Virgil steered the Thomas Flyer south and west through Old Town and across the river at Kingsbury Tract, then straight down Halsted into the Nineteenth Ward.

"Nothing like the taste of coal smoke on the tongue." Trumbull fished out another piece of Beemans and snapped the gum between his teeth. "And I thought New York was bad."

They had entered an industrial neighborhood of long brick factories and simple wood-frame houses that crouched beneath the level of the street. Sooty-cheeked children played on sidewalks while their mothers glowered from sloped porches. "This car's going to need a good wash and tightening," Virgil said as he rumbled along Halsted's jagged grooves. "Did you tell Mr. Lazar you were coming down here?"

It was true there weren't many cars in the Maxwell Street district, and certainly no luxury cars owned by one of the city's millionaires. "We're going to the most famous settlement house in the world. It should be on all of our tours. These people—" George gestured around the overcrowded neighborhood, "could be our future customers, the future inhabitants of Tidy Town."

"They don't look so tidy to me." Trumbull shifted in his seat.

"They work around the clock for pennies," George said. "Some union men I used to live with told me whole neighborhoods on the south and west sides are without plumbing. There are places where the city refuses to pick up garbage, and if a horse dies on the street it's left there to rot."

"Looks like your run-of-the-mine immigrant neighborhood to me," Trumbull said. "Dirty Slavs, dirty Armenians, dirty Italians, dirty Bohemians all stacked on top of each other. It doesn't matter who they are or where they're from, you can bet they haven't had a bath since one of their kind shot McKinley. Anarchists and flunkies. And they just keep on coming. Doubling in number every year. If we don't say enough is enough we're going to lose this country."

George had seen this kind of talk in the papers, but had never experienced it firsthand. He knew he shouldn't say another word, since this man held a brief for George's most important contract. Though he had only a general understanding of the squabbles between the Liberal Immigration League and the Immigrant Restriction League and all the other entities fighting for or against the new arrivals, his sympathies lay with the bottom dog. "I have no issue with immigrants," he said.

"So you stand with the outcasts of other nations?"

"They work as hard as you and me."

Trumbull pointed to a peddler hawking iron from the back of his wagon, then a ragpicker diving for salvage in an overflowing garbage box. "They come from the ghettos of Europe and make slums out of our neighborhoods. They're the weakest of the weak, and they're dragging us down."

Beyond a billboard for Edelweiss Beer, the vista opened up to a large complex of brick buildings surrounding an Italianate mansion. Virgil parked the Thomas Flyer at the curb and climbed out to open the door for Trumbull. When the visitor from New York hesitated, a gale of worries swept over George. Perhaps he should have taken Trumbull where he'd wanted to go and kept silent like the model employee he used to be. And what if Jane Addams was indeed home, just inside the entrance? Did George want a scene, one he himself had set in motion? And then there was Helen White, the very reason he'd asked Virgil to drive into the Nineteenth Ward in the first place. What if she really did work at Hull House? What if she were looking out one of the arched windows right now and recognizing the younger man in the back of the luxury automobile that was drawing so much attention to itself?

"We don't have to go in," George said. "We can go to the stockyards, anywhere you'd like. Virgil—" he began, but Trumbull had already delivered himself from the car and was making his way up the front walk.

George thanked the chauffeur and told him keep the motor running, then hurried toward the open doors of Hull House.

9

I made a habit of bringing my father lunch, and throughout much of that winter could count on his being away until one o'clock. I'd arrive around noon, on my break, put his food in the fridge, have a sandwich at the kitchen counter, then poke around his apartment in search of the elusive *Book of the Grotesque*. I looked in every closet, bookcase, cabinet, and drawer, cast my eyes over every Xerox and index card, turned the place over with the thoroughness of a forensic investigator. But I found nothing. Less than nothing, in fact: the title page, fragments, and folders were gone.

I usually managed to leave before my father's return, but when I couldn't get out in time he seemed unsurprised to see me, deliverer of his midday meal. Flushed and out of breath, he'd set down his cane and battered valise and lower himself onto the camelback sofa. Wing would come out of hiding and hop onto my father's lap for a scratch behind the ears. I'd bring out lunch, ask where he'd been, and the answer would always be the same: *Out to take the air, as they used to say.*

By the end of March I had searched the entire apartment and could no longer stand not knowing what had happened to the evidence I'd seen of my father's novel. I'd been watching his valise, which he carried everywhere, but it never seemed full enough to contain even a partial manuscript. So one day I got an extra key from the building manager to my father's storage cage on the twentieth floor.

The cage was empty but for three cardboard boxes. The first two were marked "CRBC" and were full of old books including, I noticed, the *Spoon River Anthology* I'd shelved in his apartment a couple months before. Most of the books were fiction titles by Sherwood Anderson's contemporaries, including Theodore Dreiser, Carl Sandburg, John Dos Passos, Hemingway, and Faulkner. I didn't think much of the books at the time; they looked like any number of editions I might have pulled from the Lakeside Library stacks or stuck under the robotic scanner.

Of greater interest were the contents of the third box, marked "BOG." *Book of the Grotesque.* I sat on the concrete floor, lifted out the pages and note cards, and went through them piece by piece, careful to leave the arrangement as I'd found it. Once again the title page sat on top, and beneath it the same fragments and manila folders I'd seen before. Below that, inch upon inch of more notes and folders: *Chicago Barons of the Gilded Age; Street, Rail, and Waterway Maps; The Panic of 1907.* Since I didn't have all day and worried that my father might stumble upon me at any moment, I flipped through the stack quickly. I did pause to skim some of the material, like firsthand accounts, dated 1906, of a day at the Union Stockyards, or biographical sketches of the advertising kings of a hundred years ago, their objectives little different from those of my colleagues at Imego.

Toward the bottom of the stack I found an accordion file marked *Old Drafts.* But the file was mostly empty; only the first section contained any manuscript. The twelve typewritten pages began:

From the window of the westbound train George Willard saw what fifty thousand new arrivals a year had witnessed. In the distance, over the corn and oat fields, a gray pall hovered like a storm cloud. He had heard stories about Chicago since he was a boy, had risen at two o'clock this morning unable to sleep or slow his heartbeat, which even now pounded in his ears with the rhythm of the wheels rumbling over the tracks.

The chapter goes on to describe the landscape from the train, the blighted neighborhoods, the grand boulevards *tracing the lakeshore like the curve of a woman's hip,* the shock and wonder George feels upon his first encounter with the *unruly metropolis.* Had I seen the chapter in workshop I would have praised the writing and period detail, but said the story was slow to trigger. I would have rolled out the old familiars: *What's at stake? Where's the conflict? Who are the antagonists?* I wondered where the rest of the book had gone, what happens in chapter two, once George is off the train, in the maw of the city.

As I was putting the box marked "BOG" back in place, I noticed just behind it a brochure I hadn't seen at first. I had a passing worry that it had fallen out of one of the boxes, but I'd been so careful—I was sure it must

have been sitting loose. I held it to the light. LIVING WITH CONGES-
TIVE HEART FAILURE, it read. THE GOOD HEARTS PROGRAM AT
LAKESIDE UNIVERSITY HOSPITAL.

I checked my watch. Well past one. I couldn't linger any further. I put
the brochure back and returned to the office, where I spent much of the
afternoon searching the Internet. I knew my father had heart disease, but
congestive heart failure put him in a whole new category. Since all I'd seen
was the brochure, no ECG results or instructions for treatment, I had no
way of knowing the severity of his condition. Stage A meant his future risk
was high but functions were fine for now, B and C could be managed with
meds and treatment, but if he'd reached Stage D, he needed a transplant, or
in the case of a seventy-eight-year-old who'd put on hard miles and still took
a drink before five: palliative care. *I have one foot in the grave,* my father had
said. Perhaps he wasn't kidding.

But I knew I couldn't mention his heart without admitting I'd been
through his things. It was enough that I'd uprooted him, made him agree to
see the cardiologist. If he wanted me to know his business, why would he
hide the boxes and brochure in the storage cage? When I asked about the
appointment back in February, he'd said his heart was *same as ever: ticking
like a bomb.* He claimed he was taking his pills, walking more than he had
in years, had cut back on butter and salt. *My last cigarette was postcoital,* he'd
said. *And believe me:* that *was a long time ago.*

So unless I confronted him, all I could do was keep an eye out for
symptoms. He did have a slight wheeze in his chest, but the raspiness dated
back to his Pall Mall days. He seemed tired on occasion and sometimes
short of breath, but not alarmingly so. I looked for veins standing up in his
neck, swelling of the ankles, but nothing seemed out of the ordinary. I even
checked the medicine cabinet every couple weeks and counted his pills to
make sure he was taking them. By that measure, at least, he was proving a
man of his word.

My attention to my father had not gone unnoticed at work. At a rare dinner out at an Indian place in the neighborhood, Dhara told me there'd been
chattering in my bullpen that my lunch breaks had been growing longer and
longer.

"Where have you been?" she asked. "I never see you in the cafeteria anymore."

I'd been off the road for much of the winter. The universities I was
assigned to were getting cold feet about digitization. Ordinarily I'd have

been all over the Midwest, following up with librarians or at the warehouse checking in with the manager. But the scanning had slowed considerably due to legal battles over copyright. Though my team was far removed from the negotiations, our calendars had thinned, and unlike everyone else in the office we had to make an effort to look busy. "I'm sorry, Dhara," I said. "I've been spending a lot of time at my dad's."

"Still bringing him carry-out?"

"He wouldn't eat otherwise."

"So Imego's his taco truck? Seriously, we ought to be careful, Adam. You can't afford to lose this job."

And that's when I told her about the heart-failure brochure. I don't know why I'd kept it to myself. I guess I felt I'd exhausted Dhara's patience, and didn't want to hear her say I was making a song and dance about nothing. "He could be terminally ill," I said.

"How long have you known?"

"A month or so."

"Why didn't you tell me before?" she asked. "We used to go over the whole day at dinner. Now I never see you."

"You're the one who works late," I said.

To my relief, Dhara had no rejoinder. She nipped the top off her samosa, and the steam rose like a mini volcano. "So you haven't badgered him with questions?"

I didn't admit I'd sneaked into his storage cage. "I stumbled across the information."

"But you don't know how sick he is?"

"He looks the same—scarecrow in a cardigan—but I think he doesn't want me to know. The brochure was hidden. I wasn't supposed to see it."

"You've got to find out," Dhara said. "If you don't want to talk to him, I will."

I was surprised she cared. She'd only seen him a couple of times, coming and going, since he'd moved in. Mutual discomfort had marked the few times they'd spoken, and privately she'd always been critical of my father— for good reason. Perhaps she was remembering her mother's last years and realizing, for my sake, there was only so much time.

"I'll do it," I promised, though I didn't know how. The prospect set my foot to tapping.

"So—I need to tell you something," Dhara began, and she paused long enough for competing thoughts to cross my mind: *I want a divorce* or *I'm pregnant.* "I've applied for that job at corporate," she said. "I've reached the ceiling here, and the Chicago office is not where it's at. Even Pittsburgh is growing more than we are. I have to take a shot sometime, don't I?"

In my heart of hearts I'd known this was coming. Still, I allowed a silence to linger in the air, a momentary sadness to pass over my face. Then I asked, "What about me?"

"If I get the position, we'll talk about it, of course. I'm sure you'd be able to find something, with the Library Project or public relations. We can cross that bridge later, and hope it's the Golden Gate."

"You know how I feel about this," I said. "I really don't want to leave."

"Let's just see how the thing plays out. Maybe you'll come around when you see what they're offering."

"I doubt it," I said.

"Your work is stalled, too, Adam. There's not a lot keeping you here."

"What about Vritra? I thought you were all worried about his health. We can't just abandon him."

"I'll make you a deal." She actually put out her hand to shake on it. "If we move to California, he can live with us for however long it takes him to get situated."

"He'd never go for it."

"What choice does he have?" she asked. I shook her hand limply, and my mind drifted for the rest of dinner.

But on the first of April I got a surprise. Dhara was working late. I was home alone having microwave lasagna, reading the *New York Times* online at the swag-leg table, when the doorbell rang. It was my father.

"Do you want to come in?" I asked. He never visited our apartment, had stepped inside the place only a couple of times.

"That's okay." He looked down at his loafers; his white tube socks drooped over the sides. "I wanted to bring you this." He leaned his ball-handle cane against the wall, reached into his corduroy sport coat, and pulled out a thick handful of cash. "You can count it, if you'd like." He pressed it toward me.

Most of the bills were hundreds and fifties. "Jesus!" I said. Instinctively, I grabbed his lapel and pulled him inside.

He stumbled into our hallway. "Easy there."

I grabbed his cane and closed the door behind him. "My neighbors are going to think a drug deal's going down."

"I'd be the oldest pusher on the block." My father leaned against the wall, catching his breath. "Is that how you treat everyone who gives you six thousand dollars?"

I held the money as if he'd put a gun in my hand. "Is this a joke?"

"It *is* April Fool's Day." He grabbed his cane from my hand and made for the couch.

"Honestly, what on earth is this for?" I asked.

"You know what it's for." He sat down with a groan. The hem of his trousers rode up his chalky legs. "I'm sorry I got behind on the rent. But this should cover January through April. Plus moving expenses. How much were those? A thousand?"

"Two thousand, but that's not the point. Where did you get this money?"

"Where did you get this couch?" my father said. "It's about as comfortable as an injection table."

"It's modern. And you're avoiding my question."

The elastic in his tube socks had broken, leaving his shins exposed. If his ankles were swollen, it was impossible to tell beneath the bunched material. "I'm not a pauper, you know."

"You've said yourself: Wall Street ate your IRA. What are you living on?" I asked.

"Why should I face this cross-examination?" He began to get up from the couch. "Do you want the money or not?"

"I'm sorry, Dad. But you have to understand it's a little strange for me to be holding this"—I waved the wad of cash like a fan—"when your house is in foreclosure."

"That was another matter," he said. "What's done is done."

"You're not going to tell me where this money came from?"

"It was mine, and now it's yours." He pushed past me and headed for the door. "You can expect my next payment on May 1, with the moving balance included and a smile for your trouble."

Not five minutes after he left, Dhara came home. "Guess who I saw in the lobby," she said.

"My father."

"Yes, the very one."

"What was he doing in our tower?"

"You're not going to believe it," I said.

"Did he tell you about his heart?" She looked genuinely concerned. "How bad is it?"

"I was going to bring that up, but instead he gave me this." I handed the cash to Dhara, told her the amount and what it was for. She asked the same question I had—"Where did the money come from?"—but I told her he gave no answer, in fact breezed out with the promise of future rent checks. "Maybe Hollywood called," I said, "and they're making *Sherwood Anderson, Volume One* into a blockbuster."

Dhara opened the refrigerator and poured herself a glass of water. "The whole thing is strange. I don't like it."

"We should be glad for the extra cash," I said.

"Sure, but where did it come from? What if he's getting himself into more trouble?"

As she was putting the Brita pitcher away, my cell phone rang. Dhara and I both had iPhones, and we had a habit of leaving them on the hallway table when we walked in from work, so when one of the phones rang we often headed over simultaneously to see who the call was for. This time it was mine, and I recognized Lucy's 617 cell number.

"Who is it?" Dhara asked, just a few steps behind me.

"*Unknown.*" I slipped the phone into my pocket, where it continued to ring.

"Could be important," Dhara said.

"No one's looking for me," I tried to assure her. "It's probably a telemarketer."

"They don't tend to call cell phones."

"Who knows?" I shrugged. "I'm sure it's nothing."

A moment later, my voice-mail notification chimed. "Telemarketers don't leave messages," Dhara said.

"We were talking about my father and the six thousand dollars he just delivered." I tried to wheel her off the subject, but she was eyeing me with suspicion.

"You look like the cat that ate the canary," she said.

"I don't know what that is," I stalled.

"Your face is red. You look guilty."

"This has to stop, Dhara." I walked past her to the living room and stood at the window watching for my father's apartment light to turn on. "I don't know what's gotten into you."

"Well, I think you do." She went to the bedroom and closed the door.

Lucy was calling to invite me to lunch. "There's a new independent book-store/café I thought we could check out. It's just down the block from my apartment. I hear they do salads and sandwiches."

I called back the next morning after Dhara had left for work. "Sounds good," I said, and we planned for the middle of the following week. "That is, if they haven't gone out of business by then."

"They're only a couple months old, Adam. What happened to the optimist I used to know?"

"9/11, Iraq, Afghanistan, the financial implosion, the end of 'the great American ride.' You'd have to be crazy to open a bookstore at a time like this."

"Would you rather get a steak near the Stock Exchange?"

"I'm sorry. I don't mean to be a downer," I said. "Things are a little funny on the home front. I won't bore you with the details. I promise to be in a cheerier mood next Wednesday."

When we got off the phone I decided I'd feel a lot better if my life weren't so full of questions: What stage was my father's heart failure? Would Dhara get the job in Silicon Valley? Did she really want me to join her out there? Where would I be in six months? Chicago? San Francisco? With or without a job? What about Lucy? Why was I even asking, "What about Lucy?" Would I find the rest of *The Book of the Grotesque*? Would I ever write my own novel? Where did my father come up with that money? Was it his to give? And where did he go every morning, on these walks?

I asked the weekday doorman in my father's tower if he'd seen which direction my father took when he set out in the morning. But the doorman said he only ever saw him picking up the mail. "You might talk to the guys in the garage," he suggested, with a vaguely sardonic look.

In photographs of the famous buildings of Chicago, Harbor City is rec-ognizable as much for its honeycomb towers as for the parked cars, back ends facing out, dotting the first nineteen floors. In Steve McQueen's last movie, he gets into a car chase up Harbor City's parking ramp and runs the bad guy's Pontiac off the seventeenth floor into the Chicago River. When I told the parking attendant that I was Roland Clary's son, he rolled his eyes. "Oh, yeah. The guy who can't stand that we're valet-only. Drives him crazy that he has to wait while we get his car."

I apologized and promised the attendant I'd try to teach my father some manners. "How often do you see him?" I asked.

"Most mornings. Nine thirty or thereabouts. I told him he ought to get the brakes checked on that Mercury. They sound like a mouse in a trap. Could be the pads. Could be the rotors."

I thanked him, and the next morning brought the Prius around and waited down the block for the white Mercury Mystique to exit the Harbor City garage. And there it was, right on time, heading down State Street. I never watched detective dramas, but I felt like an amateur sleuth on a stakeout. This made the experience unreal, and therefore easier to carry through. Had I stopped to think about what I was doing, I would have turned around and gone into the office.

We passed the old Marshall Field's building, now a Macy's, and continued down State. Since it was rush hour, traffic was tight. Just one car separated us, so I slouched in my seat and put on a pair of dark sunglasses. I probably didn't need to bother, because my father was one of the most distracted drivers I knew. He kept books in the passenger seat—never a good sign—and was forever fiddling with the temperature or the radio dial.

At Adams Street he turned right. We crossed under the El, then went over the river and the Kennedy Expressway and into the West Loop. The traffic thinned, and the sight lines opened to half-vacant new condo buildings and squat walkups crowned with water towers. At Halsted he took a left, and we passed gyro shops and grocers along the edge of Greektown, then students biking to or from class at the University of Illinois–Chicago. The Brutalist redoubt of the UIC blurred by, concrete fortress after concrete fortress, interrupted only by the homey brick encampment of Hull House near the center of campus.

Ignoring a NO TURN ON RED at Taylor, my father swung right, and not wanting to lose him I followed suit, nearly cutting off a cyclist. "Learn to drive, Prius!" a voice faded behind me. Worse insults have been hurled.

I should have guessed where my father was going well before I could smell the charred peppers and sausages of Al's #1 Italian Beef or notice the cucinas and ristorantes lining the street. The storage locker I had arranged for him stood on the west side of Little Italy. From half a block away, I could see my father pull up to the access gate, roll down the window, and punch in his code. The gate opened, and I sat waiting long enough for a light rain to pass, and listened abstractedly to NPR. The G20 summit in London had ended the day before with a trillion-dollar pledge to struggling economies and a promise to overhaul financial regulation. Closer by, a federal grand jury had charged our laughingstock of a former governor with racketeering, extortion, and fraud.

After a half hour or so my father's car reemerged and I followed him back along the same route we'd taken, until he turned north on the Kennedy. We took the expressway under a couple bridges, then I had to cut across two lanes of traffic when he abruptly exited. Stopped at a light two cars back at Division and Elston, I could see on the opposite corner the recently shuttered Chicago dive known only by its hand-painted sign—SLOW DOWN—and the neon tracing beneath it: LIFE'S TOO SHORT. Perched on a stagnant bend of the river, the colorful shanty used to cater to an odd mix of slumming hipsters, party-boat carousers, and antique barflies.

Up Elston we went. If Michigan Avenue was Chicago's storefront, Elston was its back lot. Along this thoroughfare of lube shops, tattoo parlors, contractor suppliers, warehouses, and liquor discounters, I could almost hear the music of Wilco, Jeff Tweedy's weatherworn voice.

Past an oxygen supplier up near Montrose, my father parked at a meter, opened his door, swung out one leg at a time, and with the help of his cane, vaulted himself onto his feet. I drove past and caught a glimpse of the sign—MAYFAIR BUY & SELL—then pulled over a block up. In the rearview I watched my father go inside. A few minutes later he returned, followed by a pot-bellied man with a chin-curtain beard. He opened the trunk, which mostly blocked my view, but I could tell they were rummaging around in there. They made three trips back inside, the man carrying boxes, my father trailing.

Twenty minutes later he was back on the road. He did a U-turn and headed down Elston, then turned into a Goodwill near the Vienna beef factory. He pulled up to the rolling steel door, pushed the call button, and a sullen kid in high-tops and low-rise jeans emptied the contents of the Mercury's trunk and backseat: lamps, books, records, bric-a-brac, garbage bags full of clothes, and a stack of old pictures that might have been part of the other-people's-ancestors collection.

My father took his receipt and headed home. It was a little before one when he gave the keys to the valet at Harbor City. I watched him disappear in the direction of the elevators, and instead of parking and going in to work I continued on, back toward Little Italy. I didn't know when else I'd have a chance to see what he'd been up to in that storage unit. The pawn shop explained the six thousand dollars, though he must have had to make dozens of trips. No wonder he'd been gone nearly every day since I'd moved him here.

Because the contract was in my name, paid for with my credit card, the attendant gave me a code to the gate and a key to the unit's padlock. I punched in the numbers, drove in, and parked the Prius next to 421. As the lock clicked open I had a brief hope that I would find *The Book of the Grotesque,* and that the rest of the novel would be brilliant. I would convince my father to send it to Lucy; she would publish it, and this old man, whose life had appeared to be wasted, who hadn't had a word in print in over forty years, would stun the literary world.

There was the old optimism. Alive, after all.

But when I threw open the rolling door, expecting to see the storage cage filled from front to back with my father's accumulated junk, just as the movers and I had left it back in January, I found instead a nearly empty space.

10

The soap salesman, Richard Trumbull, had already walked into Hull House by the time George caught up. The sound of a violin playing a melancholy Chopin étude filled the large drawing room, and a greeter, a long-faced woman with hooded eyes, held a finger to her lips and whispered, "The children are having a recital. Are you with the Lab School?"

"We're just visiting," George said. "We can come back another time."

"It shouldn't be long. Here—" She escorted George and Trumbull to two empty seats within a semicircle of listeners.

"We really ought to head back," George began, but the greeter didn't hear him. Trumbull sat down heavily in a Windsor chair and wiped his brow. Forty or fifty people were gathered in the spacious room of arched doorways, intricate molding, and floral-print walls. George had expected Spartan décor, but the main house of the settlement was comfortably appointed with Turkish rugs, claw-footed sofas, oak rockers, and plaster busts—no children rushing about pell-mell, but a sense of calm and casual order. Potted ferns billowed beside glass-enclosed bookcases, and a dozen young violinists from perhaps as many nations sat straight as their bows in front of a marble fireplace. Standing before them, an olive-skinned boy played a solo étude. He could not have been older than twelve, but he had a look of such concentration, and the music was so suffused with experience—it seemed impossible such a sound could emerge from the hands of one so young.

When his playing was over, people applauded enthusiastically, and a man with wire spectacles and a push-broom mustache—the violin teacher, George presumed—stood up and thanked everyone for coming. He talked about the long hours the boys and girls had put into their music, and apologized that Jane Addams herself could not be in attendance—she was giving a lecture at the University of Wisconsin. But he could say on her behalf that excellence in the arts was essential to a complete education, for music had a "civilizing and refining influence and a special place in the life of an industrial community."

Out of the corner of his eye George caught a glimpse of Trumbull, who joggled the chain of his pocket watch but did not look down to check the time.

The violin teacher continued, "For arranging this recital I should thank Helen White of the Laboratory School at the University of Chicago. Helen, would you like to say a few words?"

And there she was, standing up in the front row, not halfway across the room, and turning around straight into George's line of vision. She looked slim and attractive, in a fawn-colored poplin dress, her hair gathered into a simple knot. He felt an impulse to duck, to sneak out of the room and back into the Thomas Flyer, back to his young wife and the comfortable existence he had slid into almost entirely by chance. But he was long-torsoed and couldn't hide in the intimate crowd. Helen was saying something about partnership, about how lab schools the world over could learn so much from Hull House about bringing the arts into the curriculum. George saw that she was not wearing a ring, and recalled how the violin teacher had introduced her by her maiden name. Yet it seemed impossible that the prettiest and richest girl in Winesburg could be edging up to thirty and still unmarried. Her eyes brushed across his, and she did a double-take. The words caught in her throat, but she continued and seemed to make a point of turning slightly away from George as she praised the talent and skill of the young violinists and their teacher, who, from the look on his blushing face, had apparently fallen for Helen.

When she had finished her remarks, George turned to Trumbull and said, "Well? Shall we get going?"

The large man rose to his feet with an audible groan. "I thought you were urgent to see this great social experiment. And now you're telling me it's time to leave?"

"The point was for you to meet Miss Addams, but evidently she's on her lecture tour."

"We would have had a provocative dialogue," Trumbull said. "But we're here. Might as well take a look at her little collective."

George said that Lazar would be expecting them back at the office before too long, and with traffic the way it was in Chicago, particularly west to east, they really should be on their way. He couldn't understand why all of a sudden he felt petrified by the thought of meeting Helen White again. Perhaps he believed their moment had come and gone. She had not so much as said good-bye when he'd left town, had written but two or three times, in her boyish hand, on her mother's stationery, but that was nearly a decade ago.

He led Trumbull back toward the front door, where they ran into the greeter—and were it not for that one impediment, that final barrier between safety and danger, present and past, they might have made it all the way to the car, George might have returned to Margaret satisfied that at least he had laid eyes again on his love of years ago—and perhaps that might have been enough. But the greeter stopped them and asked, "What did you think?"

"About what?" George managed through his fog.

"About the music, of course."

"Oh, yes. It was quite good."

"Would you believe that Belio, the boy who played the last étude, 'Tristesse,' is nine years old? He only picked up the instrument at seven."

"Remarkable!" came a voice behind George. And then Helen's hand was on his shoulder and they were face to face. "George Willard! Well, I never!"

Acting as if everything was completely natural, George said, "Helen White. Richard Trumbull," introducing the two. And Helen went along. "You've met Mary?" She indicated the long-faced woman with hooded eyes. "Yes," came George's reply. He wished no end to the formalities, but before he could get his bearings Trumbull was talking to the greeter, and into their small circle drifted the violin teacher, his star pupil in tow. Soon George found himself standing alone in a corner with Helen, looking into her eyes for the first time since she'd come down from Cleveland to attend the Winesburg County Fair and they had escaped to Waterworks Hill, an evening that had glowed in his mind like a beacon all these years.

"I shall never forgive you for leaving town without saying good-bye," Helen began.

"*You* forgive *me*?"

"Why, yes. You left on the 7:45. I happened to be home that weekend," she said, "and my mother let slip that you were going away the next morning. So I got up early, but she delayed me with her yawping. I ran along Main Street, but by the time I got to the platform the train had pulled away. I saw Will Henderson there, looking bone-weary. And your father was announcing that you were going to make a name for yourself."

"I had no idea," George said. "I figured you had your own society at college, and had forgotten us poor souls back home."

"I wrote to you."

"And I wrote back."

"But there was one letter I remember you didn't answer."

"I must not have seen that one," George said. "Maybe my father had it redirected to the wrong address. I moved around a couple of times those first months in Chicago."

Helen asked George to tell her everything that had happened since their last correspondence, and he began with Ma Kavanagh's boardinghouse, skipped his run-in with the Duryea, said he fell in with an advertising firm and found he had a talent for copywriting. His hands were in his pockets, his wedding band hidden from view. "I'm still working for the firm. You know the Monadnock Building? I have a window office on the fourteenth floor," George said. "You seem surprised."

"I didn't see you in business."

"Nor did I," George admitted. "But life has its practicalities."

"Particularly here," Helen agreed. "I thought Cleveland was hard. But Chicago—good heavens!" Her face darkened a moment; then, as if catching herself, she smiled again.

George had heard stories about single women coming in from the heartland and getting ensnared in the white slave trade. Rarely a week had gone by without Ma or Nellie Kavanagh, Margaret or her mother mentioning some new, horrific case of a recent arrival abducted, brainwashed, sold into servitude in the factories or brothels. The *Chicago Inter Ocean* ran a regular column on "Missing Girls," and this summer the city was in the midst of its worst crime wave—burglaries every hour, well over a murder a day, and countless unsolved cases. George worried for Helen. "Where do you live?" he asked, a non sequitur.

"In a caravansary on the edge of Hyde Park."

"South Side. I haven't ventured there more than once or twice. How's the neighborhood?"

He must have looked concerned, because she gave a fluttering laugh. "Oh, George. Can't you see I'm all grown up? I can take care of myself." She said her building was a fortress, close to the lakefront and well patrolled by a no-nonsense Armenian proprietress and her hulking twin sons. Helen had been living there for two years, since her enrollment in the education program at the University of Chicago. She had come to study with John Dewey in the Department of Pedagogy, but in the spring of her acceptance Dewey left for New York after a battle with the university's president. She decided to go forward with her plans, but the Lab School had lost clout since Dewey's departure, so she'd been spending more and more time volunteering at Hull House, where Jane Addams was fighting the good fight for Progressive education and seeing after each student one at a time. This afternoon's recital, for a host of area teachers, was among several events Helen had planned. "Without the arts, what hope do we have for peace and equality—not to mention beauty?" she said.

George was struck by her seriousness and wondered what had happened between Winesburg and now. He asked her as much, and she told him she'd found the college in Cleveland to be little more than a finishing school—it had been her mother's choice, something she realized after her first year, when she transferred to Ohio Normal in Ada. She had trained to become a public-school teacher. Growing up she'd loved reading novels, and she wanted to share her ardor for books. But the curriculum had been too stifling. In her senior year she met a professor who had gone to the University of Michigan with John Dewey, and he urged her to study with the man who would come to be known as one of the great thinkers and reformers of his time. Dewey was a friend of Jane Addams, had often collaborated with her and given lectures at the Plato Club, Hull House's philosophy group. "Professor Dewey believes the best teachers are like artists," Helen explained. "Learned, but also with a compassion to see to the core of people, to unlock something in them, and bring out their potentialities."

"If I'd had a teacher like that," George put in, "I might still be in school."

"You'd make a very fine teacher," Helen said. "You were the artist in town, after all. Everyone knew that."

"And now I work in an office." George heard a trace of self-pity in his voice.

"What was it you said: 'Life has its practicalities'"?

"I'm happy," George insisted.

"You look well."

"I was going to say the same to you."

"My mother tells me that you're married," Helen said. "I wanted to pass along congratulations, but I didn't know where to send the note."

"How did you hear?" George asked.

"Seth Richmond. He still drops in on my parents when he's in town. He said he went to your wedding."

George took his hands out of his pockets and crossed his arms. He felt called out, though he would have got around to mentioning his marriage eventually. "My wife, Margaret—perhaps you knew her at the university. Margaret Lazar? She graduated last year."

"No," Helen said. "What did she study?"

"This and that. I can't say exactly. Is there such a thing as general education?"

"George—what kind of husband are you?"

"I know she read a lot of literature—she loves the Brownings—and she's quite taken with the arts, theater, and the like. She would have been greatly impressed with that boy on the violin."

"I meant to ask—what brings you to Hull House this afternoon? Did you hear about the recital from someone?"

George felt a momentary panic. He had come in the hope of catching a glimpse of Helen, and now, amazingly, here they were, but he could make no such admission. "I was showing a client around the city. What a lucky stroke to find you here."

"Yes, of all places."

"It's a wonder we didn't run into each other earlier," George said. "You should have called on me when you got here."

"It had been so long—"

"Anyway, this client is interested in settlement houses." George nodded toward Trumbull, who had just come back from a brief tour of the main house and was having an animated conversation with Mary the greeter.

"Perhaps the two of you would like to see the other buildings," Helen said.

Not wanting to subject her to the soap salesman's politics, George declined. "We'd better be getting back, but perhaps I'll see you here again."

"We have an excellent theater, and I could introduce you to some of the writers in the Little Room. Quite a literary scene is coming together in Chicago, and Jane is a major part of it."

George asked what days Helen was at Hull House, and she said Thursdays and Fridays, sometimes on weekends. As they were preparing to part ways, a man a few years younger than George, Teutonic and blond, with a wide gap between his front teeth, passed through the room and touched

Helen on the shoulder. "I'm running low again," he said, not stopping for introductions.

"How low?" Helen called after him.

"I could use fifty loaves, if it's not too much trouble." He waved and said, "You're a jewel," then made his hasty way out of the room.

"That's the baker, Stefan. He's overworked, so I've arranged to have some restaurants donate their extra bread."

George considered admitting that he'd seen her at Henrici's but thought better of it. Instead, he wished her well, said he hoped to catch her again sometime. "How many from our town end up in a megalopolis like this? The ones who leave ought to stick together."

"I know what you mean." That shadow of melancholy crept over her face again.

Before turning to leave, he said, "Today is my twenty-ninth birthday. Can you believe how old we've become?"

"Speak for yourself, George Willard." Helen took his hand then gave it back to him. "Happy birthday, all the same."

Back at home that evening, George was greeted with a surprise. Margaret had hired a string trio to play just for the two of them, and had borrowed Nettie McCormick's chef to lay out a dinner fit for crowned heads. Course after course arrived—broiled squab and supreme of guinea fowl, asparagus tips and Paris Sugar Corn, Russian caviar and a raft of imported cheeses, Golden Gate peaches and chocolat blancmange. After dinner the string trio took their leave, the servers retired to the kitchen to clean up, and Margaret led George to the parlor, where she unveiled a brand-new stereopticon and a set of slides of paintings from the Louvre.

"We can't let another summer pass without a trip to Europe." She kissed his cheek and peered into the viewfinder. "You can look at the *Mona Lisa* every day without leaving the house, but in nine months we could be standing this close to da Vinci's own hand."

"I can only imagine," George said.

"You don't have to imagine. We can go. Promise me you won't reach thirty without seeing Europe?"

In fact, George had never been farther east than Cleveland, farther west than the Union Stockyards. "The world has come here," he said. "We're becoming a great cultural center."

"You needn't be so provincial."

"What about work? I can't just drop everything and set sail for a month or two."

"Father won't mind." Margaret changed a slide in the magic lantern and urged George to peer into it: a large group scene of men and women in red, yellow, and blue garments in an ancient open courtyard.

"Veronese's *Wedding Feast at Cana*. You should see what an enormous canvas it is. It would take up the entire wall of our living room," Margaret said. "Some of the trip could be business. You could meet prospective clients in Paris, help grow the agency overseas. Who knows? If all goes well, we could live there for a while."

Lazar would never let George do such a thing. If he were to ask, Lazar might say it's a fine idea, but he'd send Kennison instead. George never confided in his wife his frustrations at work, and though Margaret must have known, must have heard details from her mother, they rarely talked about the office. It was the horse in the corner.

Then again, Margaret did have a talent for getting her way, and her father spoiled her. Perhaps she could convince Lazar to make an arrangement overseas. George's arc at the agency was on the descent, so what harm would it do? He could start over, in Paris of all places. What would people back home think of him then? What would Helen White think?

She wouldn't be impressed, he decided. She'd think he'd lost his way. It was when he put on airs this afternoon that she gave him a certain look—of having seen through him, of disappointment, perhaps. He couldn't go to Paris. What good would it do him to idle about European capitals and depend on his wife to translate the language and customs? He wasn't a college man, wasn't born to be a gentleman of leisure. He was George Willard of Winesburg, Ohio.

"Well, I love the stereopticon. It's a beautiful gift," he said. "And you can tell Nettie McCormick that we're keeping her chef. I've never had such a meal!"

"I'm not letting you off the hook yet. I mean it about Paris." Margaret put another slide on the plate: *Bathsheba at Her Bath*, Rembrandt's painting of the famous nude, King David at her feet. "I intend to go back to Europe at least once more before we fill this house with children. And I shall need an escort."

He knew she would keep pressing if he didn't make some gesture toward a promise. "Paris. Next summer. Okay, then," he said. "And speaking of culture—I heard the most astonishing violin recital today." He went on to talk about stumbling upon a prodigy at Hull House while taking a client on a city tour. "And of all the coincidences, I ran into a schoolmate from back home in the bargain. She helps coordinate some of their arts programs."

George hadn't meant to bring up Helen, nor had he expected that Margaret would be familiar with the settlement's theater. But to his surprise she brightened. "You know someone at Hull House?" she said. "I've been wanting to see a play there since college. Everyone says they have the best little theater in the city."

"Why did you never go?" George asked.

Margaret brushed her curls from her temples, her bracelet sliding down her arm. "For a visit to that neighborhood I would need a bodyguard."

"It's not that bad. We could have Virgil drive us," George said. "If you'd like, I can find out what's on."

That week he intended to buy tickets but was mortified to discover that the current play was George Bernard Shaw's comedy *The Philanderer.* He wondered if this was some devilish sign that he should abandon the thought of ever seeing Helen White again, but he chose to dismiss the idea—he had done nothing wrong—and continued to check the papers for the next production.

Meantime, his work life had grown ever more unpleasant. Lazar broke the news that Kennison was taking over the Nuvolia contract. Tidy Town was officially retired, shuttered like Hindman's Harness Shop in Winesburg, its moment eclipsed.

George demanded an explanation, and Lazar said it was time for *Prove They Need It.*

"What's the campaign?" George asked.

"We have an entirely new approach here, if you haven't noticed. The trick is to introduce a problem and then go about demonstrating that your product is the solution," Lazar said. "Clyde talked to some doctors and found a dozen bacteria that cause body odor. The one with the best ring to it was bromhidrosis. We'll make a big fuss about the evils of this chronic condition, bacteria that emanate from the skin. We'll say that millions don't even realize they're suffering from it. And then we'll provide the remedy. *Nuvolia: the Bromhidrosis-Fighting Soap.*"

George thought this would never work, but over time he would be proven spectacularly wrong. Within a year Kennison would bring Nuvolia back to second place, and within three years the brand would reclaim the top position. For now, George refused to believe that such a dull campaign could ever succeed. "I guess we'll see," was all he said, resignedly.

"We're lucky even to keep Nuvolia," Lazar added. "Do you want to tell me what you were thinking on your ill-begotten tour? Richard Trumbull did not come to Chicago to visit the slums or be converted to socialism."

"I thought he had a perfectly decent time."

"You thought wrong."

"Should I have taken him to the slaughterhouses?" George asked.

"Our job as advertisers is to give people what they want. If we don't agree with what they want and try to force our beliefs on them, we doom ourselves to failure," Lazar said. "Our industry is changing. You can lead, or fall behind. That is up to you."

As 1906 wound to a close, George felt increasingly that he had no choice, that he was washed up at twenty-nine. He had lost his major client, and the campaigns that fell to him were for local businesses or products on the verge of obsolescence: cylinder records, straight-front corsets, patent medicines. He did manage to keep his office, he still had a place at the conference table, but Kennison and his adjutants ran the show.

Brought low by the situation at work, George hadn't checked the papers to see what was on at Hull House since noting a puppet show and children's operetta that had played in November. But soon after the New Year an article appeared in the *Chicago Daily News* about a new book Jane Addams had written, calling for peace in a troubled time. This sent George to the entertainment listings, where he found that a play had recently opened at Hull House: *Odysseus in Chicago,* a three-week run with an all-Greek cast that critics were raving about. He brought the reviews home, Margaret said she would love to go, and on a frigid night in early February 1907, a Thursday, one of the days when Helen would likely be working, George and Margaret set out for the theater on the dodgy side of town.

11

Ravenous Bookstore & Café sat at the end of a stretch of boutiques and restaurants on Armitage, the main shopping avenue in Lincoln Park. It was more café than bookstore, with a clutch of tables in the middle, floor-to-ceiling shelves along the left wall, and on the right a huge mural of a raven on the shoulder of an especially unflattering likeness of Edgar Allan Poe. Lucy had arrived before me, and she was standing at the shelves in profile, one of only a couple of browsers. She wore a slim-fitting lilac dress and her hair loose, tumbling in a sandy sheen to her arms. She'd told me she was working from home today, so I tried to make sense of why she'd dressed down for our first meeting and up for this one.

"What are you reading?" I asked as I approached.

She smiled and gave me a quick hug, then turned the book so I could see the cover: *Jane Addams and the Struggle for Democracy.* "The Press published it a couple years ago. Have you read it?"

"I've been woefully behind on reading," I said. "But I did drive by Hull House yesterday. Does that count?"

"No—and you're missing out. Jane Addams was incredible, one of the great women of the century. And a surprisingly good writer, too. That combination of thinker and doer is so rare." She pressed the book into my hands. "I'm buying it for you."

"Lucy—"

But she was already on her way to the register, pulling her wallet from her purse.

"Let me," I said.

"I insist. Now aren't I a model employee—supporting the company's books?"

When we sat down for lunch, I couldn't help saying, "I have a good job, you know." Lucy had always paid for everything, wouldn't have it otherwise, and when I used to tell her I wasn't a starveling, she would bristle and say *There are worse sins than generosity.* "I work at Imego." I came out with it, because she was going to find out one way or another.

"I thought you were a proud Luddite. I don't remember your taking computer science."

"Actually, I'm on the books project. I was going to tell you, but I thought you might never speak to me again."

She sat back in her chair and gave me a look that said *If this is a hoax, I'm on to you.* But I held her gaze long enough for her to realize I wasn't kidding. She asked how I got the job, and I told the whole story about Dhara and Lakeside and how I wound up, almost accidentally, at one of the world's wealthiest and most ambitious companies.

"Well, this is surprising news," she said.

"I guess we're on opposite sides of the table."

"Yes, I'm here and you're there." Lucy's neck flushed red. "And apparently I'm David and you're Goliath."

"We're not out to kill each other." I picked up a menu and cast my eyes over the list of sandwiches. "Imego and publishers just signed a settlement agreement, right?"

"And a lousy agreement it was," she said. "We're looking at a future where a single company could control all the world's books. All the pricing, all the distribution. If the Internet is killing print publishing, Imego is robbing its grave."

I made an effort to appease her. "You know, we've had a slowdown at work. Libraries are nervous."

"That won't last long. How many books have you scanned so far?"

So much for appeasement. "Close to ten million." I slid Lucy her menu, but she left it on the table.

"And what about copyright? Why should U. Chicago and other presses do all the work of finding writers, editing their manuscripts, managing their neuroses, and bringing good books into the world, only to have Imego copy them and rake in the proceeds?"

"Most of the ten million are orphaned or in the public domain," I pointed out.

"But some are not, and that's troubling, especially since Imego's idea of fair use is pretty much the entire text."

"When you search, you can only read a snippet," I corrected her. "You have to pay for the rest."

"Again, why is the book yours in the first place?"

"Because Imego undertook one of the craziest, most daunting tasks in the history of civilization," I said. "No one else was going to do it."

"If I had twenty billion dollars to burn, I would have. But I'd partner with publishers and writers, not screw them." She picked up her menu, tapped it on the table, and put it down. "You're a writer, Adam. Aren't you worried about how your books will be published?"

"These days the only readers of so-called literary fiction are other writers: faculty and students, the wandering herd of MFA graduates," I said. "A 'writer's writer' used to be the name of a critical darling the masses ignored. Now the critics have disappeared along with the book reviews, the masses don't read, and a 'writer's writer' is anyone fool enough to spend three, five, forty years type-type-typing into the void."

"So you're a fool?" Lucy asked.

"The title of my thesis was *A Brief History of the Fool*. Now I prefer the term *grotesque*."

"I've seen more grotesque than you," she said.

"Like Edgar Allan Poe over there. I hope the food isn't as bad as that mural."

She relented a little at that. "I wouldn't count on it."

"And why did we come here again?" I asked.

"I'll do anything to support books."

My salad was mostly candied walnuts, my iced tea undrinkably sweet. When Lucy asked how lunch was, I said I'd met my monthly sugar quota.

"Complaining about sugar is anti-American. You ought to be ashamed of yourself."

I was grateful that Lucy had lightened the mood, glad to move beyond our little back and forth over Imego. But I felt I owed it to her, or perhaps to myself, to say how I really felt about my job. "I know I sounded like I was defending the Library Project," I began. "I've been working there for five years, so I guess I'm programmed to take the company line. You know Imego's motto: *Remember what your mother told you*. Well, I don't know many mothers who would tell their children to take over the world. And though I'm pretty sure the founders and current leadership are not capitalist wolves but true believers in making information universally available, I do worry what would happen if their stocks crashed and survival depended on the bottom line."

I acknowledged other concerns people had about my employer: privacy, censorship, control of information. These were legitimate fears, which I shared. But mostly I wanted to say that I wasn't happy there, and would leave if I could. "Though not in this economy," I told her. "I owe quite a bit of money for my MFA." I moved swiftly past the subject, since I wasn't about to revisit the debt I owed Lucy. I didn't so much as look up for her reaction. "Like everyone else these days, I'm kind of stuck," I said. "But I'm still working on that novel." I don't know why I kept telling her that I had a book under way.

"When do you write?" Lucy asked.

"Nights," I lied. "My wife is rarely home."

This hung in the air while the waiter returned to see if we were interested in dessert. Lucy suppressed a smile, and we both declined.

"I've been married little over a year," I continued. "Though we work at the same place we hardly see each other. And now Dhara decided to apply for a position at Imegoland. I guess she wants to Rollerblade to work."

"In California?" Lucy asked.

"I don't want to move there." I told her about my father, the heart-failure brochure, how I worried that he'd not survive another uprooting. I said Chicago was home; nowhere else felt as real to me. "Dhara can't see where I'm coming from. I know it's terrible, but I hope she doesn't get the job."

Lucy wasn't saying much, nor was she prompting me, so I filled the space with far-too-candid talk. I knew it was a betrayal, and I had to worry I was becoming like my father or one of those grotesques he talked about, cut off from the world. It shouldn't have been that way. I'd had my circle of friends in college, but the ones who'd come to Chicago had moved to the suburbs and nearly all had kids by now. I had a job, but worked on the margins and spent so much of my time on the road. I had a family, sickly, scattered, or gone. I had a wife. Yet in some fundamental way I was alone, and here was Lucy, across the table, hearing me out.

We paid the check, and when we stepped onto the sidewalk, I asked, "Where do you live?"

She pointed down the block in the direction of the El, then we walked along talking about the neighborhood. Lucy said she'd thought about living in Wicker Park, Bucktown, Ukrainian Village. "But those places have become as bougie as Lincoln Park. I don't care if you've got tattoos covering 80 percent of your body and the Sex Pistols blasting on the stereo, you're still charging five dollars for a cupcake," she said. "I'm running out of years to be cool, so I might as well live here."

When we got to her street, a couple blocks past Armitage Station, she put out her arms and I leaned in for a quick embrace. "I'd show you my apartment, but it looks like something out of Doctorow's new novel."

I was relieved she hadn't invited me to her place. I was married. I loved my wife. What did I have to complain about? The thought that Lucy and I could just be old friends seemed much more appealing at that moment than embarking on a misadventure that couldn't possibly end well. "I like Doctorow. What's the book?" I asked.

"It's not out yet, but I scored a galley in a trade. It's called *Homer & Langley*, about famous hoarders in New York."

"The Collyer brothers," I said. "I know that story all too well."

"Your father?"

"The very one." As we stood there on the corner of Armitage and Dayton I told her about the storage locker in Little Italy and how over the course of three months it had gone from full to nearly empty. I wanted to say I'd staked my father out, followed him across town, but I worried she would think I'd gone off the deep end.

"How sick is he?" she asked.

I told her about stages A through D, but said I didn't know. And, like Dhara, she urged me to confront him, once and for all.

"I don't mean to sound alarms," she said, "but I had a friend in college whose father killed himself—left the car running in the garage—and during the year or so beforehand he'd been casting off everything he owned, taking out insurance, getting his house in order. You used to complain all the time about your dad, but you also worried about him. Do you think—?"

"No," I said. Then, "I don't know." Whenever the thought had crossed my mind that he might be suicidal I had pushed it away. He didn't seem to have given up. He still had plenty of wit and spleen. He'd always been more angry than depressed. "He's pushing eighty. Isn't he too old?"

"I thought rates were higher at that age," Lucy said. "People take their own lives to escape the pain."

I recalled that December morning, pounding on my father's door, climbing the ladder to the second-story window, the sense of panic over what I might find.

I thanked Lucy for listening and for the good advice. She apologized on behalf of Ravenous Books & Café, and we laughed, making a vague plan to see each other again.

That night, I brought my father a grilled chicken salad from the ground-floor restaurant, and we ate dinner in front of his small TV while watching the Cubs play their third game of the season. "Is it my imagination, or have you tidied up?" I asked. His papers were in a small stack on his desk, the settees and chairs free of books.

"Are you going to watch the game or chitchat?" He turned up the volume.

"It's the top of the third, and we're up eight runs. This hardly qualifies as crunch time," I said. "I was merely admiring the apartment."

He labored to his feet and fixed himself another drink, and we spoke only of baseball until the end of the game, which the Cubs won, 11–6. "Could be our year," I said. The team had won the NL Central two years in a row, and some were predicting World Series.

"Ha!" he laughed, and continued laughing until he fell into a fit of coughs.

The next morning, at the usual hour, I pulled the Prius around and waited for my father to exit the garage. He was twenty minutes late, and instead of going into the Loop on State, he headed north, up the Magnificent Mile. He turned left on Walton and parked at the curb just beyond the Newberry Library. He got out, paid at the meter, slid the ticket onto the dashboard, then went inside. A minute later a security guard came out front with him and helped bring a small box back up the steps and into the building. I wondered what was in that box. Manuscripts? Letters? Books? My father's novel? Perhaps he was delivering it to the curator of the Sherwood Anderson Collection for a read-through.

This time I waited for nearly two hours, so long that at one point I got out of my car and sat on a bench across the street in Washington Square Park. I called into the office to let my team know I'd be working from home that morning, and I made a round of calls to university librarians.

When my father finally returned, he was trailing the same security guard, who once again helped with the box. Then he took off, up LaSalle, along the margins of the Gold Coast, to North Avenue, where he swung a left at a McDonald's. From across the street I watched him grab a book from the passenger seat and go inside. He put in his order, then shuffled with a tray to a window booth. He ate an oozing cheeseburger, just what his heart needed, while flipping the pages of the book. When he had dumped his tray he returned to the car, sipping at a drink through a straw, and continued along North to Wells Street and the stretch of shops and restaurants in Old Town. He pulled over and parked under an awning marked "CRBC." A lean, eager man with bifocals that hung on a chain from his neck rushed out to help him with the box, and they went inside.

CRBC. I'd seen the letters before, etched on the boxes in the storage cage. I did another search on my iPhone. Citizens Republic Bankcorp? Cross Roads Baptist Church? Cannery Row Brewing Company? I added the word "Chicago" to the search, and the first page to come up was Chicago Rare Book Company. An hour passed, and then another, until I couldn't avoid turning around and heading back to work. I wished I had looked in those CRBC boxes to see what was there when I'd had a chance.

A big shipment—sixty thousand books—arrived, with little notice, from the University of Michigan, so I spent the rest of the week and well into the following one working Dhara-like hours at the West Town warehouse. I had meant to talk to my father, but it wasn't until the end of April that work slowed again and I got back into the routine of delivering his lunch.

To my surprise he was there that first afternoon, then the second and the third, until, finally, I asked, "What happened to your walks?"

"Oh, I gave those up months ago. I found that driving is less stressful on the skeleton."

"I'm sure your doctor would prefer it if you got your legs moving," I ventured.

"What do doctors know?"

We sat down to eat at his dinette table, and he even managed not to complain about the food. He was good for a *thank you* maybe once a month, and this was one of those days. We were dispatching the flavorless turkey wraps I'd picked up in a rush from a coffee chain when my father asked, out of the blue, "Are you still writing?"

I could remember only a few times this subject had come up. It was my second year of graduate school before I summoned the nerve to tell him

I was in a writing program, and just as I'd expected he called it a waste of time. *These salons are a racket. They're creating a generation of dilettantes. Did Shakespeare get an MFA? Cervantes? George Eliot? Hemingway and Faulkner got their MFAs by reading Sherwood Anderson. That's all the degree is, a jargoned-up book club. If you want to be a writer, yes, you have to read your eyes bloodshot. But you also need a rare talent and a host of demons driving you.*

"I'm too busy at work," I said now. "When I get home I don't have the energy."

"It's not easy, is it?" And then, as if to distance himself, he added, "I can only imagine—sitting at a desk day after day with nothing to draw on but dreams." After a few bites, he put his wrap down and dropped his napkin onto his plate. "Tell me about what you've written?" he asked.

I was hesitant to get into it, but I couldn't remember ever seeing him quite this benign. I wondered if something was going on with his heart, a new medication, a change in dosage, lack of oxygen to the brain. He wasn't so much out of it, though, as uncharacteristically placid. So I told him about *A Brief History of the Fool,* first in the most abbreviated, dismissive way, but he kept prompting me, asking more questions, until I found myself describing the stories at length, talking about the characters—a bartender, an amateur astronomer, a diver after shipwrecks around the Great Lakes—and the curious features of the town, which as I talked about it sounded too much like Bloomington. I admitted this to my father, but he said, "Sounds more like *Winesburg* to me. But don't worry; you're in good company. In all of American literature of the past hundred years, no book has had a greater influence. Not *Gatsby, Catcher,* or *Invisible Man.* The more you read the more you'll see it's true."

I cleared the table and was getting ready to go back to work when my father said, "I'd be happy to read your book." He got up and stood by the sliding doors to the balcony, and with his back turned added, "I wouldn't be surprised if it was good."

Shaken perhaps by the unheard-of event of a compliment from my father, I declined right away. "Thanks for the offer, but I haven't looked at that book in years. If *I* have to avert my eyes, I couldn't possibly inflict it on you."

"As you wish." He shrugged.

I felt like I'd let him down, and I wanted to give him something—if not the abandoned book, at least a thought or two I'd been keeping to myself.

So I told him for the first time that I didn't like my job, that I had problems with Imego, that I wished I could get a stretch of unfettered time to finish a book. "But I'm in no position to quit, and even if I were, I probably don't have the guts."

That's when my father said, "I knew it." I wasn't sure what he meant: He knew I wanted to be a writer? Or he knew I didn't have the guts? It wasn't clear, and I wouldn't find out, not then or ever, because he proceeded to tell a story I'd heard before but never at such length, about how Sherwood Anderson, at age thirty-six, stressed by debt and a yearning to be free, to be a writer, fell into a fuguelike state and left his wife, children, and job in Elyria, Ohio, literally walked out the door of his office one November morning and four days later turned up at a drugstore in Cleveland, unshaven, still in his business suit, pants covered to the knees with mud. He didn't know his name or where he was, and wouldn't begin to recover his faculties until days later in a hospital ward, his wife at his bedside. Within two months he had moved alone to Chicago, picked up copywriting work to pay the bills, grown his hair long, and fallen in with an artistic crowd on the forefront of what would become the city's greatest literary moment.

"I'm not telling you to leave your wife," my father said. "That never worked out too well for me. Nor am I pushing the benefits of a nervous breakdown. But an artistic temperament repressed can be a withering thing."

And then he was on to another story, which I remembered as the most poignant instance of dramatic irony in all of *Winesburg, Ohio*. It occurs in the tale "Death," about the demise of George Willard's mother. In her youth, Elizabeth had artistic desires, and was even given a chance to explore them when her father, at the end of his life, gave her eight hundred dollars, a significant sum in the 1870s. "It is to make up to you for my failure as a father," he said. "Some time it may prove to be a door, a great open door to you."

But instead of going to the city, where she dreamed of becoming an actress, Elizabeth closed the door forever, and would pass the rest of her short life trapped in Winesburg. Her father had been the proprietor of the town's hotel, and against his wishes she married the desk clerk Tom Willard "because he was at hand and wanted to marry at the time when the determination to marry came to her." Her father had made her promise never to tell Tom about the money—and this wish, at least, she fulfilled. Not long after her wedding she stashed the eight hundred dollars in a tin box and sealed it behind the plaster walls of her room. She had always intended to give the money to George so that he could embark, in some big city, on the artist's life that she had denied herself. But she had grown tired and gravely ill, and in her last six days she couldn't move from her bed or speak, couldn't tell her son about his secret inheritance. My father quoted from the story: "She struggled, thinking of her boy, trying to say some few words in regard to his future, and in her eyes there was an appeal so touching that all who saw it kept the memory of the dying woman in their minds for years."

My father sat down on the camelback sofa, as if recounting the tale had exhausted him. "George might have gone to Chicago with a leg up to start the work he was meant to do. But no such luck. All he'd have had in his billfold were his last paychecks from the *Winesburg Eagle*. He would've had no choice but to join the rat race."

"And those eight hundred dollars just sat in the walls, like buried treasure."

"No one would have known to look. The secret would have died with Elizabeth," he said. "Maybe years later the hotel would have been razed, the mangled tin box hauled off and buried in the rubble of the county landfill."

All this talk of mortality made me realize I might not have a better chance to ask about my father's heart. "Last time I was in your bathroom I couldn't help noticing all the new canisters of pills," I began. "I know you hate to talk about this, but are you sure everything's okay with your heart?"

My father's expression soured. "Did I invite you to look into my cabinets?"

"The pills were out in the open, prescriptions from your last appointment."

"So you were reading the labels?"

"I was washing my hands, and they caught my eye. They looked more like the kind of collection a heart failure patient might take." There. I'd said it.

"Are you an amateur cardiologist? Moonlighting on the side? Are you a nurse? Well, you're not who I had in mind. I was thinking more along the lines of Ursula Andress."

"No, I'm your son," I said. "Pardon me for giving a damn."

"Look, I can take care of myself. I made it this far." He got up and mixed a Diet Rite and rum.

I knew I'd been foolish to think I could get a straight answer. I wanted a letter—A, B, C, or D—but all he gave me were the usual one-liners. For a while there, we were having a real conversation. But up came the old shield, out the old arrows.

"I should be getting back to the office," I said.

"What's today's date?" he asked.

I told him it was the thirtieth of April.

"Just a minute," he said, and began fumbling in his desk. Wing jumped up and expected a scratch. Ignoring the cat, my father pulled an envelope full of money from the drawer. "It's a day early, but here." He handed me May's rent. "I might not see you tomorrow, so you may as well take this now."

12

The Willards arrived at the main entrance of Hull House in Lazar's apple-green Pierce-Arrow, the most reliable winter car in his collection. George was embarrassed when Virgil opened the side door and gave Margaret his arm to help her down to the curb. Children and their laborer parents were sliding about the icy sidewalks, and no one for miles was formally attired. George had insisted that Margaret's Merry Widow hat, well over a foot wide, with a fountain of feathers, was too much for the settlement—"You'll be lucky to fit in the door"—but Margaret had said, "The theater's the theater. And really, George, are *you* one to tell *me* what's fashionable?"

Within the house, no one seemed to notice. Both drawing rooms were in use for evening classes. A chorus of singers could be heard from the top floor, and below it the scamper of feet. The greeter was so busy shepherding children from club to lesson to meal that she only had time to point her finger and say, "Next building over," when George asked where the auditorium was.

At the box office, out of his wife's earshot, he inquired after Helen, and the ticket-seller said she was working backstage that night. George had not attended much theater, but *Odysseus in Chicago* had a powerful effect on him. The set was spare, the cast made up entirely of Greek Americans from the surrounding neighborhood, men and women with day jobs as factory workers and deliverymen, teachers and clerks, yet their inexperience only intensified the performances. Though some of the actors spoke with heavy accents, George felt as if he were watching the last ten years of his life play out on stage. The immigrants delivered their lines with a longing that reminded him of his own journey, his own distance from home and desire to get back to that place—not Winesburg so much as a feeling he had there, about the people, their hopes and defeats. Tears pooled in his eyes as he watched Odysseus pine for Penelope from the snares of Calypso, and reunite at long last with his true love.

After the play George found Helen talking to the German Union baker. "You're back!" she exclaimed.

George stepped aside to make way for the Merry Widow hat. "This is my wife, Margaret," he said. "And this is Helen White, from home."

"Ah." Margaret reached out her gloved hand, and with practiced nonchalance asked, "How do you know each other?"

"Why, everyone knew your husband," Helen replied. "He was our paper's star reporter."

"Only reporter, more or less," George put in.

"He's being modest," Helen said.

George couldn't be sure of its source, but a tension hummed in the atmosphere. Did Margaret know? Was she jealous? He'd never seen her territorial side, never been in a setting where the tables were turned. Helen was the more beautiful woman, and carried herself with an ease and discretion that the younger Margaret perhaps recognized she couldn't match. And who was this baker, Stefan Wirtz, that Helen was introducing? A suitor? A lover? He gave nothing away, in his derby hat with a dusting of flour on the brim, his four-in-hand tie sitting slaunchwise about his wrestler's neck.

Everyone spoke all at once, praising the play in a flurry of words, before Helen suggested they sit down for coffee. "Stefan can arrange a discount," she said in a jocular way. But Margaret seemed to take her seriously: "We always pay full price."

In the spacious coffeehouse, with its stained rafters, diamond windows, and rows of blue china mugs, they got coffees and shining rolls Stefan himself had baked that morning. They took a table by the large, crackling fireplace, and the conversation cast about, from *Odysseus in Chicago* to the treacherous winter to the daily operations at Hull House and its myriad classes, taught by trained volunteers at fifty cents a course, including Grammar, Literature, History, Political Economy, Parliamentary Law, Latin and a range of languages, Physics, Chemistry, Geometry, Trigonometry, Music, Dance, Painting, Clay Modeling, Sewing, and the Domestic Sciences.

In its eighteen years, Hull House had grown to thirteen buildings that took up a whole city block. There were weekly classes, constant lectures, concerts, recitals, and plays, a daily kindergarten, a free day-nursery, gymnastics and a variety of athletics to keep restless children off the streets. And the coffeehouse, too, convivial and filled to capacity every evening, kept the parents away from the bars in a city well known to have one saloon for every sixty people.

Margaret seemed to have lowered her guard, though she was directing most of her questions at Stefan. In his mild accent, he enumerated the clubs on the Hull House block—the Women's Club, the Men's Club, the Newlyweds' Club, too many children's clubs to recall, and the smaller groups for gardening, stargazing, mandolin, fencing, and countless other interests.

Helen began to say, "I'm not sure where you stand politically—" when Margaret bristled, as if accused: "I'm a Square-Deal Progressive. Pro-settlement. Anti-trust. I think Roosevelt is doing a swell job."

"I only meant to mention that some of our clubs do have a mission about them," Helen said. "I have friends in the Eight-Hour Club, a group of women in local factories who push their fellow workers to hold fast to the eight-hour law. And Stefan is a member of the Arthur Toynbee Club. They discuss economics and social reform."

"We just met last night." Stefan slurped his coffee and set the cup down. "Our treasurer is a refugee from San Francisco. Lost everything in the earthquake last year. He warned us about the stock market—not that a baker has any bread to begin with—but he says a catastrophe is coming, sooner than we know."

"What does your father think?" George asked Helen, referring to Banker White.

"He's been worried since the nineties about easy credit, and thinks the speculators are paving the road to ruin."

"That's right," Stefan agreed. "This fellow from San Francisco says we haven't felt the last of the tremors. That city's in ashes. But the whole country could have another thing coming now that foreign insurers have paid the claims and their lenders have raised rates on American banks."

"Well, my father's agency is driving a roaring trade," Margaret put in. "Last year was their best yet."

"What business is your father in?" Helen asked.

"Advertising. George is his top deputy."

"I don't know about that," George said. "But I guess I'm doing okay."

"He's doing more than okay." Margaret tilted back her head, sending the feathers on her hat aquiver. She had taken off her gloves and tented her arms so that her jewelry was on display. The engagement ring was her least expensive piece, something George had noticed at parties and outings but couldn't bring himself to note. She wore her grandmother's diamond bracelet, her mother's opal and rose diamond ring, and a double-strand necklace of cultured pearl. In the auditorium and coffeehouse she looked like the queen consort come to give alms to the poor.

"Yes, I work for my father-in-law," George said, and felt compelled to add, "I've been with the agency going on ten years. I was well established by the time Margaret and I got married."

"You shouldn't have to explain," Margaret declared, and an awkward silence followed.

When the conversation turned back to the goings-on at Hull House, George grew distracted and relived his fear that no one would respect him now that he had married rich. He wondered if Helen thought he was a sycophant, or a kept man. He hadn't told her who his boss was when he'd had a chance, and now she might not believe him if he tried to explain.

But he knew he couldn't say a word, not here, not in front of his wife and the gap-toothed baker, who issued warnings about the money supply like some folksy market guru. Did he really think he was impressing Helen, living hand to mouth while vaporing on as if he had the ear of tycoons?

Back in the Pierce-Arrow on the drive home, George couldn't help confronting Margaret. He didn't care if Virgil heard every word and reported back to the Lazars. "Did you have to mention that I work for your father?"

"I didn't think it was a source of shame, George. One should be grateful."

"But bringing up the business had no bearing on the conversation."

"The German was talking bunkum and I had a clear example why he was wrong," she said. "The agency is booming, and as Father says: Busy advertiser, bustling economy."

"They might have thought you were trying to boast, to put them in their place."

"I was doing no such thing."

"The point is you made me look like a sponger."

"You're a self-made man," Margaret said. "That's one of the reasons I married you."

"It didn't come across that way."

"You're overreacting, George. Helen didn't seem to mind what I had to say."

"You probably think she's hinterland squab, another small-town dreamer like me who hopped the first train she could out of Winesburg. But her father is one of the richest men in the county. She has a college degree. She's in graduate school at your alma mater. You have more in common with her than you do with me," George said. "So why were you treating her with such disdain?"

"I don't know what you're talking about."

"You barely looked at her, and when you did it was down your nose."

"Well—" Margaret's breath clouded the windows.

"What?"

"She never answered my question: How do you know each other? Maybe you can tell me."

George was relieved to be sitting next to her in the close backseat, traveling in darkness through the ashy snow. She couldn't see his eyes, couldn't read his delivery when he said, "I told you: We were schoolmates. My friend—remember Seth Richmond, from the wedding?—used to pay her court. They were both from wealthy families, and everyone thought they'd marry, but evidently Helen took a different path." He explained how she'd gone to Cleveland for college, then Ada, and why she'd settled on Chicago. "I hardly know her, but it's always something to run into an old townie. So I figured we all should meet. I thought you'd get on fine. I still think so."

"She's pretty," Margaret said.

"I guess."

"No boy doesn't notice a pretty girl."

"I had eyes for one thing growing up in Winesburg: getting out. And here I am." He put his arm around her and pulled her close.

"She's very pretty, George."

"You're prettier," he said. "Why are we even talking about this? It's absurd." He turned her face to his. In the murky light she looked like a stranger. "Listen, Margaret. I have no interest, never had an interest in Helen White. I love you. You're the most remarkable woman I know." He kissed her.

"You're certain?"

"I've never been more sure about anything."

Tears glazed her cheeks. How could she be crying? What had brought this on? "Margaret—?"

"I'm fine. I don't know what's wrong with me." He produced a handkerchief, and she dabbed at her eyes. "I have too much time—that must be it," she said. "In school my days were filled with activity. Perhaps I have too many interests. I used to tell my mother that her friends were all peacocks or dilettantes, but I'll be one of them before I know it."

"You're only a year and some out of college. You're young!" George gripped her gloved hands.

"Oh, maybe we should just have children and be done with it."

"There's plenty of time for that," George said. He hadn't thought about children, didn't want to think about them. He had much to do, though at the moment he couldn't recollect exactly what. "And besides, didn't you tell your mother that you intended to have your own life first?"

"Oh, what she'd give to be sitting in this car! Virgil—" She leaned forward in her seat. "You're not listening, are you?"

"Haven't heard a word," he said.

"You heard me ask if you're listening."

"Mrs. Willard, I'm your parents' driver, not their spy."

"Oh, hang it. What does it matter anyway?"

George had never seen his wife so agitated. He knew the winter had been hard on her, but something tonight had loosened a spring. Perhaps her jealousy was not so much about Helen's looks or any ties she might have had to George but more about the life Helen was making for herself. Margaret had loved the play, and had asked so many questions about Hull House that one might have mistaken her for a resident-in-training. "I have an idea," George said. "The settlement is hungry for volunteers. I can't think of a better place for a bright person with broad interests."

"I've never taught."

"It doesn't matter. You can join a club or two or three. You'd be a leader in no time. And if you want to teach next term, I'm sure they can find a place for you."

"I'll think about it," Margaret said. But by the time they'd reached home, changed into their nightclothes, and climbed into her single bed, she had made up her mind.

It didn't take long for Stefan Wirtz's prophecy to come true. In March 1907, the stock market dropped 30 percent in two weeks. Interest rates climbed dramatically, banks tightened their lending policies, and loans became increasingly difficult to procure. In those spring and early summer months, scores of brokers were forced into bankruptcy; railroad and mining stocks plummeted, hundreds of speculators were run out of business, and the unemployment rate rose nearly a percentage point per month.

George's father wrote him a letter of concern: *Don't know how you're getting on out there in Chicago, but here at home we're feeling the pinch.* In recent years, despite his airy hopes for Winesburg, he had been catering less to tourists and families and more to traveling salesmen. He even turned half the lobby into a "drummers' room," where salesmen could display their wares for local merchants. But now it seemed even the drummers were drying up. *Their companies are taking them off the road. They say it costs too much and people aren't buying. Supply's at a standstill. Last week I had just one salesman in the drummers' room. One, George! But the top dogs at Rawleigh are looking to bring him home, too. . . . Don't you worry about your old man. Everyone knows Tom Willard's a fighter. I'll beat the game. . . . But if you have friends named Palmer, Field, or McCormick who want to invest in a wholesome American concern, be sure to tell them about the New Willard House.*

George shared these worries with Helen, who told him that even her father, the regional bank president, was nervous. By late summer several Wall Street brokerage houses had filed for bankruptcy, and an unsettling number of depositors had closed accounts or withdrawn their savings, to hide their money under the mattress or bury it in the yard. Stefan brought further alarm from his meetings of the Arthur Toynbee Club: The United States had been without a national bank since Andrew Jackson dissolved it in 1832, and the Toynbee group agreed that without a central bank controlling credit resources, the country was all but certain to face a major money panic.

Even the Lazar Agency had lost momentum. Reports from the Service and Performance Departments showed diminished returns each of the sixteen weeks leading into autumn; many advertisers had put a freeze on spending, and more than a dozen had either closed their accounts or gone out of business. Clyde Kennison took to the road to make personal appeals to his reeling clients, and when he was in the office could be seen pacing the halls or browbeating subordinates. George took private satisfaction in his rival's struggles, but the moment didn't last. Nuvolia was among the few companies whose profits rose during the recession, and George lost more clients over a six-month period than anyone in the agency. This did not go unnoticed by Lazar, so George was forced to defend himself: *I can't be blamed for this when I had my best client taken away. Nuvolia is still prospering because I built the foundation. And the companies that failed were already dying when I inherited them.* In September Lazar fired 10 percent of his workforce, but George survived. He knew his boss's hands were tied, knew the pinch of golden handcuffs all too well.

Margaret became a Hull House habitué. In spring she enrolled in an art history class taught by settlement cofounder Ellen Gates Starr, who was also a Browning enthusiast and took to Margaret straightaway. In the summer she worked with Starr to create a lending library of art reproductions and went around the city to interest schools in the program. Helen helped her make connections, and found her a place on the stage crew for W. S. Gilbert's *The Palace of Truth,* Leo Tolstoy's *Where Love Is,* and Shakespeare's *Twelfth Night* at the Hull House Theater. By fall she'd become assistant stage manager and had added a storytelling and a photography club to her growing list of activities.

George had learned to be careful what he wished for. Ever since his engagement he'd been hoping Margaret would find a way to fill her days, but now that he'd led her to the settlement she'd begun to think of the place as a second home; he saw her infrequently, and when he did her mind was elsewhere. At first he would come back to the empty house and wander its spaces, idle about with the newspapers, a book, the stereopticon. He took to cleaning and dusting and cutting flowers from the garden to place in rooms where he hoped Margaret would notice them. But she would return from the West Side well past suppertime, her voice hoarse from a day of excited talking, and stand at the kitchen sink eating popcorn balls or hot sausage wrapped in brown paper, waffles, or penny ice cream bought from sidewalk vendors on the drive home. *We should try to have supper together more often,* George would say, something Margaret used to urge on him. But she was too rushed to sit down for a casual meal, and when George offered to come down to the Hull House coffeehouse she said *We're both too busy; maybe some other time?*

She didn't notice the daffodils, irises, and lilies as April turned to May and May to June. Or "Carnival of Venice" on the Mira Music Box or the polish of the mahogany or the immaculate rooms. When George would point out these touches she'd say *I figured the maid had done all that.* And he would remind her that the maid only came once a week and someone had to keep up with the other days. She'd say *I know several girls who could use the extra work. Why don't you leave off and we can hire them?* To which George would reply *This is all beside the point.*

It was during a run of such weeks—he'd counted twenty-eight days since Margaret had last invited him to bed—that he arranged to meet Helen White. He had seen her several times in the company of others, always his wife and sometimes Stefan, but in August he had attended the opening of *Twelfth Night,* and while Margaret was busy backstage he had run into Helen. She was working that evening as an usher, and after the performance she introduced him to Jane Addams. He looked into the serene gray eyes of perhaps the most famous woman in America as she spoke about Shakespeare's love of the "play within the play." He nervously paid his compliments, and in the wake of her departure from the auditorium he asked Helen to lunch the next afternoon.

At Schlogl's, a venerable German restaurant a few blocks west of George's office, they talked about Miss Addams. He ordered wine, which he never did at lunch, as Helen explained the great woman's mystique: "She's the mother I wish I'd had. Of course, I have to share her with thousands of siblings. But the thing is she makes each of us feel like an only child."

"I think Margaret would say the same about Ellen Starr."

"The world is spilling over with unfulfilled, unhappy mothers," Helen continued. "And their unhappiness is their daughters' inheritance. It's funny: If you look at Jane in repose, as I sometimes have, you'd see the very picture of melancholy. It's bred into her, bred into so many of us. But what woman has accomplished more, for herself and for multitudes?"

"What does your mother think about Hull House?" George asked.

"She wouldn't approve, and I'm ashamed to admit I haven't told her. I wish I could say I'm an independent woman, but she and my father are paying for the roof over my head and my schooling and everything else. I know I need to finish this degree—I've put in too much time not to—so I can't risk a tussle with my parents. Unlike Jane, who grew up in a town much like ours, with a father much like mine, I haven't come into a fortune, can't buy up a mansion and invite all comers."

"Would you if you could?"

"I don't know," she said.

"Surely you'll have the opportunity."

"My mother is mean enough to live past a hundred, and with the way the economy is going we could all be lining up at Jane's door." In her white organdy tea dress, Helen cast a light in the dark, smoky restaurant, with its walnut-paneled walls and large oil paintings of monks quaffing brandy. George hadn't seen her this dressed up since her courting days in Winesburg and wondered if she'd made the effort just for him. "Besides," she went on, "it's one thing to volunteer part-time at a settlement, quite another to run one. Jane has no family of her own, and couldn't, given the depth of her commitment. She never married and never will."

"That's quite a sacrifice."

"One I'm not sure I'd be willing to make," Helen said. Then, as if aware of what George was thinking, she added, "I've had a caller or two, but without my mother here to bring prospects around I'm left to see to those matters myself. And I haven't the energy or the inclination."

"What about Stefan?" George asked.

"I admire his ambition—he's only been speaking English since he sailed here at sixteen, alone, with only a few pfennigs in his pockets; he knows more about money than a banker's own child. But he's so single-minded, and sometimes I feel he takes advantage of me. The bread runs have been multiplying lately. And I don't know if it's my company he's after so much as—I shouldn't be saying this—"

"What?" George prompted her.

"I don't want to be someone's investment . . . or safety net."

George couldn't help thinking the same critique applied to him. Though Helen's comment did not seem aimed in his direction, he knew he had taken similar advantage of Margaret.

A waiter appeared, and Helen ordered the rabbit stew, George the bouillabaisse and a half bottle of wine. "You know why I suggested this place?" Helen asked. George shook his head. "In that corner over there"—she pointed across the room to a large round table that for the moment sat empty—"the literary lights of Chicago assemble each Saturday. A job-lot assortment of newspapermen, playwrights, novelists, poets. Jane comes here from time to time with members of the Little Room."

"I had no idea."

"I'm surprised," Helen said. "You must be doing *some* writing. I figured I'd be reading your books by now."

"No—." His voice trailed off. Then he told her about Tidy Town, how making up characters for his ad campaigns convinced him for a while that he was doing what he'd set out to do. But he couldn't resist the siren call of money and advancement. "You have to understand I grew up in that sad hotel, haunted by my mother's disappointments. Once I had an office in the clouds, I couldn't come down."

"But it sounds as if you'd like to," Helen said.

"Why do you think that?"

"It's in your voice. On your face. Are you happy, George?"

He finished his glass of wine. "Are you?"

"That's a rotten trick."

"You're right," he said. "I'll answer the question, but you have to promise that you will, too."

"Okay."

He was close enough that he could see the wheels of gold in her eyes. "I'm happiest when I'm looking forward," he said. "And lately I haven't had much to look forward to. So, there. I answered your question."

"I shall be equally brief," she said. "I'd like to tell you I'm as happy as I've ever been. Yet I have no one to share it. And that makes me wonder if I'm happy, after all."

The waiter came. The bill was settled. And that night, while Margaret was off at Hull House learning photography, George rummaged through an old box and found the notepad he used to carry with him everywhere. He turned back to spring 1896, when he was eighteen and the future lay before him like so much open track.

13

When I brought over lunch on May 1 and my father didn't show up at his apartment, his voice saying *I might not see you tomorrow* kept coming back to me. I even stepped out on the balcony and looked down toward the river-walk, but he hadn't jumped, no sirens were closing in, and I scolded myself for imagining he'd ever do such a thing.

Headed back to work, I saw him stepping out of a cab. One foot, two foot, cane, launch. He never took taxis, so I had to ask, "Where have you been?"

He paid the driver and held his hat against a swift breeze. "I sold the Mercury. Grand theft auto, more like. Those lug nuts at the used-car lot—they fleeced me, then couldn't be bothered to ferry me home."

I was shocked by this development, but tried not to let on. "I thought driving was your new form of exercise," I said.

"They should have taken my license long ago. It says all you need to know about the State of Illinois that I'm still on the road."

"Not any more, apparently."

"That car was a needless expense. I can get around fine." He looked bowed and pale, even thinner than usual.

"I left some grape leaves and hummus in the fridge," I said. "I can follow you up, if you'd like."

He put a shaky hand on my shoulder. "I appreciate the solicitude. Really, I do. I'll tell you what. You can get the door. That would be a help."

So I let him into the building, and we parted ways. I felt at once relieved that my father was no longer driving and uncertain of what would come of this.

At the office, I was surprised to find Dhara waiting in my bullpen. She was talking to Eddie Hartley, who sat on the edge of my desk in a green-and-yellow John Deere T-shirt and an experimental beard that made him look like a shepherd in a seventh-grade nativity play. "Lord Byron," he said. "We've been looking for you. Late lunch?"

"I get my work done." I usually put up with his banter, but the very sight of him, his bony ass on my desk, his Red Wing boots kicked up on my chair, made my eyes sting. "Do you mind?" I said, and he hopped down, his uncapped curls flopping over his brow.

"You should be thanking me." Eddie jiggled the mouse on my desk, and the screen stayed blank. "You left your computer on, dude. Less of a gentleman might have switched your keyboard language to Icelandic or dragged porn sites into your startup menu. I shut you down to protect you from sinister forces."

"I'd like to think my team members are more mature than that."

"Who are you kidding?" Eddie said. "Every workplace is a den of pranksters. No one's above the fray. In the Oval Office, at this very moment, the president of the United States is sitting on a whoopee cushion."

I turned to Dhara, and was happy to see that she wasn't smiling. Perhaps the puckish charms of the engineering manager had finally worn thin.

"I'll leave you two alone," Eddie said. Then he bent down a little so he and Dhara were eye to eye, and in the most earnest voice, as if he were playing two characters and had just done a quick costume switch, he asked, "Are you sure you're okay?"

Dhara nodded. "I'm fine. I'll get over it."

After Eddie disappeared, I asked what was wrong.

"So much for Silicon Valley," Dhara said. Her eyes were red and she was sniffling. I could count on one hand the number of times I'd seen her cry. "I didn't even make the short list. I came back from lunch to an e-mail: three lines, from the marketing manager's secretary."

"I'm sorry, honey. I'm stunned." In fact, I could hardly believe that one of the stars of our office had been shut out so soon.

"Maybe we should go to the snuggle room," she said. "I don't want people to see me like this."

The snuggle room was the only secluded spot in the office—the joke was that if you were searching Imego and wanted privacy, this was the last refuge. Around the corner from the whiteboard and tucked away, it had pod chairs and deep sofas and was sectioned off with room dividers made of frosted glass. People seldom used the snuggle room except to catch up on sleep or to clamp on giant headphones and listen to electronica.

With the place to ourselves, we settled into a comfortable couch. "I know how competitive Imego is," Dhara continued, "but seriously, not even to make the first cut? I built the Books program here, remade the Marketing Department."

"It's absurd," I said.

"Do you think it's because I got my MBA at Ohio State?" She dabbed at her eyes with a Kleenex. "If my mom hadn't been sick, I would have gone to Stanford or Berkeley. I could have been out there making contacts years ago."

I wanted to say *You wouldn't have met me,* but I knew this wasn't about us, and the best thing was to keep quiet and listen.

"I wonder if it's a flyover thing. I've seen my share of anti-immigrant bias, but anti-midwesterner? That would be a first," she went on. "Do you think they have a point? If you were calling the shots at one of the world's most desirable companies, would you hire some rube who grew up in a motel in Dayton, Ohio?"

"Yes, I would. And you're no rube. You're the smartest, most driven person I know."

"You're just saying that." She sank farther into the sofa. "Maybe the flyovers are just that—a vast flatness under the clouds."

"From our balcony we can see the Sears Tower," I said. "Chicago is anything but flat. It's always been a hub of daring and innovation: We invented the skyscraper. We split the atom—"

I cut myself off because Dhara wasn't up for a booster speech. She was doing something completely unlike her: indulging in self-pity. "Maybe I'm not good enough. Maybe I'm looking for any excuse not to face that simple fact."

Still, Dhara continued working long hours, even though she said there was no one left to impress. The nation's unemployment rate had reached a twenty-five-year high; the economy had lost three million jobs already in 2009, and the year wasn't halfway through; and at Imego the first layoffs had begun, not in Chicago, but in similar "backwaters," as Dhara called them. I reminded her that the company had let go of only two hundred people worldwide and still had five hundred job postings. "We're growing, not shrinking," I tried to assure her, but she pointed out that sales and marketing people were more vulnerable, since advertisers weren't spending like they used to.

Privately, of course, I was relieved we weren't going to California, and I had to admit I'd been in denial about the possibility. When Dhara had applied, I was certain she would get the job; at the same time I never allowed myself to imagine our packing up a truck and driving across the country, deciding what to do with my father, finding a tiny apartment in the Bay Area, settling in to a new life. The prospect was too overwhelming.

Besides protecting her own job, Dhara went out of her way to protect mine, which I wouldn't have known had I not run into Eddie Hartley one day. Or, rather, had he not literally run into me. It was toward the end of May, the winter behind us, spring rains tapering off, and Eddie had begun to ride one of those self-propelled skateboards—ripsticks, they were called—not only to work but around the office. I must have stepped into his path, because before I knew it he had crashed into my hip and lay crumpled at my feet.

"Whoah!" He bounced up like a jack-in-the-box. "Lord Byron! Sincerest apologies!" He picked up his board and gave an exaggerated bow.

"Do you have to ride that thing in here?" I hissed.

"Time is money," he said. "It gets me from A to B twice as fast."

"Seriously, Eddie, how old are you? Thirty? Thirty-five?"

"I know, I know." He adjusted his Stag Beer cap. "You've been upset. I heard about your dad, and I want you to know I'm sorry—all of us around here are pulling for him. My grandfather died of heart failure last year, so I understand."

"Just watch where you're going. Okay?"

"Hang in there," he said, and loped off.

When I confronted Dhara that night, she told me I should be thanking her. "You have to admit you've been playing with fire, taking two-hour breaks, leaving early. Everyone knows there's a slowdown at the Library Project."

"So you're selling out my privacy to protect the bottom line. That's the Imego spirit!" I took out my iPhone and checked the time. It was nine o'clock, and neither of us had even thought about what to have for dinner. I collapsed on the sofa and tossed the phone onto the coffee table.

"Do you want to lose your job?" Dhara sat next to me.

"No, but I don't like the Eddie Hartleys of the world knowing my business."

Dhara put her hand on my knee. "I'm sorry," she said.

Then, as if on cue, as if to mock the rare event of my wife apologizing, my iPhone started buzzing, and there, in front of both of us, Lucy's number lit up. Dhara was looking right at the phone, and I let it ring once, twice. Very coolly, she said, "Aren't you going to answer it?"

"Why should I?" I asked.

"It's Lucy, right? Go ahead. Feel free to pick up."

"I don't want to," I said as the phone continued to vibrate the table.

"You don't want me to hear your conversation? What are you trying to hide?"

"I have nothing to hide."

"Then answer the phone!" Dhara was almost yelling now.

But by the time I reached it and held it to my ear, the call must have gone to voice mail. "Too late," I offered.

"Too late is right," came her reply. She sprang to her feet, rushed into our bedroom, and slammed the door behind her.

I stood there pleading for fifteen minutes. She said nothing. I tried to turn the knob, but it was locked. When not a sound came from behind the door I began to worry. We had two balconies—one off the living room and one off the bedroom—and it crossed my mind she might jump. Imego had turned her down for the only job she wanted; her marriage was in a rut; her mother had died, and she was estranged from her father. I slid open the living room balcony door and peered around the corner. She was sitting in our bed, flipping through a magazine. What was wrong with me?

The fridge was mostly empty, but I did manage to pull together an omelet.

"I made you dinner," I called, but she wouldn't answer. I kept trying—to no avail—then ate half the omelet while pacing at the bedroom door. After rinsing the plate, I remembered the hex key from our utility closet and picked the lock.

"Dhara—" I stepped inside the bedroom.

"Don't even." She kept her eyes trained on her *Dwell* magazine. "I'm not talking to you. You can stay at your father's tonight."

"I can explain."

"I'm not listening."

"I've only talked to her that once."

"Get out."

"I have no idea why she's calling," I said.

"Adam, if you don't get out of this room right now—"

"I'll bring the phone in here, and you can listen to the conversation yourself—"

"You're lying!" She threw the magazine across the room, and it landed at my feet, the pages splayed to a two-page spread of a beautiful outdoor hearth.

"Dhara—"

"Get out!" She shot up and headed toward me.

I stepped out of the room and closed the door.

I did stay at my father's that night. Grabbed my toothbrush and iPhone, some stray clothes from the front closet. I took the West Tower elevator down to the lobby, the East Tower elevator up to the thirtieth floor.

He answered the door in a tattered paisley bathrobe and slippers. "What's the occasion?" he asked.

"Trouble at home." I held up the toothbrush.

"That bad, eh?" He had an old book under his arm, which he slid into the valise sitting on his desk. "How about I make you a drink?"

"Do you have something other than Diet Coke and rum?"

"My mixer is Diet *Rite*. It's my Rite of Devotion," he said. "Not everybody's taste, apparently."

He took two wineglasses and a dusty Côtes du Rhône from a cabinet. He said the bottle had been a retirement gift from his department chair, but he wasn't a wine drinker and had no occasion to open it. He looked in every drawer for a corkscrew, and when he found one I popped the cork and poured us each a glass.

"To marriage." I raised a toast.

"Yes, singular, not plural."

"I should object to that," I said. "If it weren't for your third marriage, I wouldn't be here."

"To your first, and my third. Cheers."

We clinked glasses and sat down on sofas across from each other.

"Tell me why you're here?" my father asked.

I didn't want to get into it, but I was fresh from my banishment so couldn't help opening up. Though I didn't say we'd been thinking about moving to California, I did tell him that Dhara had been rejected for a job she'd wanted, and that I was on thin ice at work. I said that Lucy had resurfaced after many years and I'd met her a couple of times behind Dhara's back. "Somehow she seems to know. Maybe she's been checking my cell phone," I said.

My father sipped the wine. "Blech!" He winced.

I took a taste. "Seems fine to me. What do the sommeliers say? Earthy, with cherry and pepper notes?"

"I'll soldier on, then." He swilled the wine in his glass. "Let this be our unholy communion."

I didn't know what he meant by that, but later I'd remember it as a kind of harbinger. "Anyway, Dhara is thinking the worst. But I've done nothing wrong. Lucy and I have some common interests, that'll all. She's into books; I'm into books. There's not much more to it than that."

"You're meeting an old flame, whom your wife wants expunged from the record, if not the earth," my father said. "You're telling yourself she's a friend, forgetting how you used to lust after her with the desperation of a starving polar bear. And the memory of that lust or love, animus or intimacy or whatever mad concoction it was, still lies within you, like a dormant virus. Merely seeing her again might trigger a full-blown disease. Your wife has reason to worry. *You* should be more worried than you are."

When I wasn't willing to admit that he might be right, he cited his own life as an example. "I had to reach this state of bodily and psychic deterioration to have the long view and be able to say I made mistakes. Someone else's story would have done me little good, but perhaps you will be wiser."

Over the years I'd come to know the cautionary tale that was his life, but usually from my mother or relatives. I couldn't remember hearing it in my father's own voice, at least never at length. He had been at the University of Chicago for a year before coming home to marry his high-school sweetheart in Marinette, Wisconsin, the summer he turned nineteen. He and Gladys lived in Chicago through college, and he stayed in the city another four years writing catalogue copy for Montgomery Ward, just around the river bend from this apartment. In 1957 they moved to Ann Arbor, where he enrolled in the graduate literature program at the University of Michigan, and within three years Gladys had given birth to Michael. It was around this time that my father fell in with the Students for a Democratic Society, who were just springing up on campus. Their internal education secretary was a political science master's student from New York named Rachel Gold. She smoked Tiparillos and kept a copy of C. Wright Mills's "Letter to the

New Left" in the pocket of her thrift-store blazers. When my father got his first tenure-track job he left his wife and son and set up house with Rachel a short walk from the Oberlin College campus. "But don't cry for Gladys," he said. "She and Michael were better off without me." They moved home to northern Wisconsin, Gladys settled down with a paper-mill worker, and Michael grew up plotting his escape from the same small town his father had once fled.

Rachel would come to know a similar restlessness. In 1966 she became pregnant with Eric, and a few months later married my father at the Lorain County courthouse. After the positive reception of *Sherwood Anderson: Volume One,* she made him go on the market. "I was happy at Oberlin—best job, best students I ever had. We lived forty miles from Clyde, Ohio, Anderson's hometown. Even in 1968, with the world blowing up, I could still feel what it must have been like to live in a place like Winesburg a hundred years before. Maybe I dug in against the pull of Rachel's wanting to get to the action." But the best he could do was Indiana University. And Bloomington was no Berkeley.

Rachel lasted a year and a half in Indiana. "She brought the war to the home front, all right," my father said. "You should have heard the way that woman could curse and carry on. She was a hard-liner, and I was a floater. She wanted me to do teach-ins, join the strikes and protest marches, and when I would only go so far she called me a closet conservative." He met my mother at the IU library, where she worked in Special Collections, and though he didn't say as much, I was thinking she provided a refuge from the Rachel wars. Unlike Gladys, she had an advanced degree and was devoted to books; unlike Rachel, she understood the Midwest and could see both sides of an issue. Her temperament, too, fell somewhere in between, and for a while she provided a grounding force. Not the "twin flame" of my father's revisionist memory—she was sensible, orderly, repressed; he was obsessive, scattered, unrestrained—but the best match he found in a checkered romantic career.

The marriage lasted longer than any other: twelve years. I was born in 1976, the country's bicentennial, Sherwood Anderson's centennial, and the high point, my father claimed, in my parents' married life. Around fifth grade I started acting up in class and spending a good part of the day out in the hall. I didn't remember why I'd chosen that year for insurgency, but my father reminded me that 1986 was when a twenty-three-year-old graduate student named Sarah Roselli, "a dead-ringer for Rachel, with that same wildness about her," took his "Origins of Modernism" class. "I was fifty-five, same age as my father when he died of a heart attack unloading lumber at the Marinette docks. I'd been working on *Sherwood Anderson: Volume Two* for nearly twenty years, and I was wearing the golden handcuffs of tenure, marriage, and family. And I kid you not: on a chain around her neck Sarah wore a golden key."

My father's star had faded long before. He had the worst teaching evaluations among the literature faculty; he hadn't presented a paper or gone to a meeting in a decade. A traditionalist, he was on the losing end of the culture wars within the department, and the younger faculty saw in his affair with a graduate student a chance to pillory a member of the old guard. They had taken the fight all the way to the Standing Committee on Faculty Misconduct when Sarah urged him to hedge his bets and apply to other universities. Central Illinois made an offer; Sarah promised to follow him to Normal; and once again he chose to start over. But that summer, after my mother and I had packed the house and moved to Indianapolis, Sarah left a farewell note, moved back to her parents' in the Chicago suburbs, and eventually joined the Peace Corps. "Served me right," he said. "Worst mistake I ever made."

After we finished the bottle of wine, he turned in. I tried calling Dhara, but she wouldn't answer. I turned off the light in my father's apartment and looked across the balcony toward Dhara's and my place. I watched her go into the kitchen and make a cup of tea, work on her computer for a while. I tried calling again; she lifted the phone, saw it was me, put it back on her desk. When she went to sleep I lay down on my father's yard-sale sofa, which still smelled faintly of a stranger's dog, and watched the lights of the city play across the ceiling.

I figured my punishment would last twenty-four hours, but by Sunday morning two nights had passed and my wife still wasn't speaking to me. I tried getting into our apartment, but she'd put the chain on, and wouldn't reply when I begged her to come to the door.

I called Lucy back that morning with no intention of going out with her, but we were catching up, having a casual conversation, when she mentioned she would be attending a fiction reading that night—"Kind of offbeat, might be fun"—and did I want to come along? I was annoyed with Dhara, who was always accusing *me* of overreacting, when *she* was the rigid, irrational one.

I told Lucy if I could make it, I'd meet her at nine just inside the entrance of the bar. I did keep trying Dhara into the afternoon, and when she continued to ignore me, I sent a text: *I'm sorry. I'm ready to throw myself at your feet. But first, won't you unchain the door?* When she didn't reply, I sent another: *Please answer me. I love you. Let's go out to dinner and talk.* By late afternoon my patience had worn thin: *The punishment does not fit the crime. This isn't about me; it's about California. Seriously, can't you be reasonable?* Around seven o'clock, as I was getting ready to send another text, my father grabbed his valise off the desk and announced that he was going out to dinner.

"Would you like some company?" I asked.

"I'm meeting someone, as a matter of fact."

"A woman?"

He laughed himself into a coughing fit. "You have quite a sense of humor," he said. "I'm having dinner with a book collector. Our conversation would bore you."

"At least let me walk you to the cab."

Before I put him in the taxi, he shook my hand, held it for a surprisingly long moment, and said, "You're a good kid. If I haven't told you that before, shame on me, because it's true. Take care, won't you? Take good care of yourself, I mean." He so rarely stumbled over his words that I felt at a loss, as well. "Okay," I said, and as he was struggling into the backseat, I added, though he probably didn't hear me, "You, too." I watched the cab disappear up State Street. My father's white hair floated like a low cloud in the corner of the window.

Lucy met me at the Speakeasy, a bar and event space in Ukrainian Village that was so dark I put my hand up to make sure I didn't run into something. We settled into a booth, and the waiter suggested a pitcher of Goose Island, the beer special that night. I hadn't ordered a pitcher since graduate school, but told him, "Why not?" The room was crowded, the house music too loud, and I had trouble hearing Lucy. I kept asking her to repeat herself, and often nodded when I had no idea what she was saying.

"I've never seen so many people at a fiction reading," I all but yelled into her ear.

"I'm impressed that you can see at all."

"I can't, but it's like being outside on a pitch-black night and hearing the cicadas. You don't have to see them to know they're everywhere." The beer arrived, and I filled our plastic cups. "Maybe there's hope for our generation, after all."

"We'll see," Lucy said. She explained that "Lit Up" was part reading, part drinking game. Some in the crowd were literary, but most were here for the five-dollar pitchers. All kinds of writers—good and bad—from around the city came and put their names in a hat. The organizers picked three read-ers—randomly, or so they claimed—and each got up to thirty minutes. "I don't know why people want to put themselves through it," she said, "but the drinking part goes like this: Anytime you hear a cliché or stereotype, you're supposed to take a sip of beer."

"So the worse the writer, the drunker you get?"

"That's the idea," she said. "One reason I wanted to come is that lately they've been getting ringers. A National Book Award finalist who lives on the North Side got up there a couple weeks ago, and hardly anyone drank through his entire reading."

"I'm surprised he didn't get booed for letting their beer get warm."

"But how better to win nonreaders over to books than showing a captive audience what great writing sounds like?"

Soon a spotlight fell over the fedora-wearing emcee, who laid out the ground rules and introduced the first reader. By the time he sat down, our pitcher was empty and we'd ordered another. How he'd managed to pack so many animal-related clichés into one story that wasn't a beast fable was a feat in itself. I drank to *elephant in the room, fighting like cats and dogs, frog in his throat, hog heaven, took the bull by the horns, ate like a horse, wolf in sheep's clothing, every dog has his day,* and the coup de grâce: *hotter than a fox in a firestorm.* Before the second reader came on, Lucy leaned so close that her mouth touched my ear as she said, "If the next guy is that bad, I'll be drunk as a skunk."

We laughed, but should have been worried, because the second pitcher was gone by the end of reader two. Her story, set mostly at a hospital over the month the protagonist's mother is in a coma, featured a sampler of TV-movie tropes: the arrogant doctor, the sadistic nurse, the bratty kid sister, the midlife-crisis father, the degenerate boyfriend. The story ended with a turn that would have made O. Henry blush: the coma victim waking up and saying that what pulled her through was hearing the words, "Be positive." The nurse had the final line: "Ha!" she exclaimed. "That was just me telling the doctor your blood type: *B positive.*"

By the last reader we were too buzzed to order more beer. We did play along with cups of ice water, but the hush of the crowd and the lyric rhythm of her sentences made it clear that "Lit Up" was closing with a real writer. The story was told in a series of monologues, letters a woman wrote but never sent to the various love interests in her life. Piece by piece, a portrait emerges of an agoraphobe, holed up in her garden apartment checking job sites but applying to nothing, imagining whole lives with former lovers and various men she's met online. By the end—at some indeterminate time in the future—a family member she hasn't seen in years has come to check on her. The bell rings. But she's ill and bedridden now, under self-imposed house-arrest. The unsent letters pool on the floor beneath her. And we're left to wonder will she or won't she answer the door. I couldn't help thinking of George Willard's mother, drawing her final breaths in the last place she wanted to be.

We stayed long enough for Lucy to introduce herself to the third reader. She complimented the story, gave her a business card, said feel free to send work, but on our way to the Damen El stop she scolded herself for "falling all over the poor woman." "I don't usually drink this much," she said, looping her arm around mine. "And I shouldn't be operating these heels under the influence of alcohol." Since we'd been sitting down, I hadn't noticed the three-inch pumps, and now was feeling short walking next to her. We made our way up Damen, and she didn't let go of my arm until we put our fare cards into the turnstiles. We sat close, shoulder to shoulder, our hands almost touching, as the train rattled and pitched back toward the Loop, and I wondered what would happen when we got to Clark, the first transfer station to the Brown line: Would I walk Lucy back to Armitage and her apartment? Or would I stay where I was, continuing on to the next stop: State, Harbor City?

14

The Bankers' Panic began on October 17, 1907, when two dubious financiers failed to corner the copper market, and the institutions that lent money to the scheme, most of them already teetering from the recession, hurtled toward insolvency. Within a week one of the nation's largest trust companies collapsed and regional branches around the country withdrew their deposits from New York City banks. Amidst the rumors of bad loans and uncertain of the safety of their money, thousands of people poured into local banks to take out all their funds, sending Wall Street into paralysis and the nation to the brink of catastrophe.

The bank runs began in cities—from his office window on October 21, George could see the line at First National of Chicago stretch four full blocks—before spreading to suburbs and towns. Tom Willard stood outside Helen's father's bank for nearly an hour and withdrew his meager savings to stash in a basement safe. In the last week of October, the great Midas himself, J. P. Morgan, who had bailed out the U.S. Treasury during the Panic of 1893, asked Treasury Secretary George Cortelyou to transfer tons of gold, silver, and paper money into Morgan's private pool to stem the crisis. He gathered the richest bankers and trust officers in New York to meet at his home library, then locked the doors and said they were going nowhere until they agreed to make emergency loans to faltering banks. Hours later, an agreement was reached, and the crisis was soon averted.

Still, real output would decline the next year by 11 percent, the recession would continue for another four years, and soon thereafter, following a great fight, Congress would pass the Federal Reserve Act, creating a Central Bank to regulate institutions and maintain stability. For decades the Bankers' Panic of 1907 would serve as a warning in recessionary times, until less than a year beyond its hundredth anniversary, at the end of another age of wild speculation, when it would be spoken of again as a cautionary tale that too many had ignored.

Though most of the country survived the crisis in 1907, a number of towns, Winesburg among them, were not so lucky. Bled of its assets, Helen's father's bank would go into receivership in the winter of 1908, and Banker White would retire and put his mansion on Buckeye Street up for sale. The house would stay on the market for two years, eventually selling to an undertaker at a fraction of its former value. Though her parents offered to continue to pay for her schooling, Helen knew they were doing so out of pride. They had lost most of their savings, and she couldn't conscience depleting their accounts any further. She finished her spring classes at the University of Chicago, still two years shy of her graduate degree, and for the first time in her life faced uncertainty.

In mid-April 1908, George received a Western Union telegram from his father: *Lost the hotel. At a loss for what to do.*

George cabled back right away: *Come to Chicago. Think things over.*

Tom Willard replied: *Look for me 1 June. Must settle affairs.*

A Cleveland bank was soon to take over the New Willard House, and George's father had limited time to vacate the premises. With his name on the deed of the town's most visibly shuttered property, his liquid assets listed at fifty-three dollars, he had no choice but to declare personal bankruptcy.

Perhaps in his delirium he forgot the date when he'd said he would be arriving. Perhaps the bank asked for his keys sooner than he had planned. Either way, he neglected to inform George and left Winesburg on May 16, two weeks early—dyed his hair and mustache, shrugged into his summer suit, pinned a half-blown rose to his lapel, strode down the ramp to the train station, and greeted the conductor who'd been working this same "easy run" for as long as anyone could remember:

Beautiful morning, eh?

Going to see your son?

That's right. He's a big bug, that boy. One of the top admen in the city.

You tell him hello for me.

And that's just what he did when George opened the door to find his father, gripsack in hand.

"The conductor, Mr. Little, sends his regards," he said, then stepped into the house looking up and down. "Well I'll be damned. You're doing all right. Just fine, I'd say."

He was too distracted to notice Margaret and her parents having tea in the parlor. "You remember the Lazars," George said.

"From the wedding. Of course." Tom took off his straw hat and shook hands with everyone.

"What a surprise!" Margaret declared. "We weren't expecting you."

Tom removed a handkerchief from his suit pocket and mopped his brow. "You'll have to excuse me. I'm just off the train. What a free-for-all the Loop has gotten to be!"

"Just in for the weekend?" Harriet asked. She'd been caustic all afternoon, since her husband had convinced the family to take a drive along South Park Boulevard in his new Richmond touring car. Harriet couldn't stand his automobile hobby, found the entire enterprise vulgar. George, on the other hand, preferred these occasional jaunts to the alternative: dinner or the kinds of social gatherings his in-laws might otherwise demand of him and Margaret. At least the loud motor and city traffic could be counted on for squelching conversation.

Tom Willard set down his gripsack. "Can't say for certain how long I'll be."

"You seem to be traveling light," Harriet noted.

Tom returned his hat to his head. "I had a trunk sent around. Should be here by evening."

"A trunk!" Margaret exclaimed.

"Just a wardrobe trunk. Could have managed it myself, but I'm saving my back."

Margaret turned to her husband, and her eyes flashed like semaphores. George addressed Tom Willard: "In the cable you said June 1."

"Did I? Impossible."

"Shall I show it to you?" George felt a momentary relief that he had physical proof of the misunderstanding, until Margaret interrupted: "The point is you never bothered to tell *me*."

Lazar touched his wife's wrist. "Perhaps we should be leaving," he said and Harriet all but slapped his hand away. "We just sat down for tea. It's early yet." By which she meant she had no intention of missing any marital fireworks.

"I didn't mean to cause trouble," Tom began, and George said, "Margaret, sweetheart, I'd been planning to tell you, but each time it crossed my mind you were over at Hull House."

The freckles along her collarbone were plunged in crimson. "So this is my fault?"

"You've been busy. That's all."

"Too busy to hear that your father is moving in?"

"He's not moving in. Tell her—"

Tom hesitated. "What do you want me to say?"

"You know, about the business—"

Harriet couldn't resist stirring the pot. "We understand you're a hotelier. I hear the slump has been especially trying in the provinces. How *are* you holding up?"

Tom twisted the ends of his mustache. "You can't believe what you read in the papers. But George will tell you that I've talked for a good many years about getting out of innkeeping—and Tom Willard isn't one to pass up an opportunity."

Harriet wore a falsely ingenuous look. "An opportunity?"

"It's still in the planning stages," Tom said. "But we're on to a new chapter—you can bank on that."

George stood in curious awe of his father's self-denial. He had steered the family business, the hotel he'd inherited from George's mother, over every imaginable rock and shoal, and had finally run it aground. And here he was unwilling to own up to his failure. He could be lying in his casket, and he'd still be muttering, *I'm doing okay. Just fine. You've not heard the last from Tom Willard.*

Indeed, he would continue to make his presence felt for longer than anyone would have liked. He took the top-floor room. *Which we were saving for the baby,* Margaret told George. This became a running joke between them—*Have you checked the baby's room? Make sure the baby's room is in order*—until the joke felt too cruel and a little too true. That spring Tom got up each forenoon and dressed as if going to work. He had his bowl of farina and coffee, and made George late with his talk. He kept pressing his son to help him make contacts, but he wouldn't say what line of business he wanted to pursue. George suggested hospitality, but his father demurred.

Finally, toward the end of June, George gave in and arranged a private meeting between his father and his father-in-law. He wished he had demanded to attend, or rather that he had not agreed to the meeting in the first place, because Tom Willard boldly asked Lazar for a sizable campaign contribution. His great and secret plan was to make a late entry in the race for U.S. Congress, Sandusky County. *You could be looking at the future governor of Ohio,* he'd been known to say—and to think that *he* used to be the one telling George to *Wake up.* Here was a man with no income, no fixed address, living out of a wardrobe trunk hundreds of miles from town, his name stenciled on the walls of Winesburg's newly derelict hotel. Furthermore, Lazar was a Republican, and would never have dreamed of supporting a Democratic candidate, family ties be damned.

And so Tom Willard abandoned his political plans as cavalierly as he had hatched them. He spent the summer rattling around the house, reading aloud from newspapers and stalking his next delusion. At first George and Margaret indulged him and stayed at the kitchen table while he beat his gums over a "promising" new investment scheme. Tom's fifty-three dollars disappeared, and he asked his son for a "loan" to tide him over; this became a ritual. George and Margaret learned to speak in code to avoid saying anything that might set Tom off on a new caprice, and before long they found themselves in flight from their own home.

Margaret spent time at the stereopticon, with its pictures from the Louvre, and revisited the idea of moving to Paris for the summer. George had to admit, given recent developments, that the plan had appeal. But after a week or two Hull House reclaimed Margaret's attention, and she dismissed the idea of travel as "frivolous." She continued her work with the lending library and put increasing amounts of her own funds toward the purchase of art reproductions for local schools; she served as stage manager on Bronson Howard's *Old Love Letters* and John Galsworthy's *The Silver Box.* And Stefan recruited her into the Toynbee Club and had her awarded a new title: Director of Philanthropy.

For the first time in years, George lingered at the office at the end of the workday, but found his prospects unchanged. He had read through his old notepads, one after the next, but the entire lot of them disappointed him. Mostly he'd jotted down the daily comings and goings of Winesburg's citizens: *A. P. Wringlet received a shipment of straw hats. Ed Byerbaum and Tom Marshall were in Cleveland Friday. Uncle Tom Sinnings is building a new barn on his place on the Valley Road.* He had recorded curious quotes such as this, from the Standard Oil agent Joe Welling: *The world is on fire.* But he had forgotten the context of Joe's pronouncement, and his spirits sank upon realizing that the notepads contained few seeds for the books George hoped to write. He returned to the box of keepsakes he had stashed in his closet and unearthed a story he had begun as a teenager, a love story he'd once told Seth Richmond about. He had asked Seth to inform Helen White that George was in love with her, for he wanted to know how love felt in order to write a story about it. But he had gone no further than a few pages of outline notes and hackneyed lines. And now as summer gave way to fall he got in his mind that he ought to call around to Helen to see how she was managing.

They hadn't run into each other since the end of spring term. Helen had gone home to Winesburg for the summer to help her parents pack the family estate and prepare it for the market. She wrote half a dozen times, more than she had back in college, and George noted that she sent the letters not to his house but to his office. Was she trying to avoid raising Margaret's suspicions? Was she being thoughtful or furtive? Or was he reading too much into her choice of postal address? She said she'd planned to stay only a week or two in Winesburg, but coming home opened her eyes in ways she hadn't anticipated. She was surprised to find her parents, her mother especially, chastened by the blow fate had landed. They offered once again to pay for her degree, but seeing the toll the new century had taken on her neighbors, so many of them out of work and looking hollow on their porches, only made her more determined to do something serious with her life.

She spent her days going through old chests and closets and visiting friends she hadn't seen more than once or twice in a decade, schoolmates who had children, as many as three or four by now. *We're getting old, George,* she wrote. She took long walks through town and out between the berry fields along Trunion Pike. *I went up Waterworks Hill on a perfect afternoon to visit the fairgrounds, and I remembered going there with you one evening to flee an especially tiresome suitor that my mother had arranged. Do you recollect how we ran down that hill, got in a tangle and you tumbled and fell and picked yourself up? We were laughing and then everything seemed so quiet and still as we walked toward the valley and the lights of town.*

He did remember, of course. Which is why, in part, he suggested they meet again. She'd been back in Chicago but a week. His timing was fortuitous, she said, because a few trunks were due to arrive at her lodgings and she would probably need help getting them upstairs.

They met on a bright, humid Saturday while Margaret was at the theater working a matinee. Seeing where Helen lived eased George's worries about a single woman alone on the South Side. Her caravansary, pale brick with tall iron gates, was guarded like a citadel by the formidable Mrs. Bedrosian and sons. The building sat catty-corner to campus and the famous Midway Plaisance, part of the former fairgrounds of the Columbian Exposition.

George arrived too late to be of much assistance. The twins, Shahnazar and Norhad, thick as pillars, insisted on doing the work themselves, plucking the trunks from the ground and sweeping them up three flights of steps. George did catch a glimpse of Helen's room, and though not nearly as meager as his quarters at Ma Kavanagh's, it was modest, to be sure, a large bedroom with mullioned windows looking out toward the Midway. He was surprised to find her desk untidy, her bedding rumpled, and her clothes and books scattered higgledy-piggledy about the furniture and floor. She made no apology, though perhaps felt disconcerted, as George did, by the presence of Mrs. Bedrosian, who stood cross-armed in the hallway like a sign of posted rules, among them: No gentleman callers, especially those with wedding rings.

Helen led George along the Midway, past the campus buildings and the library to the Laboratory School, at the east end, where she had put her studies into practice. The building was locked, though they did peer into the windows at the darkened classrooms.

"Do you think you'll go back?" George asked.

"Honestly, I haven't decided. I hate not to finish something—"

"I know what you mean." George tried flirting with danger, to test her response: "Regrets can be impossible to live with."

But Helen didn't seem to catch his implication and continued where she'd left off. "I've always been one to set a goal and see it through," she said, "but over the last couple years I've had competing plans: graduate school and Hull House. Then the world turned upside down. When I went home, I realized I'd spent the better part of my life pursued by guilt: Why should I have so much when others are in despair?"

They returned to the path and continued walking east along the Midway, toward Lake Michigan. "Perhaps that guilt chased me unawares to the normal school and into teaching," Helen went on. "I'd wanted so much to be around ordinary people, people for whom pretense cuts no figure. You were one of those people, George. You still are. I envied how easily you could move between bankers and cobblers, merchants and pensioners. You had a way of making anyone comfortable, even high-mettled me."

"If I seemed comfortable in your presence, you should praise me for my acting," George said. "You had me nervous as a cat."

They crossed a thoroughfare and headed toward a lagoon. "But you know what I mean. You have a natural way about you. You don't let society tie you up in knots."

If ever that were true it no longer seemed to apply, but he wasn't about to disabuse her of the notion. They were walking close. Her voile skirt brushed against his hand. People passing by must have assumed they were married.

"I grew up behind castle walls," Helen was saying, "and though I tried to leave that behind when I went to the city, I was still Banker White's daughter. Even if no one knew who my father was, my privilege enveloped me like a skin."

"You always struck me as perfectly genuine," George said.

"I think you recognized our shared desire: We were both desperate to leave, and we knew we had to get out of town in order to create our own expectations." She pointed to a bench by the banks of the lagoon. "Is this all right?"

George offered her his hand, and they both sat down. To the left, beyond a stretch of immaculate lawn, stood the Palace of the Arts, one of the last remnants of the World's Fair; to the right, the wild habitat of Wooded Island. Before them lay the lagoon, ringed with people out to take the air, and in the distance the lake, light-spangled and beaded with boats.

"Oh, listen to me running on and on," Helen said. "I do apologize. Your ears must be positively ringing with my talk."

George put his hand on hers long enough to feel its warmth, then removed it. "I haven't had a more pleasant afternoon in a great while."

"You're kind—and patient, at that," she said. "I don't know what's gotten into me. I feel both liberated and adrift at the same time, like I'm piloting one of those boats on the lake, yet never learned to sail."

"I think you're making your way just fine."

"Well, I'm not Banker White's daughter anymore, that's for sure."

"I never felt you were. You're being too hard on yourself, Helen. I always said you were the only girl in town with any get-up to her, and that's never been more true than now."

"Chicago is full of such girls."

"Well, I don't know any."

In the silence that followed George wondered if she was going to ask *What about your wife?* But Helen only pointed out a couple of children feeding the swans, the birds nudging each other as they stretched their necks toward shore.

"I have two choices, it seems," Helen began. "I could teach and perhaps one day go back to school. Or I could put in application for permanent resident at Hull House. They have some paying positions there, and I get on well with Jane."

"What do *you* want to do?" George asked.

"What do you think I should do?"

"I bet you know what you want but aren't ready to say."

"I have a confession," Helen put in. "The first time I went to Hull House, on a field trip with the Lab School, I had convinced myself that I would see you there. I have no idea how the notion got into my head. I knew you still lived in Chicago because your father would go up and down Main Street telling anyone he passed what a big wheel you'd become. But I was afraid to look you up."

"Why?" George asked.

"It had been so many years. I figured if we were going to meet we were going to meet," she said. "But I had this intuition that it would happen at Hull House. You were an ace copywriter, so the settlement seemed an unlikely place. But I never believed the reports that went abroad about your life among the smart set. I used to see you talking to laborers outside Daugherty's Feed Store or to misanthropes like Wash Williams, who my mother tried to get fired from the telegraph office for what she called 'his grotesque appearance and prehistoric hygiene.' You were friend to the outcast and displaced, people who would be welcome nowhere more than Hull House. But I didn't see you there, so after a while I dismissed the thought that I ever would. Then, lo and behold, you appeared."

"I have a confession of my own," George said. They sat next to each other, and so, not looking into her eyes, he felt a certain boldness. It occurred to him that directly east of this bench, almost a straight line across the lagoon, the lake, the farms and towns of Indiana and Ohio, stood Winesburg. "When I saw you at Hull House that day, it wasn't entirely coincidental." He went on to tell her about Henrici's, how he'd spotted a woman across the restaurant who looked just like her, how the host had claimed he didn't know her name but did say she collected bread for Hull House. George had wanted to stop by for months, and when the opportunity arose he took it.

He didn't say his stock had fallen at work or that increasingly he felt like a coward and a fraud. He didn't say that he might well have been in love with Helen once, and found her every bit as appealing now as ever. Nor did he tell her, not yet anyway, that he had married a woman he didn't love.

"So I guess I'm not the clairvoyant that I thought I was," Helen put in.

"On the contrary," George replied. "You thought you would run into me at Hull House, and eventually you did. Your intuition was right all along."

"That's one way to look at it," Helen said.

"Have you decided what to do?" George asked.

"About what?"

"Hull House or teaching."

"Weren't you supposed to tell me the answer to that?" She gave a little laugh.

"Trust your instincts," George said. "They were right about me."

"Then I guess I shall be drafting a letter to Miss Addams."

And so she did, that very evening.

Two months later, Chicago celebrated the Cubs' victory in the World Series, unaware that the team wouldn't win another championship for a century and more. It was amidst the city's jubilation that Helen called once again on Shahnazar and Norhad, this time to help her move from the third floor of Mrs. Bedrosian's to the third floor of Jane Addams's Hull House. She joined the forty residents who lived on the property, and agreed to stay on for at least six months. She taught grammar, reading, and literature to a range of students, collaborated with an art teacher on a bookbinding class, and spelled Jane as primary Hull House liaison to the Little Room.

Later, George would not remember whether it was his idea or Helen's that he should join the literary club. He had begun filling up his notepads again, this time with observations. He went back to taking the grip to work, and most days would walk the two miles home, stopping midway at the river to watch the drawbridge open with its loud, plaintive wail. He'd write down descriptions of tugboat captains and steamer workers and of the gray-green water, befouled with flotsam and oil. He'd continue on his way and sit up at night cataloguing the faces he called up out of the dark moil of the street. He remembered something the schoolteacher Kate Swift had once said, that he should try to *know what people are thinking about, not what they say*. So into his notepad went the halting beginnings of character sketches and interior monologues, first of people he knew—Helen, his father—then of people he saw but knew not at all, like Virgil the chauffeur and the violin teacher at Hull House who positively swooned whenever Helen breezed by.

Into the winter of 1909, George had begun spending weekend afternoons at Hull House. He signed on for Helen's bookbinding class, and played the wallflower at meetings of the Little Room. He read the novels and stories of members who assembled there—Henry Blake Fuller, Elia Peattie, George Ade, Hamlin Garland, and Edith Wyatt—but shied away from the heated discussions that surrounded books such as Theodore Dreiser's *Sister Carrie,* which some considered a work of empathic genius and others amoral and awkwardly written. There was much anxiety about the salons of New York, and though certain members made a case for Chicago, George knew that the heart of literary America sat eight hundred miles to the east. With no books of his own or even published stories, he felt a bit like an imposter at these meetings, but Helen assured him that others were in their apprenticeship, too, and he could learn a great deal from the company of writers.

Margaret was not so approving. Though she never said as much, she gave the impression that she had discovered Hull House and George was horning in on her territory. She asked why he didn't attend the roundtable at Schlogl's instead, and he explained that only established writers gathered there. She asked about the bookbinding, and this put him in a corner. "If I'm hoping to publish books of my own, I want to know every part of the process," he said. She gave him a skeptical look, but didn't accuse him of wanting to spend more time with Helen White. He had never admitted to a history with her, and he was careful not to seem interested when the three were together in the same room.

Margaret had other reasons for being on edge that winter. George's father had still not found a job. He claimed to have exhausted every contact he had, mostly salesmen he'd known from the drummers' room. While George was at work, Tom Willard supposedly met with these men and their bosses, but the meetings came to nothing. "They tell me I'm too experienced," he said, and later Margaret complained to George, "*Too* experienced? Bosh! He's almost sixty. He's been out of work going on a year. He talks so much you can't hear yourself think. And he lives in a world of make-believe."

The faltering economy didn't help. The Lazar Agency was doing better than most, but that only made Tom more dependent on his son and daughter-in-law. One night, while Tom was down at the corner tavern again and had left a sink full of dishes, Margaret told George she'd had enough.

"Why don't you send him to a boardinghouse?" she said. "Ring up that Irish woman on Cass Street. Surely she has rooms to let." But George knew that having tasted the good life for the better part of a year his father would be in no hurry to pack his bags. "You can't tell an innkeeper that he's stayed too long at the inn. And I'm not about to banish my own flesh and blood," George said. "Besides—you're never here, so what does it matter?"

He didn't mean to stir up a fight, or at least he thought he didn't mean to. Margaret had yet to tell him she'd grown disillusioned with Hull House, and was feeling beleaguered and used. Ice webbed the windows; it was the time of year in Chicago when people wondered if spring would ever come.

"This is my house," Margaret said.

"You're not serious," George replied. "I make a handsome salary."

"You wouldn't were it not for me."

"I don't know what to say."

"You can admit it."

"I'll do no such thing."

"Perhaps I should talk to my father."

"Margaret—"

"Admit it."

He struggled through his shock and humiliation for exactly what he was supposed to be admitting. He'd never thought his wife capable of cruelty, and wondered what had brought this on.

"Very well." He gave in. "If it makes you happy to hear me say it: This is your house."

That night, in bed alone again, he ran those words around a loop in his mind. *This is your house. Your house. This is your house. Not mine.*

15

That evening out with Lucy, I nearly ended up at her apartment. But not quite. Instead, I came home and called Dhara, and at last she picked up the phone and let me back in. It's hard to recall the precise details of that night, in light of what would happen only a few days later. I remember following Lucy out of the train at the Clark El station, heading along the grimy corridors and listening to a trio of buskers harmonize to "You Send Me," then rumbling north over the river, the walls of the city closing in and opening up to avenues, yellow streetlights and headlights, red signal lights and brake lights streaking by.

At Armitage we got off the train, and there was a moment on the escalator where Lucy gave me what I thought might have been an expectant look. We stepped off and continued through the turnstile, then down to the sidewalk in Lincoln Park. This time we didn't stop at the corner but continued on up her street, walking close, and I felt that curious combination of excitement and nausea that precedes something perilous. My hands were in my pockets. I tried to find a mantra or some way to clear my head, and in the middle of this effort a black Jeep full of college kids, probably from nearby DePaul, came racing past, four or five obnoxious boys bent on outdoing one another, two of them standing in the back, clutching the roll bar. One yelled at us, "Fuck you!" and another added, "Fuckers!" Their cackling laughter trailed down the street, followed by a squeal of tires as they turned up Armitage. And that was all it took for me to lose whatever nerve I might or might not have been trying to gather. I don't know if Lucy felt it, too, but I sensed the mood, whatever it was, had been broken, and more than that: the Jeep, the laughter had been a premonition, some kind of warning flare.

And so we went our separate ways.

You didn't have to walk me home, she said, as if to erase other reasons we might have arrived at that juncture.

It was the least I could do.

And then I was on the train again. North/Clybourn, Chicago, Merchandise Mart, Clark, and State. I slipped into my father's apartment quietly. His bedroom door was closed, lights out. I sat on the dog-smelling couch, asking myself how many nights would I have to sleep there. I woke Dhara with my call, and had just begun my plea when she said *The door's unlatched. You can let yourself in.* I wrote a quick note to my father: *Headed back to my place. Thanks for the hospitality and the stories.*

Dhara and I kept a fragile peace those next few days. I don't recall much in the way of conversation, only that I tried to cook, clean, and compliment my way to a suitable apology.

It was Dhara who pointed out that I hadn't checked in on my father since the weekend. We both got dressed, and she headed off to work. We had planned to meet for lunch at the Green City Market, which was opening for the season that morning. Wednesday, May 6, 2009.

I took the elevators down and up and knocked on my father's door. When he didn't answer, I took out my key and poked my head in. It was seven thirty. By now he was usually padding around, but I couldn't hear him stirring, only saw that his bedroom door was slightly ajar.

I brewed a pot of coffee, got two mugs from the cabinets, and put some food out for Wing Biddlebaum. I poured myself a cup and read the *Trib* and the *Times* on my iPhone. Federal regulators were running stress tests on the major banks. Fears of the swine-flu pandemic were lessening. And John Edwards, the presidential candidate who cheated on his terminally ill wife, was defending himself against charges that he'd misused campaign funds.

By eight thirty I'd had my two cups and might not have bothered to peek in on my father had Wing not been acting strange. He ignored the food I'd put out for him, he meowed in a way I hadn't heard before—deeper, from the back of his throat—and when I was getting ready to leave I found him pacing in the foyer, as if trying to block my exit.

Slowly, I pushed open my father's bedroom door.

"Dad," I said.

When he didn't respond, I repeated myself.

He was lying on his side, halfway under the covers, facing the balcony. The light through the blinds striped his face.

"Dad!" I yelled, half-expecting him to sit up and snap back at me. I approached with a sinking feeling. His eyes were closed. He had an unearthly placid look. I shook his shoulder and thought I saw a slight heave of his chest, but when I put my finger under his nose no air came out. I touched his face with the back of my hand, and his cheek was cold.

I have no idea why, in that moment of actual crisis, when I had every reason to fall to my knees or jump onto the bed and furiously attempt CPR, I just stood there. I waited I don't know how long—a minute, five minutes—before calling 911. And instead of screaming *Send an ambulance right away!* I told the dispatcher that my father was gone. She asked me about the breathing, asked me to describe his color. Pale and gray. She told me to try taking his pulse. I fished his limp arm from under the sheets and held two fingers to the back of his wrist. "Nothing," I said.

The paramedics came and confirmed what I knew. Then the police were asking me whether the death was expected or unexpected. And I struggled for an answer. I said I'd been expecting this for years—he was nearly eighty, his health in decline—but, no, it was unexpected; he'd been more spirited lately than I'd ever seen him.

While we waited for the coroner to arrive, I went to the living room and called Dhara. She didn't answer, so I left a voice mail with the news, and sent a text as well. She returned the call right away, and was at my father's apartment within minutes.

"I'm so sorry." She embraced me for a long time, there in the hallway, with the door still open. And that's when I wept. "I'm sorry, too."

The coroner asked about my father's medical history. I told him about the heart trouble, so he looked at the labels on the pills in the medicine cabinet. He called the cardiologist, and I learned that my father had been in Stage C heart failure, functional but declining, just on the verge of Stage D. D for dying.

The next hours spun by, as I made phone calls and arrangements. I reached my half brothers in New York and Boston. Neither sounded too surprised. "I've been waiting for this call," Michael said. "I bet he left behind an incredible mess."

"Actually, no," I told him. "The apartment is clean. It looks as if a maid came through here. He was selling off his stuff right till the end. And it appears that he died in his sleep."

"Bizarre. I used to have nightmares that he'd get drunk and cross the median, crash head-on into a family of four."

This got my blood up. "He was a drinker, but only at home. He never went out," I said. "And is this really a time to talk that way?"

"I'm sorry. He could be brilliant, but he was also a pain in the ass."

Eric was no better. I'd called and allowed the news to sink in. He'd plied me for details about discovering the body, and told me he wanted to talk to his wife and kids. When he called back a couple hours later, all he seemed to care about was my father's bank account. Did he have debts? Were we going to have to pay some enormous bills—to the Feds; to the credit-card usurers? Was that foreclosure fiasco over with? Or was somebody going to come after us? "I can't afford to write another check, Adam. We could be looking at teacher layoffs across the state. And this is Massachusetts, for Chrissake. The last sane place in the country. If I get canned, what are my kids going to eat?"

"The foreclosure went through," I said. "That's all behind us. I don't know about the rest, but first things first. Dad just died. I have a lot to figure out."

"And the funeral costs?"

"He was your father."

"He didn't raise me."

"I'm not getting into this," I said.

The coroner determined that my father had died around 2:00 a.m. Body temperature falls two degrees per hour after death, so it was just a matter of counting backwards. Since there was no evidence of foul play and the doctor had said my father's heart could have gone at any minute, the coroner skipped the toxicology screening and said there was no need for an autopsy. I asked if I could request one, anyway, just to be sure—I was remembering what Lucy had said about old people and suicide—but the coroner told me I'd have to order that myself, and the base fee in Cook County was at least a couple thousand dollars.

I called the cardiologist back. I wanted to believe that my father had gone peacefully in his sleep, but a part of me wondered if he hadn't taken a bunch of pills, left them in the bathroom so no one would suspect anything, or if he had knowingly mixed too much heart medication with his usual four or five glasses of alcohol. If I let him go without an autopsy, I might never find out, so I asked the doctor how long people survived with Stage

D heart failure. But he wouldn't give an estimate, even when I pressed him. He did say it would have been months, not years, before my father would no longer have been able to get around on a cane.

"What would have happened then?" I asked.

"We'd have moved him to the hospital for round-the-clock care."

"And you told him this?"

"He knew his condition," the doctor said. "I made it very clear."

I hung up none the wiser: Either my father had died of heart failure, or he had self-euthanized, knowing full well what his future looked like: needles and tubes, doctors and nurses telling him what was good for him, when in fact nothing was good for him.

The coroner signed the death certificate. Dhara went back to our apartment to research funeral homes and arrange to have the body transferred. I gathered some papers and books that were sitting on a chair beside my father's bed, and stacked them on his desk in the living room. From the nightstand I removed his empty glass, an amber film of dried Diet Rite at the bottom. I was going to rinse the glass, but changed my mind, and moved it to the kitchen cabinet. Here was his last drink, his *Rite of Devotion*.

I went into his room and sat down on the chair at his bedside. I lifted his hand and held it for a while, something I'd never done when he was alive. Then I pulled the sheet over him and closed the door.

Sitting at his desk, I stared out at the buildings and the cloudless sky, listened to the rush-hour bustle below.

Dhara called to say she'd found a funeral director and was sending him over. "I know these things are expensive," I told her. "I'm sorry. I'll figure a way to pay for it all."

"Don't be ridiculous," she said. "I have savings. The cost doesn't matter."

She offered to take care of everything—find out if my father had a funeral plan, track down friends and colleagues.

"Where should we have the funeral?" she asked.

"I don't know," I said. "Morbid as he was, he refused to talk about last wishes and wills. When I brought it up, he called me a *grave watcher*, whatever that is."

We agreed to hold off until we'd found some kind of instructions, and if nothing turned up we'd decide in the morning. Marinette, where his family was buried? Normal, where he finished his career? Chicago, where Sherwood Anderson made his name?

While I waited for Dhara to come up, I turned to the stack of books and papers that had been at my father's bedside. At the top was his biography, *Sherwood Anderson: Volume One.* Beneath it were *Winesburg, Ohio,* and his other favorite book, Anderson's story collection *Death in the Woods.* Under that was the manuscript box I'd seen before in the Harbor City storage cage, the one marked "BOG" for *Book of the Grotesque.* I opened the box with that same queasy anticipation I'd felt walking Lucy home a few days before.

For the most part the contents were the same, and appeared to be in identical order to what I'd already been through: title page on top, then nothing but notes, fragments, and folders. In addition to that one chapter I'd seen before, about George Willard's arrival in Chicago, I found another piece my father had written, a short story, it looked like, called "The Writer's Writer."

As I was getting ready to read the story, I noticed, sitting at the very bottom of the box, an envelope. I picked it up and saw that it was marked "Adam." I've never seen a ghost, but stumbling upon my name at that moment, in that place, made me feel what it must be like. I set "The Writer's Writer" aside, ripped open the envelope, and pulled out the typed letter.

Dear Adam,

I want to apologize for any trouble I've put you through on this day and in this lifetime. I was as difficult a father as you were easy a son. I hope it was not a shock to find me. I've been combing my hair and making things presentable in preparation for what we both knew was coming. You were expecting this, yes? No one likes an unpleasant surprise. I owe you a pleasant one, after all these years, and that's what this letter is about.

But, first: arrangements. I would like a small cocktail party, but please: no toasts (I've never heard an honest toast and would hate for my pyre to be set to sea on the breezes of false praise). The party could take place in Chicago, perhaps here in my apartment (remove the body, run a vacuum, serve plenty of liquor). I've left my address book in the top right-hand drawer of my desk, and have placed asterisks by the names of those I'd like invited. A short list, I'm afraid.

About the body: burn it and do what you will with the pixie dust. In life, I scattered to the four winds, so why stop now?

Something I've been meaning to tell you: I did not have long to live. After the doctor gave this prognosis, I was depressed for days, then suddenly elated. I could finish something and finish it well. If I was careful, I would not have to go out as Sherwood Anderson did, felled by a toothpick, or like the actor—I forget his name—who died onstage in a swordfight during the last scene of Macbeth. *No, I would get my house in order. I would own my departure.*

Remember Elizabeth Willard's tin box, the one she plastered into the walls of her hotel/prison, the inheritance she meant for her son but was too far gone to bequeath? That story, "Death," had always haunted me, until I realized that I could rewrite the ending.

In the same desk drawer with my address book you will find three keys on a Chicago Cubs ring. One is to my storage locker in Little Italy, where I still have a few belongings of limited value. One is to my storage cage in this building, where I have put boxes of research material, including my abandoned manuscript for Volume Two. And the third key is to a small safe hidden under blankets and shoes in my bedroom closet. You should look there, and recall how "Some time it may prove to be a door, a great open door to you."

Farewell.

Love,
Dad

P.S. Please take good care of Wing.

I read the letter twice and was reading it a third time when a knock came on the door. It was Dhara.

"You've been crying." She helped me out of the chair. We held each other on the camelback sofa, and after a while, I handed her the letter. She read it and returned it to me.

Her eyes welled with tears. "How do you think he did it?"

"Liquor and pills," I said.

"Do you want to make sure?" she asked. "We can still order an autopsy."

"You remember what the coroner said: They're expensive."

"I'll pay for it," Dhara offered.

"He wouldn't want someone cutting him up, and the letter is pretty clear. He just doesn't say exactly how. He looked good. That's the miracle of it."

"Is the letter dated?" Dhara asked.

I checked. It wasn't. "I wonder when he wrote it. Yesterday? How long has he been planning this?"

"Since the diagnosis, it sounds like."

"I wish I'd never sent him to that doctor," I said. "This never would have happened if I'd just left him alone."

"He made his own choices. He didn't have to go to the doctor. You didn't force him. If anything, knowing that his time was limited gave him a chance to 'own his departure,' as he said."

"I can't help feeling responsible."

"But you're not, Adam. He could have had a heart attack on the street, in an elevator or some public place, a bunch of strangers circling him or walking right by. He died at home. In bed. Probably fell asleep without any pain. Who wouldn't want to go that way?"

When the funeral director and another man arrived with a gurney, Dhara showed them to the bedroom, then steered me to the balcony. We stood and watched the State Street Bridge lower in the wake of a sailboat flotilla. The sun was going down. The streetlights cast a gold glow on the river. And the warning bells rang and rang as the Clark, LaSalle, and Wells Street bridges rose into the sky.

The funeral director poked his head outside, and we arranged a time to meet the next day. After the men wheeled the gurney away, Dhara and I went into my father's room, and I pulled his comforter taut to erase the impression his body had made on the bed.

"What a day," I said. "Like a thousand days pressed into one."

Dhara put her arm around me and rubbed my back.

"Could you do me a favor?" I sat down on the squeaky bed my father had picked up at some estate sale. "Could you get the keys from his drawer and open that safe? I'd be much happier if you did it."

Dhara left the room and returned with the address book and keys. She handed the book to me, and I thumbed through the pages. Indeed he had put asterisks beside twenty or so names. I wished there had been more, and even now was wondering who else to invite to this "cocktail party."

Dhara opened the closet and removed the shoes and blankets. "It's re-markably organized in here," she said. She turned the key in the lock of the safe, which was about the size of a microwave oven. I drifted over and knelt. Dhara pulled out the contents of the safe: three envelopes, which she handed to me. On each my father had written the name of one of his sons: Michael, Eric, Adam.

I tore open my envelope. Inside was a cashier's check, made out to me, for eighty-five thousand dollars.

16

THE WRITER'S WRITER

Sherwood Anderson was the father of all my works—and those of Hemingway, Fitzgerald, etc. We were influenced by him. He showed us the way.

—WILLIAM FAULKNER

He didn't know he was dying, but at the end of this voyage from New York to Panama City on the SS *Santa Lucia,* he would be met by an ambulance, taken to a Colón hospital, then laid out on his deathbed. This was supposed to have been a new beginning, though he'd had too many of those to count over his six-and-a-half decades. He'd moved from one small town in Ohio to the next, west to Chicago like so many other dreamers, then back to Ohio again; after his breakdown, he returned to Chicago, but it seemed he couldn't sit still more than a year or two before lighting out once more: to the Missouri Ozarks, upstate New York, downstate Alabama, Paris, New Orleans, rural Virginia for a new career as a country newspaper editor. And now, with his fourth wife beside him, he planned to sail through the Panama Canal, then down the west coast of South America and settle in a town—he hadn't decided where—and get to know the people.

He had made his reputation with a book about a young journalist who got to know the people, and in the twenty and more years since this one enduring achievement he had been trying to keep pace, trying so hard, book after book—twenty-seven in all—that he'd become a subject of parody. But since easing into the country life hundreds of miles removed from the stony heart of publishing, he had found what he called *inner laughter.* In his posthumous memoirs he would say that his life had begun at just the right time, and he hoped it would end at the right time, *not carry on too far.*

His friend Gertrude Stein—loyal friend, unlike Hemmy, Faulkner, and Scott Fitzgerald—had said you had to learn to do everything, even to die. He had been thinking about death, preparing for it, for years. *When it comes,* he wrote, *there will be a real comfort in the fact that self will go then. There is some kind of universal thing we will pass into that will give us escape from this disease of self. . . . It is this universal thing, scattered about in many people, a fragment of it here, a fragment there, this thing we call love that we have to keep on trying to tap.* He had defended euthanasia five years before, when another writer, Charlotte Perkins Gilman, took chloroform after learning her cancer was inoperable. *My hat off to her. I wish I also could be assured of the same sort of clean departure, of the courage and the sanity of it,* he wrote. *The little white pill. The hell is to know when to swallow it.*

He was unaware, but he *had* swallowed something. Not a pill, and not intentionally. At a bon voyage party a few days earlier, February 26, 1941, while slugging his fourth or fifth martini of the night, a three-inch, olive-speared toothpick went down his trachea, esophagus, stomach, and intestines and thrust into his abdominal cavity, perforating his colon (so would say the medical examiner in, of all places, Colón). His demise, death by toothpick, would rival that of Aeschylus—who perished after an eagle dropped a tortoise on him, mistaking his bald head for a rock—as the most bizarre in literary history.

But the writer would never know the name of his condition—peritonitis—or that it was fatal if untreated. The first day out, the Atlantic had been rough, the second day so stormy that most passengers stayed in their rooms. He figured the cramps across his lower abdomen, his lack of appetite, must have been caused by seasickness. But by day three the spasms were coming in ever-shortening waves. And though he tried to keep his spirits up, and told the editor of the *Nation,* who also happened to be on board, that he wouldn't let doctors spoil his trip, it was clear by the time they reached the Caribbean that he was seriously ill. The ship's medic administered morphine, which did little good. His wife arranged for that ambulance to be waiting at port. And the writer, whose pulse would soon race, who would soon descend into full delirium, then a coma, plowed the watery depths of his memory.

And what arose might have surprised him, for he had spent half his life cultivating his legacy—what is a writer, after all, but gardener of his own grave, custodian of his own mausoleum? But he did not remember the reviews, the parties, the fleeting adulation, or the moment when he realized for the first time that he was a real writer, how the words of his first great story, "Hands," wrote themselves across the page on a single glorious night. He had told his first wife that he felt *like a harp that the wind blew through.* If only it had remained that easy.

Nor did he remember the marriages, their beginnings or endings. How he'd tried to be a family man and entrepreneur, selling an illusory compound that promised the "cure for roof troubles," yet nothing could keep him under one roof. He stumbled out of the door one morning, left his wife and three children, and never came back. His second wife, a sculptor with a sex drive to match his own, he stole from the Illinois poet who gave him the structure for his most famous book. So began his bohemian years: the beard, the barefoot wedding and open marriage. Yet still he felt confined. He fled east, south, abroad, and she followed. He met someone else and rushed to Reno for a quickie divorce. A few years later, remarried, miserable again, he learned of his second wife's overdose from sleeping pills, perhaps an accident, more likely not.

He would come to think of his third wife as The Princess. No place was good enough, but wherever they went the air was thick with disapproval. Her intellectual parents made him feel more like the college dropout he was than a leading voice of his generation. She endured his darkest hours, when he championed Hemingway and showed Faulkner to his own *postage stamp of native soil,* only to have both men betray him. Reviews of one book after the next came back dismissive or killing, and the day arrived—this, too, he would not remember aboard the SS *Santa Lucia*—when driving with his wife through the countryside he said in what she would describe as a strange blank voice: *I wish it were all over.* Abruptly he turned the wheel, sending the car off the road. They didn't flip, but skidded into the middle of a field and for a long while sat in silence. Then the writer, whom everyone used to call the life of the party, pulled back onto the road and drove wordlessly home.

To think that he was in his last days, on this ship, on a Goodwill tour, in the Caribbean, no less, with the only woman from whom he'd never thought of running away, might have seemed a cruel joke. But as land approached, his mind didn't pause to consider—for time was running out, and he was down to this: Chicago. 1898. Maybe '99. He'd been there only a short time. Living in a tenement. Making two dollars a day for ten hours' work in a warehouse. Lifting kegs of nails. Or was it frozen meat? He was lonely and lustful, and he'd begun looking at prostitutes on the corners, in the bars, saving his money with the intent of approaching one. But he resisted until one wet evening in March or April, winter grappling with spring, when he did stop under a windblown awning on lower Michigan Avenue to talk to a woman with painted lips and gaudy jewelry. He did not recall what she looked like, though he remembered her pale breasts billowing over her cor- set, and the scent of gasoline that trailed behind her as she led him up the stairs. This was when everyone wanted but few could own an automobile, and the fashion for women was to put dabs of gasoline behind the ears, on the wrists and cleavage. In the middle of the third-floor hallway she opened the door to her room, and inside were two beds, one empty and in the other a sleeping infant and young boy. With practiced swiftness, she rolled the bed her children were sharing—they barely stirred—into an alcove. When she returned to him she began to undress. *Here, just take the money,* he said. But she wouldn't have it: *I'm not a beggar.* He shrugged into his coat and left. Back on Michigan Avenue the rain turned to snow. On the long walk home the writer, his money thick in his pocket, began to cry.

This was his last clear thought. Not: who will cry for me?

17

The same week that Margaret forced George to tell her, "This is your house," he got an apartment of his own. He'd lost another client that morning, had endured another reproof from Lazar, and on his lunch break had wandered into the Palmer House, where he'd lived during his engagement. The same manager from three years before, Lemuel Means, still patrolled the desk, same pince-nez perched beneath his stern, heavy brow. George inquired about month-to-month vacancies, and the manager signed him up for a room on the fifth floor.

"How's married life?" Means asked, insipidly.

George was surprised the manager would remember or care. "Just fine," he said. "The apartment will be for my father," he felt compelled to add. "But you'll see me coming and going, running about for the old man and the like."

This wasn't true, though it did have a shred of veracity, to which George clung. In fact, he had decided he had to have a place of his own. An escape, where he could look out the window and let his mind wander free, where he might finish a story, then write another and another again. He had no plans of telling Margaret. Since he handled the bills in the household, if he cut expenses here and there she'd never need to know. If, for some reason, she did find out, he could say he'd rented the apartment for his father—it wouldn't take much to convince him to move in.

For a time, just having these secret lodgings gave George a thrill. He would spend his lunch break at the Mission desk in his room, and the hour would grow longer by the day. He'd stay after work, go in on weekends, and soon he was finishing whole stories, watching the characters he'd been sketching out take shape beneath his pen. One piece, in particular, had come in a white heat, and he'd revised it during the last snowmelt of the winter of '09. There came a point when he needed to share the story, so one Saturday after a meeting of the Little Room he asked Helen if she would read the manuscript and have lunch with him later in the week to say what she thought.

They returned to the same booth at Schlogl's on a Friday in late March. Lazar and Kennison were in New York that week, and Helen was on spring recess, so George figured on taking the afternoon off. When he ordered a bottle of wine, he said, "I think I'm going to need this."

"I might as well join you," Helen put in.

After the waiter left, George asked, "Is the story that bad? I guess we'll have to drink our way through my blighted hopes."

"Look who's fishing for praise," Helen said, then raised a toast. "To one of the most gifted writers I know."

George withheld his glass for a moment. "This is no time to make game of me. I'm a sensitive fellow, you know."

Helen leaned into the table. "Your sensitivity thrums on every page."

"So you liked the characters?"

"I wouldn't say I liked them. But that wasn't your objective, was it? I understood them, understood why they'd put up a certain face to the world."

"McAdams is not me, just so you know," George interjected.

In the story, the main character, a postal clerk in small-town western Pennsylvania, leaves his wife and four children and starts walking, then running, then riding the rails toward New York City. He wants to be a great tenor, an American Caruso. He has memorized some of the best-known operas and practiced his singing in empty barns around the county. But his wife can't appreciate his talent and only reminds him of the chores to be done, the mouths to feed.

Helen didn't respond to George's disclaimer, instead saying, "You've captured the way men seem to need a certain order in their lives before taking on anything beyond themselves. If they don't find that sense of purpose in time, they burrow inward, and people suffer. McAdams's tragedy lies in the particulars, the intensity of his stress, the pain he causes his family when he rejects them for his art. His flight from home is truly operatic. The long passage where you show his tortured mind sorting through past and future feels like an aria of a high order."

George made like he was going to say something—he wasn't sure what—but Helen continued: "I can't deny that my hands trembled when I picked up the pages and began to read. What if George Willard, who our town had always said would become the writer—what if he were no good?"

"Did you have trouble with the ending?" he asked.

"It ends at the beginning of something new; it's agonizing and exuberant, which seems just how it should be. He's on the train. We know he's not turning back."

"Do you think someone might want to publish it?"

"Well," Helen paused, and gave a canny smile. "I hope you don't mind, but I passed it along to Francis Browne at the *Dial* on Tuesday, and he got back to me this morning. He wants the story, George. You need only say *Take it*."

The *Dial* was the finest literary magazine in the Midwest and among the top in the country. While George sat speechless, Helen refilled their glasses. "You don't have to get back to him right away," she said.

"Good heavens, yes, he can have my story. I'll pay *him* for it. The *Dial*—my word."

"I bet your wife will be proud," Helen said. She rarely mentioned Margaret, and the comment had the feeling of a test.

"She knows about the Little Room, but not that I'm writing stories."

"Surely she'd be sympathetic. She has an interest in the arts."

"You want the truth: I haven't told her because she'd be envious."

"Why should she care? She's not a writer."

"Everyone's a writer—in the mind, if not in practice."

"I'm not," Helen said. "I've always loved to read, for companionship, for the shape of a story. And, lately, as a call to social change."

"Are you talking about Upton Sinclair?"

"Yes, and Frank Norris, George Eliot, Dickens. There's quite the fervor at Hull House, a belief that novels ought to shine a light on inequality, injustice. I'm due to teach a class on the labor novel next term. I have quite the leaning tower of books on my nightstand."

"My wife still reads the Romantic poets. But we haven't turned out like Elizabeth and Robert Browning, as perhaps she once hoped," George said. "Oh, listen to me complaining about my marriage. I'm sure you don't believe me when I say I'm not McAdams."

Helen dabbed a napkin at the corners of her lips. "You don't have four children."

"True."

"And you don't live in Pennsylvania."

"True again."

"Have you committed Puccini's most famous arias to memory, and are you willing to stand up in this restaurant and sing 'Che Gelida Manina' in full voice?"

"No and no."

"Then it seems you're not McAdams. What a relief!"

George poured the last of the wine and when the braised rabbit and bouillabaisse arrived ordered another bottle. They lingered at Schlogl's until the last of the lunch crowd had taken their leave and the waiters had begun to look impatiently in their direction.

They stepped into the bright glare of afternoon and were walking along Washington Street past the *Daily News,* the *Chronicle,* the *Journal,* the *Herald,* newspapers he might have worked for were it not for a certain accident a few short blocks from here. They passed the Opera House. "Shall we go in, Mr. McAdams?" Helen said.

"You're a terrible tease." George looped his arm around her waist, and they were walking that way for a block or two before he put his hands in his pockets at the corner opposite Marshall Field's. He had a floating feeling, not unlike the last time he had a woman in mind outside the great department store. Neither Helen nor he had said what they would do with the rest of their day, or when they would part, or how. As the drays and trolleys lurched by on State Street, George caught the reflection of himself and Helen in a bank window, and wanted to hold the picture in his mind.

"Well—there's my stop." She pointed across the street to where the westbound trolleys picked up. George knew she could have said the same at any number of stops over the past several blocks. "I had a lovely time." Her voice carried a lilt of expectancy.

"We must do this again."

"Yes," she said.

"Helen." George didn't bother to look around as he took her hand. People pushed by, but the bustle seemed to fall away. "Thank you for reading my story."

"You're welcome. And congratulations."

"I have other stories, you know. I'd love for you to look at them."

"Anytime."

"I could show them to you now," George said. A discarded newspaper rustled at his feet.

"You take your stories with you?"

"No, it's nothing like that. You see, I have an apartment in the Palmer House. We could go, if you'd like—"

"You have an apartment?" Helen asked.

This shouldn't have thrown him. Chances were she was just being conversational, but her question sent his mind scrambling for an explanation. Had she said *Sure*, or *Yes, let's go*, or *That would be nice*, had she said nothing at all and they'd just started south toward the hotel, he might not have felt the need to lie. "Margaret and I have been living apart," he said. "I guess you could call it a trial separation. But we both realize things will not end well."

"I'm sorry," Helen said.

"We were mismatched from the start. No sense getting into it. We're certainly not the first this has happened to."

"I had no idea."

At the time he was grateful she left it at that, though later he'd wonder what might have happened had she asked: *What about your job? Will you be staying on? What about your father? Where is he living now? How is Margaret taking this? She's told no one at Hull House. Are you keeping the separation a secret?* But these questions never came, nor did they occur to George as he stood there on State Street, a little drunk, a little dizzy over the possibility of taking Helen up the elevator, down the hall to room 542, opening the door, throwing open the windows because no matter what he did, no matter how often he complained, the radiators in his apartment always ran too hot.

"Welcome to the crucible," he said when they stepped inside.

They didn't make it to the windows before they were kissing.

They met on evenings when Helen wasn't working and George knew that Margaret had a performance or rehearsal. That one tumble upon his rented bed, which George had hoped would mark the beginning of something, felt like the clocks had wound back to 1895, when he was a wrought-up stripling who hugged the pillow and walked the dusky streets muttering to himself about love and war. How many times had George imagined a room all their own, her silver silhouette, the sweet exhaustion?

But the next time they met, just a week later, Helen had grown hesitant. She worried aloud that they had made a great mistake, that the circumstances—his trial separation, her loneliness—were all wrong. The questions she had not got around to asking had, in the sober light of morning, come to the surface one by one. She put them to George, and with each answer he buried himself deeper in his deception.

"No, it's not too soon for you and me. The time is now," he said. He and Margaret had come to a mutual impasse, recognized at one and the same time that they had married in foolish haste. The breakup was amicable, a relief for both of them. "The trial is over," he said. "We're as good as divorced."

And no, it would not affect his job. "I've put in too many years, and have built my own little principality."

"But you must see your father-in-law every day. It's not awkward?"

"He won't be my father-in-law for long, and I've been thinking about other work anyway."

"You'd be giving up a lot," Helen said.

"The trappings mean little to me."

"And what about your father? He's not still living with Margaret, is he?"

"He moved out when I did. I found him a snug boardinghouse in Lake View, run by a Russian widow who collects presentable aging bachelors." George hated to lie to Helen but at the same time took a secret, guilty pride in his ability to spin a tale. It was dangerous how naturally the lies and embellishments came to him.

Yet he knew the fragility of this web he was spinning. One misstep and he'd catch himself up. And with his wife and Helen walking the same grounds every day, crossing in the halls—who knows, even sitting down for coffee—his undoing seemed all but assured. He wondered if a part of him wanted to lay his own trap. Or perhaps he felt his marriage was a trap, and deception, then exposure, was the only way out. He wanted to return to that first evening when they had stumbled into the Palmer House after too much wine, but apparently Helen wanted to step back even further, to the moment before, when they were still friends from home getting to know each other again. Though they mostly met at the apartment, to talk about their days and share stories, they hadn't so much as embraced since.

One evening in early May George returned home to find Margaret at the stereopticon. "What are you doing here?" he asked. "I thought Thursdays were rehearsal nights."

"They are." Margaret slid a card into the viewfinder and lowered her face to peer in. "I quit."

"Quit the play?"

"The play. The clubs. The classes. I'm finished with Hull House."

"Finished? Just like that?"

"I'll continue to help Ellen with the lending library. She's been nothing but good to me. And I still admire Jane. But the rest of them. I don't know—"

"What happened?" George asked.

Margaret told him that ever since the bottom dropped out of the economy she'd felt increasingly like an outlander at Hull House. "At the place that welcomes everyone from every shore, I, whose family has been here some three hundred years, am the alien." George thought of her in her Merry Widow hat that first time they went to the Hull House Theater, recalled the care she took with her habiliment each morning before venturing into the slums. Unlike Jane Addams, who dressed in plain clothes and sensible shoes and despite her fame blended right in, Margaret announced her class with every click of her rhinestone heels. George knew not to say as much, though he'd dropped hints before.

"What was the turning point?" he asked.

Margaret removed the stereopticon slide she'd been looking at and set it on the table. She turned to face him. "This morning I attended what I thought would be a meeting of the Arthur Toynbee Club—we were meant to discuss tariff reform—but the gathering turned out to be a most unsubtle ruse to extort a staggering donation from me."

"Extort?"

"Not technically, but you should have seen them put the rush on. There were people in the room from outside the club—fund-raising officers— some I'd never even met. They circled their chairs around me, and this meeting had nothing to do with the country's economics, only with my own—or, rather, my father's."

She said that Stefan, whom she'd thought was her friend, had done a study of the Lazar family and found it was worth some eight million dollars. George had figured that his father-in-law was a millionaire, but not eight times over, and he paused at the thought of one day coming into all that money. What if he just endured his loveless marriage, carried on a secret life with Helen for years and years? If he could get a few more publications or finish a book, he could quit the agency and tell Lazar he was setting up an office in the Palmer House to become a full-time writer. Surely, Lazar would understand, having taken that route for a time before steering down the titan track. And so, too, would Margaret. What woman of culture would not want to say *My husband is a man of letters*?

George was castle-building in this fashion while Margaret leafed absently through the box of stereopticon cards. "You wouldn't believe what Stefan turned up," she continued. "He knew the value of our house, the amount in my savings account. He'd made a 'conservative' estimate that I could afford up to 5 percent of my net worth, and handed me a folder that included his calculations and a breakdown of how Hull House would spend the money over a ten-year period. Your friend, Helen—"

At the mention of her name, George awoke from his reverie.

"Helen's room and board, plus that of some half-dozen lodgers, would be funded through my generous donation. And the rest would go to the theater. Can you believe the cheek of it?"

George knew that most residents were subsidized in part or full through a similar passing of the hat, and that Jane Addams had given away her entire fortune and all proceeds from her books. But the coincidence, if it was a coincidence, of Margaret being asked to pay for Helen's keep made his heart gallop. He wondered if Stefan had his suspicions and was trying to send some kind of message. "I guess I'm not that surprised they would approach you," George said, in a measured voice.

This was the last thing Margaret wanted to hear. "So I see you're on the side of the extortionists. But try putting yourself in my position. I've spent two years among these people, volunteering my time and enthusiasm. And now it seems that right along the smiles and courtesies, the friendships I thought I had made, were toward one end alone. I'm starting to think that my position in the theater was given me in the hopes I'd one day open my purse."

"That can't be true," George interjected. "You've done a superlative job."

"You're not there. You've never seen the looks I get, from the stagehands and the bit players, the ones who think *I should be managing this play*," she said. "And I bet by making me Director of Philanthropy, Stefan and the lot were hoping my first big haul would be from very own accounts."

"I think you're overreacting," George put in.

Margaret ignored him and pulled out another slide from the box. She tucked it into the magic lantern. "Take a look," she said. It was *Wedding Feast at Cana*. "So what do you think?"

"Paris?" George asked.

"We're not getting any younger."

"You're just upset," he said. "But I'm sure it's all a misunderstanding. Sleep on it. You'll get up tomorrow morning and realize your friends are still your friends and they only meant well."

But a trust had been broken, and Margaret never did return to Hull House, except on occasion to see her friend Ellen Gates Starr, who unsuccessfully urged her to reconsider. With the morning, too, came George's realization that having his wife at home cut both ways. On the one hand, she wouldn't be crossing paths with Helen and the treacherous Stefan Wirtz, but on the other she would be keeping an eye on George's arrivals and departures, asking after him and expecting him for dinner and outings. He urged her to work full-time on her lending library of art reproductions in the hope that this would get her out and about, and though she tried for a time to fill her days with that one activity, so much thinking about art only sent her back to those infernal stereopticon cards, and her grand plans for a tour of Europe.

George did his best to avoid the subject, though it wasn't long before he found himself sitting at a table in Harriet Lazar's parlor with his wife and a gabbling travel agent, who went on about the writings of John Ruskin and how the greatest treasures of Europe were to be found in Italy—and no, three months would not do; it would have to be six, minimum, even to skim the surface of all the continent offered; and why wait until next summer when they could travel in the fall, when the lines weren't as long, the heat not so oppressive? Harriet hovered like a kestrel and swooped in at the slightest stirring, as when George suggested that perhaps his wife might travel with her mother or a friend, or even alone in the most hospitable places. He could meet her in London or Paris for a month before sailing back. There was so much to do at the office. But Harriet knew what had become of George at the agency, was aware that any functionary could take over his contracts ably for six months, a year, forever. *You're on an extended honeymoon*, she said. *Might as well enjoy it.*

Seeing no way out, George gave in, and agreed to sail on September 15 from New York to Liverpool on the RMS *Cedric*. He couldn't picture himself in Europe, couldn't imagine that he would actually board that ship and cross the ocean. He had no idea what he would tell Helen, only knew that he would put this off for as long as he could. When Margaret got a bee in her bonnet she was nothing if not persistent. She filled her hours with planning the itinerary, and soon after Decoration Day, the tulips, lilies, and irises abloom in the yard, she enrolled in a drawing class at the Art Institute. She presented George with six leather-bound daybooks, one for each month of the journey. "I'll do sketches, and you can write about our adventures," she said. "You always wanted to be a writer. What better way to start?"

He hadn't told her about the stories he'd been writing, but now he saw an opportunity. He was under way with his first novel, he explained, and if he could just have these next few months uninterrupted to work on the book he could finish before the trip, perhaps even hand-deliver the manuscript to an editor in New York on the way out to sea. "But I'm going to need a quiet place to write."

"What's wrong with here?" she asked.

"My father," he said.

"He leaves *me* alone."

"He must be afraid of you. No such luck for me, though. He'd be in my ear all day." And that's when George proposed that he get a small apartment in the Palmer House, where he once lived, just for these three months. "A writer's garret," he said, "where I can stop after work and finish my novel."

"Some garret," Margaret teased.

But happy and distracted with her planning, she put up no resistance.

18

A week and a half after my father died, thirty or so people gathered at his apartment for the cocktail party he had requested. I served Diet Rite and rum to those game enough to try it, and stocked the bar and fridge for everyone else. Since only a half dozen of my father's asterisked friends had said they would come and I couldn't stand a sad turnout, I invited a few people from the MFA whom I'd lost touch with, and Dhara brought in some coworkers, plus her father and stepmother from Dayton. It had been two years since I last saw the aunt and uncle I'd lived with after my mother died, but they came, as did my father's sister and her kids, cousins I'd met long ago at a family reunion, all down from Wisconsin. My half brothers made it, too, though I was disappointed that they didn't bring their wives and children.

"Do you know what it costs to fly six people halfway across the country?" Michael asked, unprompted, soon after he and Eric walked in. "Fifteen hundred bucks, minimum. And that doesn't include lodging."

"It's not my concern," I said, and left at that. I did feel bad about my brothers' money troubles, and wondered, not for the first time, about the contents of their envelopes. Had they received an inheritance, too? Or was I the only one?

I had already deposited my check in a savings account. I'd never held so much money in my hands before, and I wanted it out of my sight—so I wouldn't lose it, so I didn't have to think about it, so it could sit somewhere while I tried to make sense of all that had happened. I had also ordered the cremation, and Dhara talked me out of getting the most expensive urn.

"What would your father have done?" she'd asked when the funeral director stepped out of his office to let us make a decision.

"He'd have gone with a yard-sale vase or maybe a coffee can," I said.

So we bought a pewter urn, which now sat on a console table, along with candles and three photographs I had of my father: in front of the Christmas tree with his sister while his father was fighting in the Pacific Theater, at Michigan in cap and gown at his doctoral graduation, and a head shot the news service at Central Illinois took for an article about his retirement.

Just enough people had come to make my father's apartment feel close and intimate. Thundershowers were in the forecast, but it was a pleasant evening thus far, warm and breezy, with an undercurrent of cool air. Everyone took a turn stepping out onto the balcony to watch the sun fade in the windows of the Leo Burnett and the Kemper, Hotel 71, and other buildings across the river. Some said they'd never seen such a view—fifty stories from the street, a full panorama of the Loop—and a few, like Dhara's father, stayed close to the sliding doors.

"He's afraid of heights," said Lali Patel. Dhara had already complained about her stepmother's wearing white to a funeral. *It's not really a funeral,* I had tried to explain. *Still,* Dhara said, *could she be more vernac? She has no education and she dresses like an aging Gujarati J.Lo.* I reminded her that at least her father and stepmother came, made the five-hour trip for a man they'd met only once. *It means a lot to me,* I said, *tight slacks and all.*

Lali was a close talker and if that wasn't disconcerting enough, she wore blue contact lenses and looked right into your eyes as she shared intimate details. "You should have Jagdish tell you about his prostate," she said. "This is supposed to be the best cancer. They get in. They get out. And you're back to normal in weeks. Not true!"

"Lali—" Jagdish tried to interrupt.

"You had a cancer scare?" Dhara asked her father in consternation.

"It was nothing."

"You do look skinny," Dhara observed. It was true. He had lost his potbelly and some of the chubbiness in his cheeks; his gold-framed glasses seemed larger on his face, and the swoosh of gray at his crown had spread across his hair.

"He wears special underpants now," Lali said. "And the operation has presented other challenges—"

Dhara turned to her father. "I wish you had told me."

"I called."

"You left a message, but you said it wasn't important. I assumed you were just checking in."

Lali spoke for her husband. "He wanted to talk to you. He was asking me for days, 'Did my beti call? Why won't she ring me back?'"

"If I'd known you were in the hospital—"

"I'm okay. Okay?"

"I'm sorry," Dhara said.

Lali wouldn't let it go. "Even if he wasn't sick, you should have called him back."

"Lali, betu—" Jagdish said. "It was a misunderstanding. She was busy at work. She works very hard, my daughter."

"And you're feeling better?" Dhara asked.

Her father nodded.

"Don't look at me," Lali said, when Dhara did just that. "He tells me nothing."

"I'm fine." Jagdish peered into his empty glass, then turned to me. "Could I trouble you for more sparkling water?"

When I went to get him some, he followed me inside, leaving his wife and daughter on the balcony. I topped off his glass and told him how much I appreciated his making the trip. "I know it can't be easy to leave the motel for the weekend. You have a 24/7 job."

"Ajit is holding the fort. He's doing better," he offered, though I'd made no mention of Dhara's brother's past troubles. "He's seeing someone about his temper, but he doesn't want to stay and take over the family business. He wants to travel the world. 'Not in these times,' I tell him. Then he threatens to join the Navy. Sometimes I wish that Dhara had never left."

"She learned a lot growing up at the Dynasty," I said. "She's the best businessperson I know."

"It's in her blood," Jagdish said with a laugh, and went on to say what I'd heard him mention several times over the years, that in the days of the old caste system the Patels were Vaishya, the merchant caste, renowned for their entrepreneurial skills. Dhara had always dismissed her father's old-school immigrant nostalgia and his claim that she was "born to sell."

He told a story about Dhara's childhood ventures. "Most kids have a lemonade stand, but my beti was not ten years old before she was making a fine profit." Though her family never had the time or money to go anywhere, she had figured out that those who did travel on the interstates rarely ate well, and preferred not to stop. So she made an arrangement with the best sandwich place in Dayton and with her mother, who was a good cook, and was able to offer three kinds of wraps: American, Italian, and Indian. She called her stand Wrap & Roll, and on summers and weekends she could be seen smiling under the banner she had designed herself—three wraps hugging, waving their flags of origin. Some of the money went to her college fund, but most she put in an envelope marked "Vacation" at the back of the motel office safe.

"We went on holiday three times. Once to Chicago and twice to Sandusky: Cedar Point," Jagdish said. "I got sick on a roller coaster called *Mean Streak*. But my children had the time of their lives. Dhara paid for everything: admission, food, lodging, gas. Twelve, thirteen years old—she insisted! And I remember after that last time she said, 'Next stop: Disney World.' But then her supplier went out of business; high school began, with so many activities; and her mother became ill. But Dhara always had a way of making and saving money, and if I had paid her a decent wage for all the hours she put in at the motel she'd be rich by now."

"She's doing okay," I told him. "She has a good job."

"Oh, I know. I'm very proud of her. Imego is the best company in the world. She grew up at a place where two highways meet. Now she works at the center of the information *super*highway."

If Dhara were in the room she'd tease him for using a term that was a decade out of date. If my father were here, he'd say a lot of good that superhighway has done us, and quote T. S. Eliot's line about everyone in the modern age "distracted from distraction by distraction." For my part, I had learned something about Dhara that made me understand her a little better. Perhaps she did have commerce in her DNA, and was driven by something beyond her control. Wouldn't life be easier if I believed that, accepted it, and knew that there were things about my wife that I couldn't and shouldn't change? And if I didn't complain about her long hours and California dreams, perhaps she might better appreciate my own modest ambitions.

As Jagdish and I headed back toward the balcony, he stopped at the photographs of my father. "I'm very sorry," he said. "You're too young to lose both parents. We should—all of us who have children—remember that it's harder on the ones we leave behind."

Dhara was stepping inside the apartment with her stepmother. Lali was calling after her, "You're in your thirties. Young in many ways, not so much in others. I can tell you this because I waited too long myself, and look at me—no offspring to receive these stunning good looks." She flicked her hair.

"I'm serious, beti. Don't be like me, girl. You have the beauty *and* the brains."

Dhara laughed and gave me a look that seemed to say *how did this woman end up in my life?* But there was something bemused in her expression as well, as if the edge had been taken off and she was seeing Lali in a somewhat different light.

I left Dhara, her father, and stepmother to talk, and spent the rest of the party circulating through the small apartment. I caught up with my old MFA friends, only one of whom, Paul Shriver, was still writing steadily. He wasn't the most gifted stylist in our cohort, but he could tell a good story, and most of all he had stuck with it, even published short pieces in some of the better journals. Six months ago he had taken a buyout at a Schaumburg PR firm, and instead of looking for work right away launched into a novel he'd been sketching out for years. It was nearly done, and whether or not it ever saw the light of publication, he said that getting the story out of his head and onto the page was the best thing he had ever done.

I heard the first peals of thunder while I was talking to my aunt and uncle about their kids, my cousins, who had both gone to Washington after college to work on Capitol Hill. Kathleen asked if I'd heard from Lucy, and I told her about the job at U of C Press but left it at that. I hadn't spoken with Lucy since that night on her street when the idiots in the Jeep yelled at us and I headed home. She had left a voice-mail message at the end of that week, but I couldn't remember what she'd said or even if I'd listened to it. I hadn't called her back, hadn't told her about my father, but now I had this strange feeling I ought to call her soon; it seemed we had something to square away.

The last of the guests left just before the rain began. Only Dhara and my half brothers remained. Michael and Eric began putting glasses in the sink and tidying up, but I told them we'd take care of it.

"You've done more than enough already," Michael said. "I can only imagine all the cleaning you had to do to get ready for this party."

"I already told you the place was immaculate, more or less as you see it."

"That's right. You did," he said, but I could tell he didn't believe me, and must have been wondering why I would still be covering for our father.

The wind whistled through the metal balcony; the rain splattered against the sliding glass doors. My brothers were getting ready to leave, but I told them they might as well wait out the storm. "Plus," I said, "there's something I want to show you."

In my father's bedroom, Michael and Eric stood behind me and Dhara watched from the doorway as I opened the safe and pulled out the two envelopes. A couple days before, I had gotten into my mind that I needed to know if my brothers were getting an inheritance and, if so, was it less, equal, more? And what had my father written on their notes? I had planned to hold the letters up to the light, even thought about unsealing them. But the better part of me resisted, and this moment was in fact the first time I had touched the envelopes. I handed them to Michael and Eric, then left the room to give them privacy. Dhara followed me and softly closed the door.

The rain lashed the windows. I locked the sliding doors to the balcony. Dhara and I continued to clean up the apartment, listening for my half brothers' reactions, but the storm muffled their voices. After a while the door opened, and Eric came out shaking his head. "Just wow," he said.

Michael, behind him, sat down on the camelback sofa. He tossed the letter and the cashier's check on the cushion next to him. From where I stood I could see the amount: fifty thousand dollars.

"What did your letters say?" I asked my brothers, hesitantly.

Michael answered first. "This is verbatim," he said. "*I made mistakes. I wish I could have done better. I hope you'll forgive me.*"

"Same as mine," Eric said.

Michael scratched his cheek. He'd had a beard for most of his adult life but he had a habit of touching it as if it were irritating him. "Something's not right," he said. "Where did the money come from? I thought Dad was in foreclosure. Wasn't he supposed to be broke?"

I admitted that I was confused, too. "But I think he had some valuable books, and I'm pretty sure he sold them."

"Books!" Michael laughed. "Who would pay, what, $150,000 for books?"

I wasn't about to tell him that I'd gotten thirty-five thousand more than he and Eric and so the total, in fact, was one eighty-five.

Eric leaned on the edge of our father's desk. "We should be grateful," he said.

"I wouldn't start spending it until you know where it came from." Michael pocketed his check and envelope.

It was at this point that the creaking began, a sound under our feet like an old man in a rocking chair going back and forth, back and forth. Having lived in Harbor City for a while, Dhara and I were familiar with that old man in the rocking chair. It was the high groan the building made, the friction between the concrete and reinforcing metal, as the towers swayed ever so slightly in heavy storms like this one. My half brothers, Michael especially, looked terrified, just as I was a few years ago when I first heard the sound.

I tried to explain. Dhara said, "It's an outdated building. We hear this all the time," but Michael was spooked, and the color had drained out of Eric's face, too.

When the worst of the storm passed, the rocking slowed to a muffled creak, then stopped. Michael and Eric got ready to head back to the hotel, but before they left I said I had something else for them. "I know you're surprised that Dad made all these arrangements. But on the day I found him I came upon a letter that might explain it." I had Xeroxed the letter and sealed into separate envelopes a copy for each half brother. "Here," I said. "You don't have to read it now. We can talk tomorrow, if you'd like."

They took the envelopes, thanked me, and left. Dhara and I went home to our apartment and put out food for Wing Biddlebaum. The orange tabby now lived with us but had barely ventured out of our bedroom closet, where he spent his days sleeping on my shoes.

The next morning we met Michael and Eric for breakfast across the river at their hotel restaurant. They asked the same questions that I'd put to the cardiologist, about how far gone our father's heart was at the point when, it appeared, he opened the medicine cabinet and washed down too many pills with Diet Rite and rum. I had worried that my half brothers might be angry—at our father for going out this way, or at me for not getting an autopsy to make absolutely sure. But after a long conversation full of assorted stories about their childhoods, little glimpses they'd each had of our father before he disappeared from their lives, Eric summed up his and Michael's feelings best: "The fact is, I didn't know the man, so anything he did, during his life and at the end, should have come as no surprise."

Along with the pewter urn, the funeral home had given me some small boxes made of decorative paper in case we wanted to divide the ashes. That morning I had poured some of the "pixie dust" into plastic bags and put the bags into two boxes, one for Michael, one for Eric. I asked if they would scatter the ashes in New York and Boston, and they said if that's what he wanted they'd find a decent place. Then we paid the bill and went out into the bright, warm morning. I led everyone down the steps to the riverwalk, the pavement still glossed with rain from the night before. After we'd passed a group of tourists and let a couple water taxis and motorboats float by, I took the urn out of my shoulder bag.

The river used to flow west to east, but a little over a hundred years ago civil engineers reversed it because pollutants were spilling into Lake Michigan, the source of the city's water. If I had shaken the ashes into the river before the reversal, which would have been right around the time George Willard was arriving in Chicago, a speck or two might have caught a ride on some flotsam and traveled a current up the coast, around the bend of Green Bay, and come in with the tide to the shipyards of Marinette, Wisconsin, my father's birthplace.

But now the river flowed west.

Michael, Eric, and I each took a turn scattering ashes. We watched the dust catch the wind, then settle on the surface of the water before floating on, past the Loop and the railroad yards, through the Chicago Ship Canal into the Des Plaines River, which met the Illinois, then the Mississippi, then spilled down to New Orleans into the Gulf of Mexico, out to the Caribbean Sea, through the Panama Canal, then along the west coast of South America, to wash up on the shores of a town where everything was strange and new.

19

Throughout June 1909, George was trying to live for the moment. He did not want to think about September, when he was due to board a train to New York, then a ship to Liverpool. Margaret had already gone to her father and asked him to reduce George's hours so he could finish this novel, and Lazar, who would do anything for his daughter, acquiesced. In the past, George might have been upset with his wife for making such arrangements on the quiet, but he'd grown accustomed to the scornful looks of his coworkers and could endure still more if it meant leaving the office at three o'clock.

He did manage to get some writing done, but a novel seemed a daunting endeavor. For now the best he could do was to set his stories in one place, a small midwestern town not unlike his own, at the turn of the twisting century. When he finished a story he would give it to Helen, pacing before the fifth-floor window while she read it sitting in a wingback chair tantalizingly close to the bed. What he'd give to share that bed with her again, to bend down and kiss her pretty neck. But she gave no signs of willingness, said *I'd better not* when he offered a glass of wine, and he had to wonder if he had destroyed a fragile possibility, if they would ever have a chance again.

After a number of such evenings Helen began to ask why George insisted that they meet in his room and made efforts not to be seen with her in restaurants or crossing the lobby.

In truth, he wanted the intimacy, loved the feeling of bringing her to this place, of playing at making a home. But he didn't tell her this. "You said it yourself," he explained. "It's too soon after my separation, so we'd be wise not to go out in public. And that manager, Lemuel Means, he has more eyes than Panoptes. Our agency puts clients in this hotel, and I wouldn't want Lazar hearing that I'd taken up with someone else before Margaret and I parted ways."

"You might have thought of all that before," she said. "I told you we made a mistake."

Two weeks would pass before they'd see each other again, an eventful two weeks that would bring further complications to George's life. One evening he returned to the Gold Coast house to find his father waiting for him in the front hallway. "I'm going home," he said abruptly. His packed trunk sat in the parlor. "I'm on the first train tomorrow morning."

"What happened?" George asked.

"The New Willard House has been sold and scheduled for demolition. Apparently our friends and neighbors are up in arms. They need me, and I aim to step into the breach." Tom Willard said the town elders were surrendering all that made Winesburg unique by selling the land to an outfit that was building drive-up filling stations across northern Ohio. "The streets used to belong to the people, to friends coming and going, to children at play, but this would mean the end of all that. Automobiles clogging downtown. The beast of motordom crushing lives under its wheels."

"Maybe there was no choice in the matter," George said. "Our town has been sliding for years, falling off, more like, since the Panic."

"You don't just give up safety. You put up a fight." Tom Willard shook his fist. "And you don't sell your character to the first four-flusher. They're tearing down your heritage, son."

At another time, George might have been sentimental about the place, but it never was a home, just a room looking over the train tracks at the end of a mostly empty hallway. And he had his memories, ghosts of his mother and of the many transients who even now were filling the pages of his notebooks and stories. For better and worse he carried the New Willard House with him, and so had no great feeling for that shell he had left behind. "How long will you be gone?" George asked.

"Could be a week. A month. If we win, I might stay," he said. "Your old editor Will Henderson is putting me up for a time. I'll keep him in gin for a cot."

And like that, he was gone.

But it wasn't another day or two before Margaret was saying, "Now that your father's not here to distract you, do you need to keep your writer's garret? What are you doing there that you can't do here?" Something in her voice and the focus of her gaze gave George a shiver. "Seems a bit plush, don't you think?" she added.

"Knowing my father, he'll be on the next train back," he replied. "He has as good a chance at stopping this demolition as he does of winning a seat in Congress. And I know Will Henderson won't put up with him for long."

But Margaret was watching the calendar, and perhaps watching her husband, too. "We can talk about this another time," she said.

George wondered if he hadn't contrived this situation in order to generate drama in his life, the kind of drama he might someday write about. There had been times in his youth, in the days when everyone in town said he would become a writer, when the person acting out his life seemed secondary to the one recording it. His notepads meant more to him than anything in the world, and now he wondered if, after an absence of more than ten years, he was coming back to that old self for whom the story was all. He didn't stop to think how he might regret what he was doing to these women, one whom he probably loved and the other who had given him security he never could have imagined growing up. He only knew that for all the trouble he had set into motion, he had never come as close to the fire of life.

But at the end of those two weeks Helen called at the Palmer House on a Thursday, one of the rehearsal nights when they used to meet. George closed the door behind her, but she did not venture more than a step or two into the apartment. "We need to talk," she said.

"Of course—" George gestured toward the settee.

"Not here." She wore a silk brocade gown and a plumed hat. A scent of White Rose formed a nimbus at the threshold. He had never seen her looking so well turned out.

"We really should be cautious." George lifted her hand. "Surely you can see my position."

She pulled her hand away. "We're going out, so you'd better put on your jacket and tie. Business attire should do just fine. I've made a reservation at Henrici's on Randolph."

"They all know Lazar over there," George said.

"That's your concern. Not mine."

"Helen—"

He tried to reason with her, insisted on knowing what was on her mind. But she would not go into it until they were at the restaurant. When George suggested they exit the hotel separately so as not to be spied by the Palmer House Pinkertons, she refused. In fact, as they passed the front desk, where

Lemuel Means made a show of looking busy, she reached her arm around George's waist and kept it there until they were out on the street. In the taxicab she let go and they rode in silence to the theater district.

At Henrici's, they were greeted by the same bow-tied host from a couple years before, when George and his young wife had celebrated their anniversary and he saw the vision of Helen White. For a moment the host seemed confused, assuming no doubt that Helen had come for boxes of bread, though he might have wondered why she was dressed so elegantly. "I don't believe anyone from Hull House put in an order," he said.

"We're here for dinner." She slipped off her gloves. And when he had turned a suitable shade of crimson, she gave him the name of the reservation.

George tried to avoid looking at the slender, fastidious man, but Helen introduced the two.

"Yes, I know who you are," the host said. "Will you be expecting others?"

"No," Helen broke in. "The reservation is for two."

At the table, after Helen had been seated, George whispered to the host, "We're old friends, she and I."

"Of course," the man replied.

After he had left, George and Helen spoke nearly in unison.

"Embarrassed to be in my company?" she asked.

"So I see you're trying to get me sacked," he said.

"I have one question for you, George: Do you take me for a fool?"

"I don't know what you're talking about."

"Did you really think I wouldn't find out about Margaret? We work in the same building, for gracious sake. Did you think I wouldn't hear that she quit to plan some grand tour overseas, not as a new beginning to her life without you, but as a kind of marital renewal?"

"That's not why she quit," George said, pathetically.

"How long did you think you could go on like this, living with your wife while keeping a room in the Palmer House to use as a snuggery? Do you take me for some babe in the woods?"

"It's not at all like that—"

"Isn't it, though?" Helen clutched her gloves like gauntlets. "I wonder how long this has been going on, how many playthings have come before me."

"No one came before you," George said. "You're the first, the only woman I've ever loved."

"Oh, sure."

"I've never meant anything more in my life."

Menus appeared and were quickly put down.

"I should have listened to Seth Richmond years ago," she continued. "Here I was thinking you were the deep one, when it was Seth all along. He used to complain about everyone in Winesburg who talked and talked, nothing but piffle. It was you he meant, George." She told him of a time when they were seventeen or eighteen, desperate to leave, how Seth had come to her one night to report that George Willard was in love with her. "'He's writing a story,' Seth had said. 'And he wants to be in love. He wants to know how it feels.' Is that true?" Helen asked.

"I loved you then, as I love you now," George said.

"That's not what I asked. I want to know if you were playing at being in love, using Seth as your messenger and me as your dupe."

"I don't remember the incident."

"I do, and I can tell you it was a fine prelude to where we are now," Helen said. "You're still playing at being in love, using me for I don't know what purpose: material, perhaps. Something to write about. But I'm no longer a girl. I have a life. A real life. Among people with real troubles."

"Perhaps I wasn't being truthful," George offered.

"*Perhaps!*"

"Okay. I'm sorry," he said. "I'm in a bind, you see. I want to leave my wife. We're not right for each other. You can see that. I think *she* can see that, too."

"I wouldn't be so sure, George. As we speak she's planning a trip to Europe. Were you ever going to tell me? Or would I call over to the hotel one day and find that you had left?"

"I was going to tell you. I just needed to find the right time. Just as I need to find the right time to talk to Margaret, to tell her we can't go on like this."

Helen put her gloves in her purse, and again sent the waiter away when he came by to inquire about drinks. "You're afraid that if you leave your wife, you'll lose your job. You want to be a writer. You always have. But you're faced with the age-old conundrum: how to make a living at something you love. I can't help you out of this. And you'll come to regret that you thought I could."

George opened his mouth to speak, but found nothing to utter.

"Remember how I teased you and called you McAdams, the character from your story who hoped to become the American Caruso?" Helen continued. "I don't think you realize how much you were writing about yourself. In your case you'd be leaving all that wealth behind. In McAdams's case, four children. Either way, a terrible loss. I think you're going to leave, George. By this time next year you'll be living in New York."

He reached out his hands for hers, but she drew them away. "I need you, Helen," he said. "I want to stay. I want to be with you."

"I don't think so."

"You wouldn't have me?"

"I don't think you want to be with anyone," she said. "Or, rather, I think you desperately want to be with someone, then as soon as you have her you wish for nothing more than to be alone."

This thought would weigh heavily on George's mind. He and Helen managed to get through the dinner at Henrici's, but it would be the last he'd see of her for weeks. He held out hope that she would forgive him, but she made no promises. He knew he had broken her trust, perhaps irreparably.

Throughout the heat of July, Margaret continued her planning, and in between questions like *Should we skip Pisa?* or *Do you want to be in London for the Imperial Exhibition?* she would mention that ever since Tom Willard had left, the house was *quiet as a moonbeam.* "You might as well do your writing here," she suggested.

George wanted to hold on to the apartment because Helen might yet return, and he dreaded coming home and facing a wife who, for all her airs, did not deserve this treatment. "I just want to finish my novel," he said. "And look—" He produced from his pocket a letter he had received that day. "My father seems to be getting nowhere with his civic protest. The demolition is continuing as scheduled. My birthplace will be rubble by the end of the month."

"I'm sorry," Margaret said, but wouldn't let it drop: "If your father returns to Chicago, why don't you let him live in your garret, and you can write here?"

"I was thinking he could stay at the house. Then he could watch over matters while we're gone."

"Come home, won't you?"

"I just need one more month," George said.

And, reluctantly, she dropped the subject.

Not a week later, Tom Willard cabled to say that the Castalia Wrecking and Shoring Company had begun its work.

It seemed only a matter of time before he would be arriving once again with his trunk.

At the office George fulfilled his obligations and little more. Lazar and his backscratchers were forever seeking new ways to *Prove They Need It,* and to George's bewilderment his old contract, Nuvolia, had become the top seller in the land thanks to Kennison's dull, unvarying, ruthlessly effective technique, the same no matter what it was employed to sell: identify a problem (body odor, dandruff, foul breath), attach a clinical name to it, and claim that only one product could provide an effective solution. No room for nuance or for secondary selling points: "You can't chop a tree in two by hitting it every time in a different place," Kennison would say. And it seemed he could do no wrong.

Besides soap, he laid claim to the best-selling cereal, biscuit, and scouring powder. He could take a routine step in the manufacturing process and turn it into advertising gold, as he did with Stroble Beer. Though many breweries used steam to clean their bottles, no one saw this as a potential selling point until Kennison focused on the one detail that set Stroble "apart from the rest": "Taste the *Steam-Cleaned* freshness."

So much for the artful turn of phrase, the clever, cadenced pitch. With Kennison out front and Lazar driving the team, advertising had become a science, the copywriting department the province of laboratory technicians. George continued to wonder how he had lasted this long.

The Western Union telegraph arrived on the first of August: *Eureka! Box of money found in rubble. Authorities determining rights of treasure trove. Likely going to most recent deed-holder: Thomas Willard. I told them they hadn't heard the last of me!*

A week later a letter came in the mail:

> *Dear George,*
>
> *My darkest hour has become my brightest. With these eyes—and I'm not ashamed to tell you they shed tears—I watched the New Willard House fall roof by wall by beam to the ground. It seemed the whole town came out on the first day. People I hadn't seen in years, some I'd never seen before, squinting into the sunlight as if they hadn't left their rooms since the last century. You should have seen the spectacle.*

*Five bodies deep on Main Street. So many hands clapped my shoulder
I woke up the next morning bruised. And you should have heard the
racket those workers were making with their sledgehammers and pneu-
matic guns. Bang! Crack! Boom! Pow!*

*A few days on, and most everyone had gone home. But not your old
man. And not Will Henderson either (he's so strapped at the Eagle he
does all the reporting himself). It must have been the sixth or seventh
day when they found the tin box. They'd put up scaffolding to protect
the street, torn off the roof and blasted away the brickwork. They'd
ripped out the plumbing and had sundered just about all the partition
walls when I heard a call go up. "Looks like something's plastered in
here," one of the wreckers said. I went as close as I could to get a good
look at them tearing away the wall with their crowbars. The foreman
knelt down and pulled out a tin box, and damned if he didn't open
the thing right there. Lucky it wasn't windy that day or the dollar bills
would have scattered all over town.*

*You can imagine the scene I made. This was my hotel, so that box,
that money was mine. And right next to me stood Will Henderson, his
pencil poised to write upon the pad of public influence. We met with a
bank representative, who said it was his fiduciary responsibility to unite
lost property with its original owner. And though my claim was clear
as day, I had to wait for the state court's confirmation. I'm writing you
to say the tin box and its contents, all eight hundred dollars, are now
mine.*

*I don't know what I'm going to do. I need some time to think. I've
taken out a room above the shoe-repair shop on lower Main. I've had
a lot of dreams, George. Maybe now I can put them in order and see
them through.*

> *Yours, paternally,*
> *T. Willard*

20

The week after scattering my father's ashes I visited the Chicago Rare Book Company in search of the lean, eager man with chain-slung bifocals. He was easy to find since he ran the shop by himself, and during the hour and a half I spent with him I was the only patron to walk in. He introduced himself as Hardy—I failed to ask if this was his first or last name—and indeed he could have passed for a minor character in a Thomas Hardy novel, a vicar perhaps: pale, angular, and fidgety. We sat by the picture window that looked out on the main drag of Old Town, and I asked him if he knew my father, Roland Clary.

"I won't soon forget him," he said. "He came in out of the blue one day with some of the most valuable books I've seen. I bought as many as I could afford, and I put him in touch with a private collector in Highland Park for whom money is no object."

"How much are we talking about, if you don't mind my asking?"

"You should probably discuss that with Mr. Clary," Hardy said. "I don't generally share those details."

I told him about my father's death. "I'm his executor," I explained. "And I'm trying to settle accounts."

"I'm so sorry." Hardy touched my hand, then quickly withdrew it. "I only saw him a couple of months ago."

"He had heart trouble."

"I know how that is. A heart attack got my father last year. This used to be his shop," he said. "And I know about settling accounts, too. My dad kept no records. His ledgers were all up here." Hardy pointed to his bald head. "The shop didn't always look like this." The books stood sentry on dusted shelves, and the place had that almond aroma of old paper and glue, along with the fresh scent of wood polish. "My father was not the most orderly person."

"Sounds familiar," I said, and passed along my sympathies.

Hardy went into a back room and brought out an old laptop computer. He put on his glasses, clicked open some windows, and went over the transactions one by one:

Death in the Woods *by Sherwood Anderson. Hardcover, first edition. A few chips along the top edge of the dust jacket. Otherwise, good condition. $2,200.*

Dark Laughter *by Sherwood Anderson. Hardcover, first edition. Excellent copy in a fine unclipped dust jacket. $3,500.* "This was the book that Hemingway parodied in *Torrents of Spring,*" Hardy said. "So much for that friendship."

Winesburg, Ohio *by Sherwood Anderson, rare first edition, signed by the author on the front free endpaper. Original dust jacket in fine shape. Tight binding. $8,500.* "The amazing thing about this one is that your father came into the shop with *three* signed first editions of *Winesburg.* The other two were in even better shape. I appraised them at $9,750 and $11,000, but could only afford the one."

Spoon River Anthology *by Edgar Lee Masters, first edition, first issue, slight age-toning to the white jacket and modest chipping at the crown. $3,200.* Hardy peered over his bifocals and continued his running commentary: "Not only did Anderson borrow the structure of *Spoon River*—interrelated stories set in a small midwestern town—he also stole Masters's girlfriend and married her."

The list went on, including first editions by John Dos Passos and several writers of the Chicago Renaissance, among them Dreiser and Sandburg. "All told, I paid over thirty-five thousand dollars." Hardy closed his laptop. "Your father must have come in here four times over the course of a couple months, so I gave him four checks in varying amounts."

"Do you remember what other books he brought in?"

"Do I remember?" Hardy said. "It about killed me that I couldn't buy all of them. He had a first edition of Hemingway's *In Our Time,* one of only 170 printed by Three Mountains Press in 1924. Very good condition. I'd put it at fifty thousand. And he had two rare books by Faulkner: *Sartoris,* a signed first edition worth fifteen thousand. And the crown jewel: a first edition of *Soldier's Pay* that Faulkner inscribed to Sherwood Anderson himself. What's even more remarkable about the *Soldier's Pay* book is that Faulkner thanked Anderson for being, and I'm quoting here, 'the father of my generation of writers.' Also interesting: the inscription date was after they'd had their falling out, so the book is a kind of olive branch. I remember your father saying that Faulkner probably sent it to Anderson's publisher, but it's possible the book never got into Anderson's hands, because this was during one of his crisis periods, when he and his third wife were moving around a lot, from New Orleans to San Francisco to rural Virginia, with a bit of Europe mixed in."

"How did my father wind up with such a book?" I wondered aloud.

"I asked him the same question. And you know what he told me: 'I am the Sherwood Anderson Collection. Eventually everything falls into my hands, and sometimes I'm lucky enough to find a real gem.'"

"Wow," I said. "So how much do you think that one was worth?"

"My conservative estimate—" Hardy took off his glasses and let them fall to the end of the chain. "$85,000."

"Good Lord." I remembered the last time I saw my father alive, how he said he was going to have dinner with a book collector, then took off in a taxi. That must have been the big spender who now owned his treasures. "I can't wait to tell my brothers about this. They laughed when I guessed where the money likely came from."

"Books are a rare thing," Hardy said. "Nothing in the world compares."

Before I left, he showed me a couple of the copies my father had sold him, including the edition of *Winesburg,* with Anderson's own signature, a sharp cursive like choppy waves. Seeing the ninety-year-old book reminded me to stop by the Newberry to ask if anyone knew about my father's missing or suspended novel project, *The Book of the Grotesque.* Dhara and I had already searched the storage locker in Little Italy and found nothing. We'd checked the cage in Harbor City and turned his apartment over. And still all I had was a stack of notes and fragments, false starts, and that one curious little story, "The Writer's Writer."

On my way home from the Chicago Rare Book Company, I stopped at the Newberry and talked to the curator of Midwest manuscripts, white-haired, cigarette-voiced Alice Wyman, who said she'd met my father a couple of times but mostly knew him by reputation. I hesitated to ask what that meant, and she didn't elaborate. She did pass along her condolences, though, said she'd read the obituary in the *Chicago Tribune,* which ran only because I called the editor, a self-acknowledged history buff, and won him over by reminding him of Anderson's ties to Chicago.

Alice said that my father had recently visited the Newberry and wanted to check the accuracy of the appraisals he'd gotten on some books. "Since we're not a commercial outfit, we couldn't be much help," she said. "But we were able to bring in an expert to help verify the signatures. And it was worth the trouble, because one of those books was not only rare but historic." I said I'd heard, but she nevertheless repeated what Hardy had told me about Faulkner's inscribed copy of *Soldier's Pay.*

That night I wrote my brothers a long e-mail with the subject line: *Father of us all.*

Dhara and I had been getting along better than we had in months. She had taken off time at work, made many of the funeral arrangements, and on her own initiative had gone to the Harbor City rental office, closed the books on my father's apartment, and called in movers to take his furniture and belongings to the storage locker in Little Italy. Our search for *The Book of the Grotesque* had captivated her, and it was Dhara who first suggested that if a complete manuscript never surfaced I should assemble the notes and see what they added up to.

I'd grown tired of sneaking around, so before arranging to meet Lucy, I told Dhara where I was going and why. She knew about the college fund Lucy had pulled together for me, but she had never made a big deal of it. "If you'd rather I not see her, I'd understand."

"It's okay," she said. "I'm not going to stop you."

"She's just an old friend."

"I know she is. And you probably think I've been irrational to be bothered by her return. You knew her in high school. It was long ago and far away," Dhara said. "But Lucy's father is a millionaire many times over. She doesn't have to work. She and the guy she ends up with could live comfortably on her trust fund for the rest of their days. When her parents die, she'll come into a fortune. She could live in Europe. She could buy a small island somewhere. And I know what you really want to do, Adam. You've said it, and I'm sorry if it didn't seem like I was listening. You want time enough to write a book or many books, and how better to have that freedom than by marrying rich?"

"I never had an interest in doing that."

"You don't need to convince me. I'm sure you've been thinking I'm jealous, so there: you know my reasons."

"I want to meet Lucy so I can pay her back," I said. "I didn't want her money then, and I don't want it now. She's a decent person. Under different circumstances you could be friends." I could hear the condescension in my voice and felt a slight sting of shame, even as I continued, "But she can't help where she came from, and has never had to find her own way. She's generous, sure, but without ever making a real sacrifice."

"Is that any way to talk about the love of your life?"

"Dhara—"

"I'm kidding. You don't have to say it."

But I said it again anyway, and I didn't forget it when I met Lucy for lunch at a gastropub across from Millennium Park.

We had only just settled into a booth when she said, "I'm still mad at you, Adam. You might have returned my phone calls." So I told her about my father, and she felt terrible.

We spent most of the lunch talking about him. I told her about the pills and liquor, said she had been right about the warning signs. "I guess I should feel worse that I hadn't anticipated it, but the truth is I'd been worried about him for a long time, and I'm certain he wanted to do this." I said there were clues in a story he wrote called "The Writer's Writer" that I found when it was too late—"Did you know that Sherwood Anderson considered suicide, once intentionally ran his car off the road?"

When the coffees came, I told Lucy about the rare books and my surprise inheritance. "It must have given him a weird satisfaction to imagine my brothers and me opening those envelopes. He had lived half a life, written half of another man's story. So here, finally, was a conclusion, and even a small legacy."

"What are you going to do with the money?" she asked.

"That's why I wanted to meet you today," I said. "Last week I wrote a big check to pay off my graduate school loans. And now I want to settle up on the college fund."

"It was a gift, Adam."

"I never asked for it, and I never gave you anything in return."

"I was happy to do it," she said.

"You have to be honest with me, Lucy. I need to know how much I owe you."

She tried to brush off the subject and move on, but I grew frustrated, and she must have realized, finally, how serious I was.

I had brought my checkbook, and I wrote her a check right there for fifteen thousand dollars, the amount Lucy had contributed above and beyond our friends' donations. "I know this is awkward." I avoided her eyes. "But it means a lot to me not to owe anyone."

"I guess I understand," she said. "Self-reliance is its own kind of currency."

I slid the check across the table. "You've done more for me than you know." She started to say something, but put her hand to her mouth.

"Thank you," I said.

With a faint shake of her head, she slipped the money into her purse.

We finished our coffees and paid the bill, and as we were getting ready to leave, Lucy said, "And what about your novel, *The Book of the Grotesque*—how's it coming along? You predicted you'd be finished by the end of summer."

"Did I?" I asked. Somewhere along the way I'd forgotten. "Well, it's early June, and summer is long. I guess I've got my work cut out for me."

We hugged at her bus stop on Michigan Avenue. The southbound CTA bus pulled up to the curb, and the doors swished open.

"Take care," I said.

"See you." She gave a little wave as she stepped onto the bus. After she sat down she looked over her shoulder and waved a second time. As she headed toward her office at the University of Chicago, I wondered when I'd see her again and recalled a story she once told me about having dinner in Boston with two older writers who had grown up in the same state but now lived on separate coasts and hadn't talked or seen each other in thirty years. At the end of a boozy evening one of the writers, who carried a cane with a duck-head handle, put his hand on the other's shoulder and said, *We need to be in better touch.* And the second writer, a once beautiful woman, now hunched and frail, replied, *Oh honey. We're always in touch.*

Lucy didn't have to explain what that meant, because somehow, being my father's son, I guess, I understood right away. A book is a letter to the world, and to read is to be in touch. So for all those thirty years the two writers had been carrying on an intimate correspondence, the enduring friendship of writer and reader. I imagined Lucy picking up a book that I had written one day. Perhaps then we would understand each other a little more.

That night, Dhara came home with the news that a number of jobs had opened up at corporate, positions with Imego's soon-to-launch eBookstore.

"They need people now, and we're both perfectly qualified."

I must have looked skeptical, because she quickly added, "I know this isn't the first time I've said that, but I spent all day talking to people, and everyone says we're exactly who they're looking for."

The buzz around the lava lamps was that Imego would be partnering with independent bookstores, allowing them to sell Imego's scanned books from their own websites for a share of the profits. I wasn't ready to buy the hype, but Dhara told me about a trade magazine article that quoted prominent booksellers who said Imego might well become the savior, rather than the villain it had been, in the online retail wars.

"I know your feelings about California, but a lot has happened since this last came up. We don't have to apply if you don't want to," she said. "I'd be lying, though, if I told you I didn't want another shot."

"When are applications due?" I asked.

"Middle of June. And they're moving fast on this."

"Let me think about it," I said.

Over the next couple weeks I didn't think much about California. I meant to, but each night when I came home from work I found myself digging into the box marked "BOG" and obsessively reading through my father's typewritten pages and disconnected fragments. I assigned the scattered notes to the folders he'd already begun—*Leaving Winesburg; Turn-of-the-Century Chicago; Street, Rail, and Waterway Maps; The Golden Age of Advertising; Chicago Barons of the Gilded Age; The Panic of 1907; Anderson and the Chicago Renaissance; Secondary Characters and Other Grotesques;* and *George Willard.* I started new folders—*The Lazar Agency; Hull House; The Lab School; Characters from Home; Characters from Chicago; Helen White; Margaret Lazar; Tom Willard,* and a new folder for *George Willard,* because the one my father had begun was overflowing.

I filled a whole legal pad with character profiles and ideas, dropped my own notes into folders full of what-ifs: *What if George, in a rut at work, married the boss's daughter? What if Helen White worked at Hull House? What if Margaret wanted to take George away on a European tour? What if George steered his wife toward Hull House?* Along with the what-ifs were open questions I knew I couldn't answer just yet: *Will George get back with Helen? Will he stay in his marriage? Will he choose art over commerce? Will he stay in Chicago?*

The weekend before applications to Imego's eBookstore were due, Dhara sat down at the swag-leg table, where I had spread the notes and folders. She'd shown remarkable patience with me, hadn't complained about the mess I'd made of our small apartment, hadn't asked about California.

Until now.

"Well? Are we going to apply?"

"Yes and no," I said. "Yes, you are going to apply. But, no, I'm not."

She didn't seem surprised or upset by this. "So if I get the job?"

"We go."

She didn't have to ask what I was going to do. She knew already, had known for a long time, since well before I asked her to marry me and she said yes. "You're going to give your notice and write a book."

"Just as you need to take another shot, so do I."

She didn't give me a hard time about leaving one of the world's most coveted jobs for one of the most uncertain. I had a story to finish, a collaboration really, between my father and myself. It occurred to me that all novels are collaborations of a sort—between the writer and his influences, the real and the possible.

Dhara said she was going to polish up her cover letter and went into our bedroom to work. I made myself a cup of tea and put out food for Wing Biddlebaum, who came sauntering up to his bowl.

Back at the table, I opened my laptop and started a new folder titled *The Book of the Grotesque*. Pulling the stack of files closer I found a stray note card that my father had written but not put away. It was a quote from Sherwood Anderson:

When you are puzzled about your own life, as we all are most of the time, you can throw imagined figures of others against a background very like your own, put these imagined figures through situations in which you have been involved. It is a very comforting thing to do, a great relief at times, this occasionally losing sense of self, living in these imagined figures. This thing we call self is very often like a disease. It seems to sap you, destroy your relationship with others, while even occasionally losing sense of self seems to give you an understanding that you didn't have before you became absorbed.

I placed this note card next to my computer and opened a new document. Sitting there looking at the blank screen, I was startled for a moment by Wing, who jumped onto the table, stepped into my lap, curled up in a ball, and began to purr.

21

How he found himself on an eastbound train leaving Chicago was a story he would write time and again in the coming years. It was a story he'd already written, already lived—leaving an ever-narrowing place for a seemingly open one, slipping out under the cover of darkness, running away.

It was September. That much he knew, because his trunk was mostly packed, the house as good as ready for the half year he and Margaret had planned to be away. If he had stayed another week he might have stepped onto this same train and continued to New York, then boarded that boat.

Helen had called him McAdams. She had predicted this. Or had her prediction become a self-fulfilling prophecy? He hadn't thought he would flee, still wouldn't use that word. No, he was not escaping—he was going home. Like his father, he just needed some time to think.

After he had read Tom Willard's letter, he tried to go about his days as if nothing had changed. He went to work, put up with whispers in the halls as he was slipping away early. *So, you're writing the Great American Novel? Kennison said. More power to you! I can tell folks I knew you when you were just a flunky at a hype shop.*

George had sat at his desk in Palmer House and tried to write. But nothing came. He went down to the lobby, where Lemuel Means shot him a glance that said *I saw that woman put her arm around you. I've seen her many times. You're a married man. My boss's wife runs in the same circles as your mother-in-law. And I'm just the kind of company drone to ring up Bertha Palmer and tell her what I've witnessed.*

No doubt he'd already done so. And the host at Henrici's as well. And the breadmaker Stefan Wirtz, who had surely said something to Margaret. And they weren't the only ones. Lazar, who had once claimed to be the last to know what was happening on the home front, met George with the steeliness of a stand of clouds before a storm. Margaret had been spending more and more time at Harriet's, going over last-minute details but also caught in the coil of mother-daughter separation. She wanted to show the face of the free woman, setting out on the adventure of her life; at the same time she wanted her mother to feel guilty for letting her go, jealous at having to stay behind.

For her part, Harriet had been making eleventh-hour threats to join the party, meet up in Paris or Rome or even accompany them from the start. It must have dawned on her that this might be her last chance to travel with her daughter. And how could she not be on hand for the great secret laid bare, the confrontation played out on the streets of a European capital? For wasn't that how betrayals were so often revealed, on unfamiliar ground, awash with strange voices and sights?

Whether his affair would have come to light in Chicago or abroad, he wasn't going to face it. He was on a train. Nothing to see but the spilled ink of night, the conductor calling out the stations: South Bend, Elkhart, Waterloo.

Earlier that day he had paid a visit to Hull House. Unannounced. He went through that open door—the greeter must have stepped away—and there was Jane Addams herself at the threshold of her octagonal office.

We met once. George Willard, he'd reintroduced himself. *It's awfully quiet today.*

The great woman, in her gentle voice, told him it was Sunday.

I'd clear forgotten, he said, then asked after Helen. And Jane herself—one of the most famous people in the world—climbed the stairs to the apartments on the third floor and led Helen down.

They talked in an empty classroom with Italian and English phrases still scrawled across the chalkboard. Helen opened the windows. It was close and hot. The sun beat down on the courtyard bricks.

Why are you here? she asked. *You might have given me some warning.*

I need to talk to you.

You look a fright, she said. *Have you been getting any sleep at all? You've skinned your knee. How did that happen?*

He looked down at his trousers, where he had ripped a hole in one pant leg and frayed the other. He didn't remember falling, but once he'd had in mind that he needed to see Helen he had all but hurled himself across the city, by grip and then on foot.

The knee was bleeding, so Helen fetched bandages and disinfectant from the nurse and set about cleaning the gravel-studded abrasion.

Thank you, but I can do it myself, he said.

You're in no state. She flicked away the gravel, dipped a cloth in iodine, and made quick, careful swabs.

He winced. *I came here to let you know that I've left my wife.* It was the last lie he would tell her. Or was it a lie? Perhaps he had as much as left already. *I love you, Helen. I'd marry you in a twinkling if you'd have me.*

She placed gauze on the wound and bandaged it. *You don't know what you're saying.*

I do. We grew up together. We can grow old together, too.

But you haven't grown up. That's the trouble, she said. *If you had, you wouldn't have lied to me, wouldn't have thrown your wife over after two years of marriage—right before a trip abroad, no less! If you were a man, you wouldn't be in this state.*

He'd been sitting in a chair, but now dropped to his sore knees. *You're right! I'm a thoughtless fool. I do need to grow up. I'm going to write a book. That's what I have to do. Write until I can see myself clearly. Maybe then I can make amends. I can come back to you, and you'll reconsider.*

Stand up, George. You're ruining your bandages.

I don't care. I just want to know if you'll let me hold on to a little hope.

Fine, if that helps you. She took his arm and guided him back into the chair. *But you treated me badly. And others, too. I won't forget what you did.*

I was wrong. People do change, you know.

We'll see, she said. Then she left again and came back with a tall glass of water, which she handed to George. *You need to drink this.*

He was thirsty. He gulped the water down. *If you won't have me now, perhaps you'll help me,* he said. *Remember on the Midway how you asked what you should do with your life—stay at the Lab School or move to Hull House? And I told you to follow your instincts, and here you are? I need you to return the favor.*

He told her about his father's letter, the tin box in the rubble, how by some miracle this man who had come to a blank wall in his life was of a sudden in the money.

Where do you think the box came from? Helen asked.

I have no idea. It's not my father's, or he would have said so. He claimed it had been on his property, so it ought to be returned to him. Maybe a thief stayed the night and had to leave in a rush. But the box wasn't in a closet. It was plastered behind a wall. Intentionally *hidden.*

Perhaps it was your mother's, Helen said. *Women have been known to stow what money they can, under the mattress, in a vase. Behind a wall? Anything's possible. She might have been saving it for life without your father, if that ever came to pass. Jane Addams is only one example of what a woman can do given some measure of financial independence.*

But my mother had no income. I don't know what savings she would have been hiving up. It's a mystery, George said. *So I need to know: Should I stay or should I leave? I can't write here anymore. I have a desire like never before to strike out for some new place. But I'd be starting from nothing.*

Maybe your father will open his treasure chest.

You know my father. He thinks only of Tom Willard.

I don't know what to tell you. I think you already know what you're going to do. You knew before you stumbled in here. You've known for a good long time.

You could come with me, Helen! Or I could get where I'm going, and you could join me there.

George—She gestured around her to remind him they were standing in the place where she'd found her sense of purpose.

I know, he said. *It's just that*—

But she embraced him before he could say whatever next might have come to mind. He dried his eyes on the shoulder of her blouse and promised himself that Helen White had not seen or heard the last of him. Here in Chicago they had reunited under the wrong circumstances, but one day he would make up for it; he would rewrite this ending.

Back on the weather-beaten streets, he leaned his way toward the grip, then the Palmer House, then his room, where he packed his valise. He told himself he could send for the trunk later, though how likely was it that Margaret would release his belongings, after what he was putting her through?

Checking out. He handed Lemuel Means his key.

Disappointed with the amenities? the hotel clerk said, no doubt with a sneer, but George wouldn't give him a response. He paid the bill, shouldered his bag, and set out for Dearborn Station.

On the train he tried to write a letter to Margaret, but he crossed out the sentences one by one. Everything he set to paper came off as false: *I never deserved you. You were always too good for me. I was unworthy to undo your shoestrings. It was my fate to fly too high, yours to be married to me in my time of crisis.*

He put his paper and pencil away, closed his eyes and listened to the rumble of the train, the clang of the brazen bell, the conductor calling out *Toledo, Woodville, Winesburg.*

Strange to be stepping onto the platform in his hometown to find a chain-wire fence where the New Willard House once stood. The lighting was poor, the moon hidden behind clouds. He would have to wait until morning to take in the spectacle. He checked his pocket watch: 11:30 p.m. He headed down Main Street to the shoe-repair shop and pulled on the door under the sign that read:

REPAIRING BY MACHINERY
WHILE YOU WAIT
POPULAR PRICES

The door was locked. He rang the bell to the apartments, but no one came down. Perhaps his father was asleep. But he had never gotten much rest, accustomed as he was to innkeeper's hours. George rang the bell again and waited. A warm wind blew up and rustled the leaves of the maples. Not a soul stirred on the streets.

After some time he stepped back and called out, *Tom! Tom Willard! Are you up there?* But no reply came, and the second-story apartments remained dark. Clouds passed overhead, and the new moon appeared, reflecting on the repair-shop window.

George sat at the curb and waited, wondered where he would have to sleep the night: on the bench outside Hern's Grocery, back at the railroad station, under a tree by the banks of Waterworks Pond? What a sight he'd be for his former neighbors—curled up like a bug, trousers torn, the soot of the city casting shadows on his face.

As he thought of places where he might better conceal himself, a figure appeared down the street, and even at a distance George recognized the square shoulders and brisk walk.

"Great ghosts!" his father exclaimed. "What on earth are you doing here?"

"Waiting for you. Why, it's well past midnight."

"So it is, son. But I believe it's you who owes an explanation."

"Perhaps we can talk inside," George said, and followed Tom Willard up the stairs to his meager lodgings, which smelled of old leather and shoe polish.

In the musty room, lit by a single overhead light bulb, George and his father talked. It didn't matter that they had never spoken about anything more serious than politics or the weather, had never talked about Elizabeth Willard's death or the failure of the hotel. Something in his father's letter had left an opening: *I don't know what I'm going to do. I need some time to think . . . I've had a lot of dreams, George. Maybe now I can put them in order and see them through.* This wasn't the old Tom Willard, the big talker ever ready with a snappy answer.

George began by saying that he had pursued Margaret out of fear he would lose his job; he'd been surprised by her interest, could hardly believe she would marry him. He recalled the visit to the ring counter at Marshall Field's, the proposal and wedding, and he realized as he was speaking that his father, too, had married up some thirty-odd years before.

Tom Willard sat and listened as George told him about Kennison and *Prove They Need It* and his diminished role at work, about seeing Helen White at the restaurant, then Hull House, how she had encouraged him to become a writer, just as many in Winesburg had when he was a young man working at the *Eagle*. George didn't know how to explain what had happened next with Helen, so he said, "I got myself into a bind, made a mess of things and lied to people. There's no going back to my marriage or my job."

"What will you do?" his father asked.

"I could use some sleep," George said. "Perhaps I'll know in the morning."

The sun sifted through the dusty windows and spilled over the floor, waking George from a sound sleep. He got up and made coffee for himself and his father, showered, and put on his one change of clothes. When the telegraph office opened for business, he was waiting outside the door.

He wired three messages:

To Lazar: *I hereby resign my position, though I deserve to be fired. You gave me every opportunity, and I sincerely regret squandering your trust.*

To Margaret: *I am going away so that I might look in the mirror and explain to myself why I have done the things I've done. I wish I*

*could make up for my cowardice and inconstancy, and perhaps one day
I shall find the right words of apology for the suffering I have caused
you. I'm sorry is not enough. Even a whole volume would surely not do.*

To Helen: *You were right. I am McAdams.*

He swung by the railroad station to check the eastbound schedule, then returned to his father's lodgings.

"Well?" Tom Willard asked.

"I'm going to New York," George said. "I'll be on the 12:05."

"And what will you do there?" Tom did not seem surprised.

"I still know my share of admen, some who could look beyond what happened at the Lazar Agency. But I want to avoid that kind of work for as long as I can," he said. "I don't care a pin for a fancy title anymore, and I don't need my hands on money all the time. I wish I could have a few months to sit at a window in a small room and dream up a good story. How about you?"

Tom stood at the window and looked out upon the street. "I'm packing up for Sandusky next week," he said. "I showed my face at the County Democratic Headquarters, and they need all the help they can get over there. The pay is rotten—volunteer, really—but that tin box should see me through for some time."

"And Congress?" George indulged him. "Still thinking about making a run?"

Tom twisted his mustache, the gray roots showing through. "I'm too old," he said. "We finally got ourselves a good candidate, Carl Anderson. Used to be a traveling salesman, then mayor of Fostoria. He's young, energetic. He could keep the seat for years."

As George was folding his traveling clothes and packing his valise, his father went to the closet and came back with an envelope. "You might need this," he said.

George opened the flap and looked inside at the stack of ten-dollar notes, probably enough to live on for a year. He made a gesture at giving the money back, but his father put up his hand.

"It's yours," Tom insisted.

"I have no claim on that tin box."

"Sure you do."

George wondered for a moment if Helen had been right, if the box had belonged to his mother and his father somehow knew this, maybe knew it all along.

Then Tom said, "I kept a tally all those years you used to send money home—for repairs and upkeep. There's not a dollar in there that you didn't earn."

"It's awfully generous of you."

"I might have said the same." Tom checked his watch. "Well, you ought to be going now."

They took the short walk to the station, and George considered how different this departure was from the first one, thirteen years before. It had been spring, the green tongues of young leaves just tasting the air, and now it was autumn, the leaves soon to flame and fall away. He remembered the clerks sweeping the steps out front of their shops, but now half the stores in town were shuttered or for sale. Sylvester West's Drug Store, Winney's Dry Goods, Myerbaum's Notions—all gone. Ed Griffith's saloon was still in business, but Jerry Bird, who used to sleep past noon sprawled against the wall outside, must have taken his last drink. That first departure, everyone had come out to say *Hey you, George. How does it feel to be going away?* But few people busied the streets this Monday, and those he did see he didn't recognize. They nodded at Tom Willard but looked suspiciously at the stranger walking next to him.

At the chain-wire fence, George and his father stopped and wordlessly surveyed the site where the New Willard House once stood. There was nothing to see. The wood, carpet, wallpaper, furnishings had been hauled away. All that remained was fine rubble and dirt, weeds sprouting around the perimeter of the foundation. But just inside where the entrance used to be, George spotted some pieces of cut glass winking in the sunlight. He squeezed through a hole in the fence and picked up two of the pieces, which he recognized as beads from the lobby chandelier. He pocketed one and handed the other to his father, who thanked him and looked away. "Salvage," George said. Then the two men walked down the small ramp to the station platform.

Half a dozen people sat on benches or stood waiting for the train to Cleveland, the connection terminal to the trunk-line railroad that ran clear to New York.

"I ought to be going," Tom said. "I have a noon appointment." He clenched his jaw, as if he wanted to speak but was holding something back. "You be sure and let me know where to find you once you've settled in." He clapped his son's shoulder and gave him a firm handshake, then turned and disappeared.

Not a minute after he'd left, the locomotive came around a bend and made its way down the track. George stepped on and settled into his seat, checked his jacket pocket for the envelope of bills. He took out his pencil and notepad and stowed his valise.

The whistle blew, the train pulled out of the station, and as the platform slipped away he looked down lower Main Street and in the middle distance saw his father facing in his direction, scanning each window as the passenger cars slid by. George waved, but Tom Willard must not have noticed. He stood there on the sidewalk, hands in his pockets, perhaps fingering the bead from the lobby chandelier.

As the train picked up speed and drove into the countryside, his figure grew smaller and smaller until it was just a dot, like a pencil point on a blank piece of paper, a place for the story to begin.

ACKNOWLEDGMENTS

I would like to thank Michael Griffith for selecting this novel for the Yellow Shoe Fiction Series. He's an incredible editor and writer, and I feel lucky to have had a chance to work with him. Michael also selected an excerpt, "The Writer's Writer," for the *Cincinnati Review*. My agent, Lisa Bankoff, has been a constant supporter, advisor, and advocate. Many thanks to everyone at LSU press, especially MaryKatherine Callaway, Rand Dotson, Lee Sioles, Susan Murray, Mandy McDonald Scallan, and Erin Rolfs. I am also grateful to the Purdue College of Liberal Arts for a grant that provided me with a semester off to complete this book. As Director of the Creative Writing Program at Purdue for eight years, I worked with wonderful colleagues and students, and I appreciate their kindness and camaraderie.

As part of my research I read a number of turn-of-the-century novels and stories by both known and forgotten Chicago Renaissance writers like Hamlin Garland, Henry Blake Fuller, Elia Peattie, Frank Norris, Upton Sinclair, Edgar Lee Masters, Willa Cather, and Theodore Dreiser to get a sense of what Chicago was like when it was the fastest-growing city in the history of the world. I found the reporting of George Ade to be particularly helpful, and drew on one of his sketches, "The Mystery of the Back-roomer" (republished in the University of Illinois Press's *Stories of Chicago*) as well as on Julian Street's *Abroad at Home*. Of course, no book had a greater influence on me than Sherwood Anderson's *Winesburg, Ohio*, a longtime favorite that became an obsession. At various points in this novel I quote from *Winesburg* and from Anderson's *A Story Teller's Story*. I also use quotes from Kim Townsend's *Sherwood Anderson: A Biography* and Walter B. Rideout's *Sherwood Anderson: A Writer in America, Volumes I and II*. In each case, I have used quotation marks or italics to attribute the material.

I am grateful always for the love and support of my family in D.C. Most of all, I want to thank Bich, first reader, collaborator, partner, friend.

PORTER SHREVE is the author of three previous novels: *The Obituary Writer* was a *New York Times* Notable Book, and *Drives Like a Dream* and *When the White House Was Ours* were both *Chicago Tribune* Books of the Year. Shreve is coeditor of six anthologies, and his fiction, nonfiction, essays, and reviews have appeared in *Witness, Salon,* the *Chicago Tribune,* the *San Francisco Chronicle,* the *Boston Globe,* and the *New York Times,* among other places. He has taught at several universities, including Michigan, Purdue, and the University of San Francisco. A native of Washington, D.C., he spent a number of years in Chicago and the Midwest, and now lives with his wife and children in the Bay Area.